DEDICATION

To My Family

THE
IMMACULATE

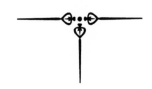

MARIAN MCMAHON STANLEY

BARKING RAIN PRESS

The Immaculate

Edited by Melissa Eskue Ousley (www.melissaeskueousley.com)

Proofread by Barbara Bailey (www.barkingrainpress.org/barbara-bailey/)

Cover artwork by Craig Jennion (www.craigjennion.com)

Barking Rain Press
PO Box 822674
Vancouver, WA 98682 USA
www.BarkingRainPress.org

ISBN Trade Paperback: 1-941295-47-9
ISBN eBook: 1-941295-48-7
Library of Congress Control Number: 2015952743

First Edition: May 2016

Printed in the United States of America

9 7 8 1 9 4 1 2 9 5 4 8 9

CHAPTER 1

ister Mary Aurelius walked with slow, steady steps as the massive brick buildings around her gathered shadows in the winter dusk. A deliberate, sharp-eyed crow in her black habit, she crossed the wide emptiness of the shuttered Immaculate Conception school complex.

Time was short now, and her health wasn't all it could be. When she'd taught here long ago, they'd secretly nicknamed her Spike because she could be tough as nails. She prayed she still had it. Just enough for one last unfinished task, one more mission. God give her the strength. Once that was done, she could depart this world, if not with a peaceful mind, then at least with the knowledge that she'd done everything within her power to bring justice.

But for now, just to walk in her old schoolyard once more was a gift. She'd slipped away from the party at the Irish-American and come here to revisit her memories at the school. Someone would notice her absence soon. Nuns weren't supposed to travel alone like this in her day. You always had to have another sister with you.

She'd come down from the Motherhouse on the North Shore with Sister Bernard, who never broke the rules and would worry about her wandering off to the Immaculate alone. Aurelius grinned. *Can't cage the wily blackbird.* She could take care of herself.

She was getting old, so there were ghosts. The ghosts of children at recess as she walked across the schoolyard. She could almost hear the voices, the laughter, the rhythm of the jump ropes, the sound of balls bouncing against the pavement. If she closed her eyes, she could still see the way the boys' white shirts, carefully ironed by their mothers, escaped their navy blue slacks and flew in the wind, the ties askew. And the girls' long legs in their pleated skirts—blouses out, hair wild, braids loosening.

She pulled her shawl against the wind as she approached the southwest corner of the girls' grammar school. Taking off one of her black knit gloves, she felt the red brick. Still slightly warm from the late winter sun, though it was getting to be nightfall. She shivered at the sharp chill in the air. Did she imagine she still saw chalk dust on the bricks where the erasers used to be knocked and cleaned? *Ah, that was such an honor. To be chosen to clean the erasers for Sister. Only the best girls and boys.*

Aurelius laughed quietly as she turned the corner. Then, she stopped. Stopped in the cold and sudden silence. In the partial darkness, back by the wall and the benches where the nuns used to sit, stood a tall figure. Hearing her steps, the man slowly turned his face from the shadows. Mother of God, she must be having a strange dream. For a moment, she could see the face the world knew. Then in the dim light, a face all wrong.

No words were spoken. The man stood very still. Then he nodded once, only a small nod, just the barest gesture. But with that she knew her time had come. Her heart froze and she called up her courage. The old nun reached her hand out for the wall again, feeling the familiar red brick, touching the children's presence one more time even as she met his eyes and murmured the Confiteor in preparation for death: *Qua peccavi, opera et omissione, orare pro me.* I have sinned greatly in what I have done and what I have failed to do, pray for me.

She hadn't completed her mission. But she knew who would.

Outside the window of the Lufthansa Lounge at Boston's Logan Airport, planes lined up for departure on the Terminal E international runway, their wing lights flickering steadily in the darkness.

Rosaria O'Reilly had already moved into her personal travel bubble. Soft travel clothes, a black cashmere wrap, and light canvas ballet flats. She'd packed a change of wardrobe in the carry-on bag beside her for the inevitable travel emergency in her current business territories—Central Asia, Africa, and the Middle East.

The pink *Financial Times* peeked out of one corner of the bag, along with the *Journal*, and quarterly sales reports for the high-end athletic shoe business she worked for. A faint sound of Urban Mandolin jazz escaped the earbuds tucked under her dark hair. Sitting as far away from the CNN monitor as she could, Rosaria was annoyed to see another monitor installed behind the bar, this one tuned to local news. Frowning at the intrusive screen, she felt her cell phone vibrate and pulled one earbud out to answer the call.

"O'Reilly." She reached for her mug of tea on the side table. "Hi, Dimitri." Rosaria could feel a little headache starting above her left eye. She listened for a few moments before responding.

"Yeah, I heard the pricing he wants. Not going to do that." She raised her voice briefly to head off what was clearly an objection by her regional sales manager at the other end of the call. "Dimitri, he can't move that much product in his territory. He'll just let it flow over into the Russian gray market and kill our pricing there. Stash is a big account, but you know, a trader—it's in his blood. He won't be able to resist it."

Rosaria closed her eyes, leaned her head back and listened, mandolin jazz soothing her nerves through one earbud, keeping her grounded. "Yes, yes. Big order. New York calls me every other day for the numbers—but we're not doing this for him." She stopped talking to listen for just a moment, then interrupted. "No, he is *not* Genghis Khan. He's just a big distributor for Central Asia looking to score by taking advantage of our pricing structures." She hesitated and laughed. "Okay, maybe he is kind of Genghis Khan, but he's workable."

The voice on the other end was insistent.

"Look, Dimitri. It's a business problem. It will have a solution." Rosaria rubbed her forehead. "Maybe there's another way to satisfy him. Add a piece of territory to keep him busy and out of trouble. I'll be in Istanbul tomorrow for the day with Ergun, and then I'll meet you in Almaty. We'll deal with it then."

She took a deep breath and glanced over at the TV monitor behind the bar. The weatherman, standing in front of colorful graphics, was predicting temperatures in the twenties, with a wind chill factor in the teens, as a developing news story crawled across the bottom of the television screen. *Elderly nun murdered on grounds of shuttered Immaculate Conception School in Malford.*

Rosaria stiffened for a moment. She cocked her head and turned to face the monitor. Then, tea mug still in hand, she rose from her seat, leaving her cell phone on the table. She walked behind the bar to the front of the television, gently moving the startled young bartender out of the way as she reached up to raise the volume. A real-time video feed appeared under the angry slash of a red *Breaking News* banner. A young man in a blue Channel Four down jacket stood on the street in front of the Immaculate Conception schoolyard.

Malford Police Chief Nicolo Cullen appeared in uniform, looking reassuringly bulky and determined, surrounded by reporters. "The nun is identified as Sister Mary Aurelius, a retired sister of the Jeanne d'Arc order, the teaching nuns that staffed the Immaculate Conception School when it was active. As of now, we are not aware of the reason for Sister's being on the school grounds at that time. We do know she was killed at this location."

The words from the television seemed to be coming from a far distance, through some vast, watery space, before reaching Rosaria and hanging suspended in the small airport lounge. "Bludgeoned to death." She stretched her fingers toward the headline on the television as if she could touch the words to feel their strangeness, their awfulness. She heard a soft, low keening sound. Was that her?

"A person of interest, a man of no known address but with links to the neighborhood, is now being questioned."

Rosaria couldn't absorb the rest of the report as she stood, a frisson of shock, confusion, and fury moving through her body. She had dropped her mug of tea, the brown liquid splashing her slacks and those of the bartender, also transfixed, perhaps more by Rosaria than the news on the screen.

"Christ," he said. "Who would do something like that?"

Rosaria was not sure how long she stood there.

"You okay, ma'am?"

She raised her hand to him to signal she was okay, even though she wasn't. Turning from the television, Rosaria walked to her seat where she collected her travel bag and her cell phone. The phone still had Dimitri's name on the screen. She could hear his bewildered voice asking for her. Rosaria shut off the phone and walked out the door of the lounge.

Later, she couldn't remember walking through the terminal and getting into a cab. She did dimly recall telling the cabbie to drive to her apartment at Trinity Wharf, and then calling her assistant to make sure her bag got off the Frankfurt/Istanbul flight and that the Turkish distributor knew she wouldn't be in his offices the next day.

She also remembered texting Dimitri the message that he had to handle Genghis Khan by himself. She could almost hear the cry of despair across the time zones.

Riding through the lighted Ted Williams Tunnel and down Atlantic Avenue, Rosaria felt outside the flow of time, that odd stasis we experience when the world has been altered in some fundamental way.

Aurelius. Spike. Her teacher. More than that. Her life's anchor, meeting a brutal end in her own schoolyard.

Rosaria's chest rose slowly and regularly with full, even breaths, and her hands rested on her travel bag as the cab sped through the Boston streets along the waterfront. She felt nothing different except for a gentle tingling. A tiny electrical current coursing through her body, a light charge carrying the message that something was changing. And in the far distance, a low, almost imperceptible roar of something larger, something darker coming toward her at its own pace across the flat, wide, wet sand.

The cab slowed for a light and some late night diners crossing the street from Tia's on the Waterfront. Couples arm in arm, probably headed back to the suburbs after a night out in the city. Rosaria's fingers traced the lock on her bag as she gazed out the side window of the cab at the arches of Christopher Columbus

Park, glittering with thousands of fairy lights. She felt her eyes smart, but—no—no weeping.

Rosaria's apartment at the end of the wharf, in a refurbished granite block warehouse from the 1800s, had always felt like her fortress. Now, she dropped her bag inside the door of the apartment, and stood for several minutes in front of the large windows facing the harbor. She watched planes taking off from Logan into the night sky, hers among them.

After some time, she poured a glass of Jameson neat. Drink in hand, she lowered herself into a large green reading chair in front of the long windows and put her feet on the chair's ottoman. Her hands felt cool on her forehead as she rubbed them back and forth, eyes closed, sipping the Jameson and feeling its familiar warmth in her chest.

Rosaria ignored her cell phone for ten minutes or more before reaching into the pocket of her sweater and pulling it out. Multiple calls from Dimitri and one from Nuncie. Maria Annunciata DiStephano, the baker's daughter, her childhood friend from the Immaculate. Nuncie and Rosaria bonded early in school because they'd both been given weightily devout names by pious mothers, one Sicilian and one Irish. Names cherished by the nuns and a continuous source of amusement to their classmates. Rosaria punched return call and Nuncie picked up immediately.

"Can you believe this? Jesus Christ."

"What do you know?" Rosaria asked.

"Not much. They're holding Joey Mucci. But he says he just found the body."

"Joey Mucci. God." Rosaria leaned back and closed her eyes.

"I'd like to kill the son of a bitch with my own hands."

Yes, Rosaria thought it likely that Nuncie could, with her delicate, terrifying frame, kill the son of a bitch who murdered Sister Aurelius. "Kill Joey?"

"Whoever did this," Nuncie said. "You think it's really Joey? I can't see him doing this."

"Why not?"

"Remember Joey? He was a harmless little guy, even if he was weird as sin."

"He's not a kid anymore, Nuncie. He's a man. A big man. Maybe he's not so gentle anymore." Rosaria stopped to sip her drink and could feel the whisky smoothing the edges so that she could function. She wanted to function. "Anyway, who's got the lead here? Who's got the case?"

"Gelenian. Leo. Remember him?"

"Yeah. Isn't he, like, twelve?"

"We all used to be twelve, Ro. He's grown up and I hear he's pretty good."

"We'll see. Where are you?"

"Still in Gloucester." Nuncie, unmarried and early retired, lived about thirty-five miles north of Boston in a waterfront home always filled with craft projects and the smell of something mouthwatering cooking on the stove.

"Do you feel well enough to drive down to Malford in the morning?"

"Of course. I'm fine. I'm not an invalid, you know."

"Okay, okay. I'll meet you in the Square. What's good there now?"

"Place called The French Connection across from City Hall. About 9:30. I can miss the traffic coming down. But what do you think you're going to do when you get there?"

"I don't know. Something."

Rosaria closed the phone and refreshed her glass before returning to the chair. A ragged tennis ball sat near the foot of the chair's ottoman. Archie, her West Highland White Terrier and owner of all the ragged tennis balls that littered the apartment, stayed with Rosaria's ex-husband, Bronson, in the South End when she traveled. Right now, she could have used the comfort of the shaggy little dog beside her.

Or someone, something.

CHAPTER 2

eo Gelenian ran his hands through his short dark hair as he hurried down the hall of the Malford police station. He stepped back to avoid colliding with Detective Wesley Johnson, who was carrying a plastic chair down the narrow hall.

"Where's Mucci?" Leo asked.

"Conference room."

"Conference room? How come?"

"Got his posse with him." Johnson turned to Leo with a half-smile on his broad, dark face. "His brother Vinnie, Father Hanrahan, that old guy helping out at the Immaculate now, and," he lifted the plastic chair, "this is for Danny Milano, the family lawyer."

Leo looked down the hall to see the elderly lawyer straightening his tie before entering the conference room. "Jesus, Grand Army of the Republic. Just what we need. It's good that he's got a lawyer and his brother with him, but what's with the priest?"

Johnson shrugged. "Vinnie says he has to be there. The guy being around keeps Joey *settled*, whatever that means."

Leo rotated his neck several times in a futile attempt to loosen a painful stiffness before he started toward the conference room. Outside the door of the room, he stopped to ask Johnson, "What's the tech haul look like?"

"Usual shit. Vodka, Bud, Red Bull empties, Dunkin' Donuts crap, a few condoms in the bushes, Zippos, matchbooks, pizza box from Pietro's, couple of Du Mauriers cigarette butts that are kind of interesting."

Leo raised his eyebrows. "Du Mauriers? Canadian. They aren't sold around here."

"Beats me. We're checking up on distribution."

Leo nodded and opened the conference room door. "Good. Okay. Let's go."

The previous night, Jack Rafferty had made a 911 call to the Malford Police from the yard of the Immaculate Conception school, long closed due to archdiocese consolidations. Jack and his wife Pearl had been cutting through the schoolyard after a fiftieth anniversary party at the Irish-American when they'd found Joey Mucci sitting against the wall of the old girls school next to a dead nun. Joey was holding one end of the nun's rosary, singing *Immaculate Mary*, the hymn from the old May processions, in a high, weird voice. A kid's voice from a big man.

Joey was still singing softly when Leo pulled up in the cruiser with Wesley Johnson. Pearl Rafferty sat next to Joey, rubbing his back and weeping as he sang. Joey Mucci, the slow, beautiful boy that they'd all gone to school with at the Immaculate, leaning against the brick wall with a dead nun in front of him. Jack Rafferty stood beside them, stomping his feet in the winter cold, watching for the police.

Other vehicles started to arrive—medical examiner Heaney, and a van of crime techs. Yellow crime scene tape was rolled out, harsh lights were hooked up. Wesley gently helped Joey Mucci up and brought him to the back of the cruiser. An officer took the Raffertys' statement and sent them home for the night.

Leo squatted on his long legs and leaned closer to the old nun's body. When Heaney walked over, Leo moved to the side, leaving some distance between himself and the medical examiner. He knew from experience that Heaney was more comfortable with the dead than the living. More than once, Leo had seen the man wince and shift his position when a breathy, bulky cop leaned close beside him to inspect a body.

"Slammed her on the top front of the skull first. Then, it looks like she fell, facing the wall of the school. He hit her again on the side of her head to finish her off. See the mortar in the blood beside her head?" Heaney pointed to the small pieces of mortar around the nun's broken skull. Small, gravelly debris spotted the blood, grown viscous in the winter cold. "But he really didn't have to do the second blow. She was probably on her way out after that first hit."

"Looks like a solid hit," said Leo. "Big stone."

"Right, a blow with a good deal of power. She's a tall lady for her generation. It took a big person to hit the top of her head with a stone of this size." He pointed to the gray granite block beside the body. Tiny sparkles flashed from where bits of mica in the stone caught the crime scene lights.

"This is not a small stone. Of course, he's a big guy and, if he was in some kind of rage, it wouldn't have been a problem for him to take this from the wall and hit her with it."

Heaney turned to the crumbling granite wall behind them—a wall with one achingly empty spot in the top row of stones. Then he shrugged and turned again to the body before him. "But that's not for me to say."

Leo looked up. "What the hell was she doing here?"

Heaney ignored the detective's question. "Not much hair and bone on the stone itself because she was wearing that thing on her head. Hair and bone pretty much embedded in the cloth."

"Coif," Leo said. Heaney looked at the detective. "It's called a coif, the white cap under the veil. Nuns used to dress that way. She wasn't young, kept the old habit."

Heaney returned to his work, uninterested in anything beyond the tangible remains before them. "Well, it's sure as hell not white now," he commented as he gazed at the nun's blood-soaked cap and neck wimple. "Blood, lots of blood. Must have taken a while for her to finally give up the ghost after she was out." Heaney gestured to the pools of blood on the pavement and the heavy spattering on the brick walls.

"Yeah, not surprised. She was a tough one."

Leo stood and looked around him. He remembered when he went to the Immaculate as a kid. The nuns used to sit on the benches in this part of the schoolyard on their rare breaks from duties during recess and lunch. These days, teenagers sometimes hung around the two sagging benches against the deteriorating stone wall, usually after school. At night, drugs and sex were occasionally sold here, but for the most part, the young people stayed away after dark.

Leo walked slowly around the crime scene from the perimeter, his leather coat open to the winter wind. Soon, they would have gathered what they could, and it would be time to move on to the next stage. Interviewing all the neighbors and the guests at what they'd heard was a party for Tom and Dot Daley that afternoon at the Irish-American. A party where the nun and some other retired teachers had been guests. It was unclear why the nun had left the party and walked to the schoolyard. It was also unclear if she'd come by herself or had been accompanied, possibly by Joey Mucci. Somebody must have noticed an elderly nun in an old-fashioned black habit walking along Lloyd Street late on a Sunday afternoon.

Leo heard the media arriving and was relieved to see Chief Nicolo Cullen's department SUV pull up. He'd take the lead on communicating with the Mayor and the Cardinal, leaving Leo and his team time to do the real work.

In Leo's line of work, it was usually straightforward. A drug deal gone bad, a jealous boyfriend, an unpaid debt. Once, even a fight over a TV remote. No great mystery, except perhaps to wonder at the depths of human stupidity and depravity. This case too looked sadly straightforward. The demons in the off-kilter, peculiar man who was Joseph Mucci had finally broken loose, and told him to kill an old nun walking through the schoolyard one winter twilight.

After Leo briefed Chief Cullen, he walked over to an officer standing by the building. Leo lifted his chin slightly in greeting. "Victor, How's Mucci?" Officer

Victor Suarez gestured to the cruiser, lights still flashing, exhaust visible in the bright, artificial light of the crime scene.

"Hard to get anything out of him. He's pretty out of it to begin with, and he's way over the top tonight." Leo knew that Victor had brought Joey Mucci into the station at least once or twice—after calls from merchants—to talk to him about loitering around stores in the Square.

Leo nodded. Joey had been sliding deeper into a murky abyss for a long time. It hadn't always been that bad. Just a little slow, just a little off. A beautiful child. Then, somewhere along the way a silent, slithery thing with tentacles had reached up from a deep, dark hole and pulled Joey Mucci down.

He was younger than Leo, but Leo could remember seeing Joey change. One day he'd seen Joey in the schoolyard, walking alone near the chain link fence, his head and upper body shaking with some weird tics. Leo knew then that Joey had gone to another place. As Joey got stranger, his classmates were sometimes cruel, the way they can be with the different, with the odd. Joey's brother Vinnie had protected him as best he could, but Vinnie couldn't be everywhere.

"What's his story?" Leo asked.

"Mucci just found her this way. Thought it was a pile of black rags, but then he saw those nunny shoes sticking out. He recognized the face. Knew it was Sister Aurelius from the Immaculate."

"He see anybody?"

"Says there were shadows. Not much to work with. Maybe you get can more out of him." Victor stopped to give Leo a direct look. "Looks bad. He's gone and he's buzzed. You'll smell it on him. Looks to me like he finally went off the rails and hit her with a rock. God knows why. Nobody knows what goes on in his head."

Leo took a deep breath. "Okay, I'm going to see if I can get anything more out of him. Keep those reporters out, and don't let anyone—I mean anyone—near us."

"Got it. For what it's worth, Leo—and I don't think it's worth much, given the source—but Mrs. Rafferty doesn't think Mucci did it. She thinks he just found the body. Her husband's not buying that—says it looks pretty cut and dried to him."

"Yeah, well, okay. Nice people and good input, but they don't get to make the call."

Leo turned and headed for the cruiser. He opened the door and climbed into the backseat. "Read him his rights?" he asked the officer in the front seat.

"Yep."

"Okay, thanks." Leo gestured to the officer to leave the vehicle. As the policeman moved heavily out of the cruiser, Leo briefly heard the buzz of activity outside. Then, the officer closed the door and it was quiet again.

"Joey?" There was no movement or sound except a shoulder moving slightly away and heavy, tearful breathing. The air was sour with alcohol and dried urine.

"Joey? It's Leo. Leo Gelenian. Remember me from school?"

A tiny nod of the head.

"You doing okay?"

Another tiny nod.

"What happened, Joey?"

Joey shook his head and then turned to Leo. Dark, swollen eyes, blotched face and mucus rolling down from his nose. Leo could see a few gray hairs in the dark curls. A ruined, handsome boy of a man. Leo took a Kleenex packet out of his pocket and pulled out a couple of tissues. There was a momentary hesitation. Then Joey took the tissues and wiped his nose.

"Tell me what happened, Joey."

Joey shuddered and started to sob. "She was dead."

"Right, she was dead. Did you hit her, Joey?"

Joey whimpered and suddenly came alive, shaking his head side to side. "Can't remember. She was dead. No, no, no." He held his head in his hands, moaning. "Can't remember. Can't remember."

Leo put his hand on the man's shoulder. "Okay, okay, Joey. Take it slow."

Joey took a series of gasping, wet breaths, then slowly his breathing became heavy but more regular.

"So, you see anybody else around there?"

"Shadows." The big man's face was anguished. "Shadows."

"Uh, huh. Shadows." Leo leaned back "Did you see a person? I'm thinking a person, Joey, not shadows."

"No, no, no." Joey started to shake his head again. "Said before. Couldn't see."

"Okay. What were you doing there, anyway?"

"Going to catch the bus. Went to Vinnie's for some cash. Went to Vinnie's and going back to the House."

"Martin de Porres House by the Common in town?"

"Yeah, they gave me a room upstairs. Throw me out now." Joey's eyes looked frightened.

"Why would they do that—because you found a murder victim? I don't think so."

"Just get in trouble all the time. Buzzed again. They said I could do this thing," Joey stopped to inhale a long, moist breath, "but I can't do this thing." He was quiet for a moment and put his head in his hands. "Get so confused." He looked up, straight ahead. "She was good. A good person."

"You have her in school?"

"Yeah. Spike, Aurelius. The guys were mean to me, but not when she was around." A soft laugh. "Afraid of her."

"Were you afraid of her?"

"Yeah." He stopped, looking uncertain. "No. I don't know."

"Sometimes I was scared of her, Joey. Liked her, but you know...."

Joey looked up and nodded, "Scary sometimes, Leo."

"What way scary?"

"Strong." Joey closed his fist and shook it. "Strong."

"Yeah, she was."

Joey was quiet for a few moments, inhaling in deeply. "Let me carry the Blessed Mother statue one time—you know, in the May procession. All the music and all the pink and white flowers. The ones we made from paper. Remember that? You were there too."

Leo nodded and smiled.

Joey was calmer, almost dreamy now. "When things are really screwed up, I like to remember that. Then, I don't feel so bad." Joey started to softly sing the old hymn again. "*Our hearts are on fire. That title so wondrous fills all our desire. Ave, ave, ave, Maria, Ave, ave, Maria....*"

"That's all right, Joey. I remember it. We're going to take you to the station now. Okay?"

Joey nodded miserably.

Leo put his hand on the man's shoulder again. "I'll see you there."

Joey turned his face to Leo and said softly, like a child, "Okay, Okay."

Leo stepped out of the cruiser. He signaled for Victor and another policeman to get into the car to take Joey to the station.

"Go out the back gate and down that one way over there—Lloyd Street. Use the side door at the station. I don't want a damned media circus. He'll go into total meltdown and we'll get nothing from him."

Behind Leo, the blue flashers on the police cruisers broke the darkness. Powerful crime scene lights cast a cold illumination on the tableau in the schoolyard. Heaney kneeling by the body, the photographer documenting details, and the ghostly, white-suited crime techs taking measurements, bagging everything they could find.

At the center, a silent Sister Mary Aurelius lay with her secrets, black and bloody robes now dark wings spread out on the schoolyard. The winter sky that night was filled with stars, flickering votive candles over a tough old nun.

Joey's story didn't change at the police station later that night. He'd found the nun just after he left Vinnie's. As his lawyer, Danny Milano, pointed out, Joey was on his meds, had a reasonably good record at Martin de Porres, seemed fine at his brother Vinnie's, and had no reason to kill the nun. On the contrary, Joey really liked the nun. Finding the body of his old teacher, of course, had knocked him seriously off balance, and he wasn't at his best when he was found with the body.

The lawyer sat back in his chair. "Sure, Joey was acting crazy," he said, stretching his arms to the side in appeal. "He's sensitive. He gets upset. Who wouldn't?" Milano sat back in the chair and hit the table with the flat of his hand for emphasis. "But Joey just found her body when he was taking a shortcut through the schoolyard to get the bus. I don't know how you could even consider Joey a person of interest."

But that was the term they did use for Joey. Not a *suspect* but a *person of interest*, who could be very helpful to the investigation. Someone they wanted to stick around. Someone everyone would assume was the suspect.

Father Hanrahan called the Saint Jude's Halfway House across town and somehow got Joey a room in the crowded facility. Leo saw Joey's brother Vinnie give the priest a grateful look. He could never bring his loopy brother, a "person of interest" in the murder of a beloved nun, back to stay at his house with the kids. His wife would bar the door, as she should.

As Joey's brother, his priest, his lawyer, and the Malford City detectives discussed what was to be done with him for now, Joey Mucci sat staring into space, gently trembling.

CHAPTER 3

till aching from a restless night's sleep in the green armchair under her travel shawl, Rosaria pulled her gray Mercedes coupe out of the Trinity Wharf garage into a light morning fog. Traffic never really went away in Boston, but this morning it moved smoothly along Commercial Street as she drove toward the Charlestown Bridge.

To Rosaria's left, the North End—Boston's treasured and heavily gentrified Italian enclave—was in full morning swing. Double-parked cars clogged Hanover Street as drivers ran in and out of bakeries and small shops to do quick errands. Old men, some with Frank Sinatra hats, sat chatting at iron tables outside *caffe* bars, collars turned up against the winter cold.

Rosaria rode in a sheath of silence. No NPR, no music. Just silence. She drove over the locks and dams of the Charles River and past the jumble of Charlestown on her right, topped by the Bunker Hill Monument and the steeple of Saint Mary's church. Another rough neighborhood, this time Irish, rediscovered and gentrified.

She cut through East Somerville's crowded blocks of triple-deckers and small shopping malls bordering Route 93, veered off onto Route 28, and crossed the placid grayness of the Mystic River before diving into the exuberance of Wellington Circle with its multiple lanes, complicated turnoffs, confusing lights, and combative Boston drivers. Her sleek car negotiated the rapids smoothly, exited on the other side of the Circle, and entered the city limits of Malford.

Malford, her hometown that had always felt too small for her, a place where she hadn't been able to breathe. Senior year, Rosaria's high school boyfriend had given her a gold cross on a delicate chain, the customary gift that in those days preceded an engagement ring and the life that would follow. For reasons she couldn't understand at the time, Rosaria's throat had constricted and she had started to cry uncontrollably. Stunned and hurt, the boy had left without speaking and never called again. Later that week Rosaria applied to college in New York.

A weak winter sun had emerged by the time Rosaria reached Malford Square, the light now a watery gray. She spotted the new French Connection shop opposite City Hall, and thought perhaps she could see Nuncie's dark blond hair through the large front window. Faintly embarrassed to be driving the expensive car she'd bought on impulse after a good bonus year into her old neighborhood, Rosaria pulled the Mercedes into a parking place around the block behind Malford Trust. Aurelius would have given her the business about this car, and rightly so.

The French Connection was a bright, fresh presence in the city square with its patchwork of establishments. Variety stores with oversized advertisements for lottery tickets and the Keno game, prepaid cell phone cards, and Western Union services to Brazil and India. Small restaurants, dress shops, beauty salons, and insurance agencies. A CVS anchored the middle block and served as a modern general store with groceries and sundries, along with prescriptions and over the counter medications.

And nail salons, a perplexing number of nail salons. An abundance of nail salons seemed to be a signature of commercial districts in struggling old cities. *Why was that?* Rosaria wondered. Perhaps lavishly colored acrylic nails made everything else easier. You could look down and get a sweet little lift seeing those fine, bright tips, maybe with a flag or flower design, when you were riding a crowded, overheated bus to work.

Rosaria walked into The Connection, chilled from the winter air in spite of her fur-lined coat. One side of The Connection was devoted to fragrant cheeses, wines, and a selection of gourmet delicacies. Even in her distracted state, Rosaria wondered who frequented this new shop and how it survived in Malford. Somebody clearly didn't do his demographic market research here. But then how to explain the knot of customers already in place in front of the counter? Fascinating.

The other side of The French Connection offered coffee, croissants, baguettes, and pastries. The rich, restorative smells made her feel somewhat better. In the center of the shop, customers sipped their coffee at small marble-topped tables and looked out long, ornate windows at the activity in the Square.

Through the crowd, Rosaria saw Nuncie at a table across the shop and caught her eye. Nuncie put down her coffee cup and rose. The two women embraced with all the unsaid words of a long friendship and shared grief, Rosaria inclining her tall frame to wrap her arms around her petite friend. Then, they both took a deep breath as Rosaria took off her coat and sat down.

"How're you doing, honey?" asked Nuncie.

"Lousy. And mad, goddamned mad." Rosaria looked away, annoyed, as she felt her face redden and her eyes start to tear up. Nuncie nodded, and reached over to cover Rosaria's hand for a moment.

After a while, Rosaria looked up and squared her shoulders. "And you. How are you feeling? You're good for another week, right?"

Nuncie had been diagnosed with her cancer eighteen months before, and when Rosaria wasn't traveling, she kept Nuncie company during treatments at Massachusetts General Hospital. Though Nuncie refused to talk about the disease or her treatment in more than the sparsest terms, the steady river of that dark reality coursed under every conversation and exchange the two friends had. Today, Rosaria couldn't help but note her friend's further weight loss and faintly yellow skin.

"Fine. Good for another week." Nuncie didn't meet Rosaria's eyes as she spoke, but glanced out the large window of the shop. "Oh, look. The in-crowd arrives at City Hall."

Rosaria regarded her friend for a moment, admiring her gift for leaving behind uncomfortable personal topics. Then, she followed Nuncie's gaze out the shop's window toward the entrance to City Hall.

A black Cadillac Escalade with tinted windows had pulled to the front of the Hall. Out of the passenger seat, Monsignor Owen McDermott emerged, crisp in a tailored black suit with only a camelhair scarf around his neck and leather gloves to ward off the winter cold. A heavyset, dandyish Roger O'Toole, Director of the Malford Housing Authority, carefully angled his surprisingly dainty feet to avoid ice patches as he climbed out from the back seat.

And from the driver's seat, Malachy Sullivan of Claddagh Properties emerged in a brown barn jacket and Burberry scarf. Sullivan hopped out of the car and gracefully negotiated the mounds of snow along the sidewalk, reaching back once to take the Monsignor's arm and steady the older man on the icy walkway.

"Shouldn't Monsignor be ministering to his parish right now?" Nuncie asked, leaning her face on her hand as she looked out the window.

"Don't think he gets bogged down in messy situations, at least that's what I've heard."

"From who? Aurelius?" Nuncie smiled.

"She was always a good judge of character."

Rosaria felt a hand on her shoulder and turned to see Bridie Callahan in a French Connection smock. A sweet girl getting past her prime in a life of poor choices. Bridie gave Rosaria's shoulder a squeeze. "So sorry about Spike, Rosaria. I know you were close. Like a second mother."

"Thanks, Bridie. Yeah, it is hard." Rosaria reached up and held Bridie's hand for a moment.

It was true. Rosaria's loving and older adoptive parents, gone now, had been a tough fit for the child she had been—a bright, too active girl. "A handful" was how the neighborhood described Rosaria in those days. "Who do you think you are, missy?" her mother had exploded in exasperation, on the occasion of Rosaria's unauthorized solo bus trip to Boston "to see the park" when she was in fourth grade. A Boston police officer finally found her sitting on a bench with several amiable homeless people near the Frog Pond.

Rosaria still felt the guilt of these memories weighing on her. For everything she'd put her poor, good, and loving parents through as a child. But, it was her solo trip to Boston that brought Sister Mary Aurelius, one of the younger nuns at the Immaculate, into her life. Sister had received permission then from Rosaria's distraught parents to take the bold and curious child with wild curls under her wing, to see if she could help. And it was there that the girl had flourished and found her real emotional home.

Rosaria stayed close to the nun her entire life. Recently, Aurelius had told Rosaria that they had had enough talks over the course of her life that Rosaria would always know how Aurelius would feel about an issue, even after the nun was gone. Rosaria remembered a sense of deep panic when she'd made that comment. Of course, Aurelius was getting old and wouldn't be around forever, but Rosaria had almost lost her breath at the time.

"Look at Sullivan's car with the tinted windows," Nuncie commented. "Like he's in the Secret Service or something. I thought they were illegal."

"Nothing's illegal for Malachy Sullivan," Bridie said. "Can't you see where he parked? Mayor's spot." She put her hand on her hip. "Tell you a funny story." Bridie drew in her breath before she continued, preparing to tell a good anecdote. "So, my cousin Claire says her neighbors complained the other week that his damned monster car takes up nearly half their street when he parks there. People couldn't get by. The streets over in Chelsea can be so narrow, you know."

"Ridiculous car," commented Nuncie.

"Well, yeah, but so when Claire marches out to tell him to get his damned car out of the way, they start talking, he turns on that charm and, get this, she ends up moving *her* car back so that he can park in *her* driveway. 'He's really not a bad guy' she says," Bridie threw her hands up and gave a short laugh. "That man has the touch."

"Guess so. A smooth one, chock full of it—always was," Rosaria said.

"So, anyway, what can I get you?" Bridie asked.

"A large black with two shots of espresso."

"Well, that'll get you going now, won't it? Okay, dear. Be right back."

There was a brief silence as Bridie went for the coffee. Rosaria rubbed her hand across her forehead, her eyes closed. "What's going on, Nunce? I don't believe this. Joey Mucci?"

"I know. He was always off, but I never thought he could do anything like this." She shrugged. "Happens, I guess."

"Yeah, it happens. Does he live with his brother? I'm not up on things anymore."

"God no, Vinnie's wife would never have him around. You know how it goes. And he's a big man—kind of scary when he gets that dark look. They tried to get him help and set him up with jobs, but nothing worked out. He's mostly at Martin de Porres House these days. Comes out sometimes to hit Vinnie up for a couple of twenties when the wife's not home. Someone saw him sleeping on the grates in back of the library at Copley Square a couple of months ago, before he got the room at the House. Breaks your heart."

Rosaria gazed out the long windows of the shop, lost in thought. When she turned back to Nuncie, she saw her friend looked preoccupied, hesitating before speaking. "What's up?"

Nuncie shrugged. "Maybe nothing. Just remembered something when I was on my way here. Something was going on with Aurelius."

"What do you mean—something was going on with Aurelius?" Rosaria frowned.

Nuncie put her coffee cup down and leaned forward. "So, I went to the McCarthy wake the other week. Mrs. McCarthy. You remember Dara McCarthy—the guy who disappeared on a trip to Alaska years ago? Anyway, his mother. So sad."

Rosaria nodded impatiently, rotating her index finger to tell Nuncie to get to the point.

"So, Jamie was there." Sister Katherine James—Jamie to old friends. "She told me something had been really bothering Aurelius. I didn't know if it might have been private with her family, maybe old regrets. Jamie thought this was different, but Aurelius wouldn't say any more about it."

"Any hint?" asked Rosaria.

"No, Jamie sensed it was something heavy, though. She just couldn't get Aurelius to open up except to say she had one last mission to complete."

"One last mission?" Rosaria knitted her brows. "One last mission? What's that about?"

"Jamie didn't know. Aurelius wouldn't say any more. You know how closed up she could be when she didn't want to talk about something."

Rosaria felt a sharp pang. If she'd been in touch with Aurelius in recent weeks, she certainly would have shared whatever this was about. Knowing this was almost a physical pain in Rosaria's chest. She'd been so causal about letting the days and weeks go by without talking to Aurelius. And even then, such superficial phone conversations—hardly worth the time. She should have made the effort to drive up to the Motherhouse when she was back in Boston, taken the old nun to lunch, or maybe on a ride to the beach or back to Malford. Just have a cup of coffee with her and really talk about important things, things that mattered. Or just sat with her, even if they didn't talk. Now, she was gone. No way to make it up to her. God, she wished she could make it all up to her, but she'd missed her chance. All too late now.

She looked up to see Nuncie reading her face. "Stop it, Ro. Stop it right now. You were very faithful to her. Don't go down that rat hole. There's nothing you could've done."

A long sigh and a pause. "You don't suppose whatever was bothering her has anything to do with what happened?" Rosaria asked.

"Why would you jump to that?"

"You never know. You just said she had a mission. The police should be aware of this."

"What for? They'll blow it off, and they'd be right to. I just thought you should know about it."

"Let's let the police decide about it." Rosaria started to pull her things together. "You can to talk to Leo Gelenian. Tell him what Jamie said and, while we're there, we can find out from him what's going on with the investigation."

"What the hell is Leo going to do with a comment like that?" Nuncie paused. "And as for getting the inside story about what's going on," she stopped again for a moment before continuing, "why would he tell us? We're not family, Ro."

Rosaria stared at Nuncie without speaking.

"Okay, okay." Nuncie touched Rosaria's hand apologetically. "You're as good as family to her, but I don't know if they'd understand that."

"Finish up and let's go."

Leaning over his desk, Leo gave Rosaria and Nuncie a cursory glance before turning back to an open folder. "Thanks for stopping by, ladies, but we have to make it quick. Case review in five minutes," he said.

After the *ladies* part, Rosaria stopped in the doorway and, without speaking, stood staring at Leo through narrowed eyes. Leo looked up and, with a raised hand acknowledging his gaffe, gave a small, conciliatory smile. "Come in, come in."

Detective Sergeant Leo Gelenian's office was spotless and orderly, standing out in a row of small offices filled with untidy paper piles and stray, unwashed cups. The acrid smell of burnt coffee at the bottom of a neglected carafe in the nearby workroom penetrated the air. The only decorations in Leo's office were a calendar from the Armenian Cultural Society and an old picture of Aran and Mary, Leo's parents, and his sister Virginia, now a doctor living over in Watertown with her husband and two boys. A vision of a monk's cell flashed across Rosaria's mind. His office needed only a plain wooden cross on the wall to complete the image.

Leo gestured to two department-issued chairs in front of his desk before swinging his lanky body into an old, well-polished wooden swivel chair behind the desk. Rosaria recognized his chair as the one that Aran Gelenian, Leo's father, had used in his office at the shoe factory, where he was the accountant for years and where Rosaria had worked summers as a teenager. She remembered Leo visiting his father's office as a young boy, swiveling round and round in that chair.

Rosaria continued to stand, but had moved from the doorway and leaned against a sidewall. Nuncie sat in one of the two dull orange chairs in front of Leo's desk. Rosaria noticed that Leo had neatly repaired the cracked plastic on one chair with matching colored tape.

Leo's dark eyes were sober and impatient. "Ro, I'm sorry about Aurelius. I know you were close friends." Then he straightened his back. "I'm jammed right now with this. Nuncie said in her call that she had something I should know. So, let's go now. What's up?"

Rosaria spoke first. "Joey Mucci?"

"Well, yeah. Guy sitting there with the body. He has a history. That's what you'd expect, right?"

"Where is he?"

Looking uncomfortable, Leo dodged her question. "Hey, let's get around to what you have to tell me, huh?"

Rosaria gave him a hard look.

Leo paused and then relented. "Downstairs. He'll have to stick around as a person of interest. Father Hanrahan is arranging a room for him at Saint Jude's," Leo said. "Now, please, what've you got?"

Rosaria nodded toward Nuncie who turned to Leo. "Spike had talked to another nun up at the Motherhouse about something bad that she had to make right before she died. Something heavy on her mind."

Leo checked the cell phone on the corner of his desk. "Everybody has something they want to make right before they die, right? Anything specific?" Rosaria noticed his right foot was starting to tap a nervous, impatient tattoo.

"She wouldn't talk about it, but Jamie felt it was something serious." Nuncie paused. "Spike used the word *evil*."

Now Leo's foot was still. He looked at Rosaria and Nuncie. "Evil. Really? Used that word?" After a long moment, Leo's right foot started its nervous tapping again. He dropped his broad shoulders and spread his hands out. "Shit, you know her. That could be anything."

A frown of exasperation crossed the detective's brow. Rosaria could imagine Leo's thoughts. An open and shut case in his lap, with his superiors and the Mayor all over him to lock it in with Mucci. No time for conjectures and random peripherals. "Look—she was probably outraged about income inequality. Always out there on one cause or another. So we don't know, and now she's dead and can't tell us."

Rosaria flinched at his easy use of the word—dead. *Aurelius dead.* "Seems like something to check out, Detective," she said.

"Yeah, thanks for taking the time to tell me about this. Appreciate it." Leo gave them a quick smile and started to gather his things.

"Feels as if you should check it out soon while it's fresh."

"Hey, lady, you let me do my job," Leo snapped. Rosaria stiffened and her eyes widened as she looked at him. "We'll decide what needs to be checked out and when. And, sorry, this new information doesn't make the top ten on my to-do list right this minute." Rosaria and Leo stared at each other briefly before Leo yanked a long yellow legal pad in front of him, crooking his elbow as he poised to write with his left hand. "Okay, tell me which nun and where she is."

Rosaria paused before responding, then enunciated every word slowly, while she stared at Leo. "Sister Katherine James. Jamie from the Immaculate. Up at the Motherhouse in Maudsley. "

"Okay, we will talk to her, but not right now. Too much else to check out and tie down." Leo put down his pen and looked at them. "Look, we have to stay on point here today. An old nun that almost everybody loved has been murdered." Leo's voice was rising and his index finger punctuated each point on the desktop. "In a Catholic city, at the school everybody and his brother went to, including the Mayor and Chief Cullen. And me, for Chrissakes. Media, city hall, the archdiocese all over us. It's intense. We have zero time for side chases, especially with Mucci downstairs right now."

Leo stood. "Listen, I have to go. Thanks for this. Appreciate it," he said again, before ushering them out of his office.

Rosaria and Nuncie walked down the steps of the station. "Always thought he was a smart kid. When did he get so short-sighted and thick?" Rosaria said. "He should give more weight to Aurelius's conversation with Jamie. It was like he's dismissing her. Makes me furious." She slapped the iron railing on the brick stairs.

"They have a protocol, Ro. Let's face it, what I had from Jamie is pretty random, and Leo's right, she was probably talking about some social justice issue." Nuncie sighed, "They'll almost certainly have an open and shut case with Joey once they charge him. The best anyone can probably hope for is an insanity plea. No one will argue with that."

Rosaria stopped on the sidewalk and faced her friend. No one would argue with that, but it didn't make it right. "That's the way it'll probably roll out. But someone should follow up on Spike's comments. I need to know, just even for myself, what was bothering her. I'm going up to talk to Jamie."

The two women moved to the side to let a group enter the police station. Nuncie shivered in the cold and pulled up the collar of her fur coat. "Seems like the wrong time to be asking people questions when the police have their own investigation going on."

"Well, there's no investigation going on up at the Motherhouse right now, and maybe somebody should be checking that out."

"Don't do other people's jobs for them, Ro."

Rosaria was looking at her watch. "I will if they won't. Look, I have to go pick up Archie at Bronson's now."

She ignored Nuncie's eye roll at the mention of Bronson's name. No love lost there. She wished she'd listened to Nuncie and, yes, Aurelius, before she made the leap with Bronson Fuller. Not one of her better decisions. Early in their marriage, Bronson, an economist and scholar of some repute, had been enchanted by what he'd called the "spunkiness" of this bright, beautiful girl from a shoe factory town. That was until the spunkiness had turned to drive and matured into professional successes that sometimes competed with his own. Then, not so enchanted. Their heavy schedules had allowed the marriage to limp along for years until they finally dealt with the inevitable and officially divorced, held together now only by a small white dog they both loved.

These days, the ever youthful-looking Bronson, with his prodigious charm and adorable shock of straw-colored hair, lived in a South End brownstone with a succession of attractive, accomplished—but not too accomplished—youngish women, the latest of whom would brightly greet Rosaria when she picked Archie up. Lisa or was it Alyssa? DeCordova or the Museum of Fine Arts?

Rosaria looked up and turned to Nuncie. "Why don't you stay at Sevi's tonight?" she asked. Nuncie's brother Sevi ran the DiStephano family bakery across from the Immaculate Conception school complex. "I'll come by about nine tomorrow. We can be up at the Motherhouse around ten. I'll call Jamie to tell her we're coming."

"Who said I was coming with you?" Nuncie gave Rosaria a sharp look.

"Pick you up at nine." Rosaria smiled.

"Shit."

CHAPTER 4

eo Gelenian and Monsignor McDermott faced each other from two heavily upholstered armchairs in the rectory parlor. "Oh, Sister had strong opinions, God rest her soul, and we had our differences," Monsignor said. "The woman could exaggerate the smallest thing, and could pick a fight on a dime. A pugnacious woman. Yes, that's the word. Pugnacious."

Leo mused that the cleric had always looked like a movie version of a statesman—maybe an ambassador or a prime minister. There was that distinguished mane of silver hair, just a bit too long and swept back, and the aquiline, patrician nose. But then there was the mouth with its strong, crooked teeth. Teeth that suggested a certain kind of childhood. Now, one could see the barely visible thin braces of late-in-life orthodontics. It was hard for Leo to imagine that such thin strips of metal could contain the power of those teeth.

Yes, Monsignor McDermott had stopped into the Irish-American that afternoon, but only briefly, just to say grace and to bless Dot and Tom and their family. Great family. No, he didn't see Aurelius leave—and he couldn't imagine why she'd go off to the Immaculate by herself. Of course, at that age, they tend to have the hardening of the arteries and all. They get confused about things.

Leo looked up from his notes. "What kind of things would Sister exaggerate, Monsignor?"

"Oh, you know—everything." He waved his hand in the air. "The time she raised a ruckus over that new development up near the Middlesex Fells because it was too close to some little swamp. Or the time she said straight out that I was anti-Semitic. I think I made some comment about the number of Hebrew teachers and students at Malford High. That's not anti-Semitic, is it, Leo?"

"Some might think so, Monsignor," said Leo. He thought it likely that many of the priest's older parishioners were comfortable with these casual bigotries.

The monsignor leaned back in his chair and gave Leo a sour look. "Well, it wasn't. You sound as bad as her. You people."

Leo knew Aurelius was not Armenian, so that he assumed the Monsignor's "you people" was referring to troublemakers in general, not their racial grouping.

"Can you think of any reason why anyone would want to harm Sister?"

The priest took a long breath and responded slowly with exaggerated patience. "God, no. Not with deliberation. Sister could be an extremely difficult woman, and she caused a good deal of unnecessary trouble in her day. I can't say we ever got along—quite the contrary. God knows, I personally tried with her many times, but she was just such a fractious personality, it was impossible. Would anyone actually murder her for all that? No, I don't think so. It seems to me this was random violence—a frenzy of rage from an unstable man. Nothing to do with Sister herself."

"You think Joey Mucci is capable of this?"

"Of course, what else would I think?" Monsignor McDermott steepled his long fingers. "He's a deeply troubled man. Again, I doubt that he had anything against Sister, though some might, but I can see how he'd go off enough to do her in. Everyone thought that man was harmless. I didn't. I always thought there was something inside him that would explode."

Leo shifted in his seat, and his eyes caught two white boards on the sidewall. Looking closer, he could see that one was tracking the combined standardized scores for the boys' high school, with a satisfying upward trajectory. Rows of college decals and names on the second whiteboard recorded college admissions. Boston College and Holy Cross dominated the list, with a smattering of other names: Stonehill, Merrimac and Saint Mike's, and Saint Anselm's. There was one entry for Harvard—Edmund Devaney—the pride of the parish. Red stars punctuated the names of boys with scholarships—almost the entire list.

Leo saw the Monsignor's face soften as he followed Leo's gaze to the board. "We've come a long way. It's a pretty good-looking record, isn't it?"

"Yes. It is, Monsignor. You've done good work there." Leo knew of the priest's dedication to the boys' parish high school, separated years ago from the rest of the Immaculate complex. The high school had a strong reputation for academics and college placements. Monsignor McDermott had a right to be proud.

"A special interest of mine, Leo. You know, I take a group every year on the college tour." The priest smiled broadly.

Leo remembered that and the fact that, for some reason, his parents would never let him go on those special little trips, college or otherwise.

"We all pile into the Claddagh Properties van that Malachy Sullivan gave us and off we go. But so much more needs to be done to get these boys where they belong. We're raising the money now for more science faculty, a new chemistry lab, maybe a robotics team. I know we can compete with the best if we have the resources."

The priest put his hands on his knees and leaned toward Leo. "I know what it's like for many of these boys. They haven't had the advantages. Malachy understands that as well. That's why he's so generous. He was one of the boys who pulled himself up. His family lived in public housing. Had nothing, as my family had nothin'. Then, as I say, with just that little extra help, he pulled himself up through sheer hard work and will." The Monsignor's jaw moved slightly forward. "Level the playin' field. That's all we want, Leo." He sat back in the chair, pulling on the cuffs of what looked to Leo like a very well-cut suit, nodding to himself. "To level the playin' field."

Leo noticed the dropped g's, the tiny slips of a rougher accent. An accent tamed and refined over the years, but ready to crawl out when the Monsignor let his guard down, when he was excited.

"A few didn't take the college route. You remember Pete Blanchette. He had a scholarship to Holy Cross, but he decided not take it. Went right into the Marines after graduation and today he's a lobsterman up in Gloucester. An honest living, but what a shame. Bright boy. Good head on his shoulders." The Monsignor paused then and continued more deliberately.

"But, you know, about Aurelius. She really didn't understand those boys at all—especially Malachy and Dara McCarthy. Aurelius always saw something where there was nothing. She could be twisted like that."

Leo remembered Dara McCarthy and Malachy Sullivan. He thought Aurelius understood those boys quite well.

The priest chuckled. "More than once I had to stand up for the boys. McCarthy, God love him, you probably know he disappeared on a fishing trip to Alaska. Very sad, we don't know where he is. But Sullivan, he's a brilliantly successful businessman and citizen."

"Yes, that's what they say."

Monsignor McDermott gave Leo a wintry smile as he stood and strode to the door. "Okay, Leo. You have everything you want now? I think we can bring this to a speedy conclusion, sad as it is. The Cardinal has called the Mayor, you know."

Leo knew this from Chief Cullen. He could feel an intense hierarchical pressure to get this ugly murder case wrapped up. That meant Mucci.

"You shouldn't delay putting that poor man away, Leo, before he hurts anyone else." He nodded to himself with a set jaw.

"We still don't know if he did this, Monsignor. He says he just found the body."

Holding the door to dismiss Leo, the priest said, "Take my advice and do what needs to be done, and quickly."

Those words would echo in Leo's mind more than once in the coming weeks.

CHAPTER 5

osaria looked over at Nuncie. Face still that menacing yellowish cast, but a certain rosiness today. Maybe a little makeup, maybe a little excitement in spite of herself. "Your color looks good today."

"Shut up."

The Mercedes was a silvery fish in the restless school of cars headed north on Route 128. In the car, the two women rode without talking, each lost in her own thoughts. A stone of sadness had lodged in Rosaria's chest. Not a smooth stone from the beach, rounded and buffed by waves and time. No, this was a piece of raw granite from one of the quarries in Rockport. Heavy and jagged, cutting when she breathed, when she thought.

Nuncie broke the silence. "Spike ever give a thought to recruiting you? Not that she'd ever even try with me—lost cause."

"Oh, she mentioned it once or twice. Wasn't for me. She was good about it even when I left the church in college. Just said that I was always in her prayers and left it alone."

Rosaria glanced in the rearview mirror, and started to move into the passing lane. A red BMW well behind her gunned its motor and sped up, cutting her off. She moved quickly to right the car and avoid another vehicle coming from behind in her own lane.

"Did you see that idiot?" Nuncie hit the dashboard with the palm of her small hand. "Jesus Christ." It took Nuncie several miles before she recovered her equilibrium, though Rosaria murmured only a soft "jerk" as she righted the car.

Nuncie settled in again and looked over at Rosaria. "I wonder why she went into the order herself. Sharp as a tack. She could have done anything."

Rosaria had asked Aurelius that question several times, but never had been given a direct answer. "Not sure. Born before her time, I guess. In her generation, she would have been some senior guy's really sharp executive secretary, when she should have been running the place. But nuns were different. They could get an education, they had important work, and they had some stature in the community. Not a bad choice for a smart woman in those days."

As Rosaria told Nuncie some of Aurelius's history as she had been told it, she felt a heaviness. So hard to be talking about her mentor's well-lived and generous life. All past.

Aurelius had been born Mary Agnes Burke into a working class family in Lowell, the oldest of five. Mary Agnes's mother died young and her father needed her to run the house. So, as a young girl herself, Mary Agnes ran the house and raised her brothers and sisters. The Sisters of Jeanne d'Arc had always helped in those hard days when Mary Agnes and her father were struggling to keep the family together. Mary Agnes never forgot that and in her early twenties, feeling the call herself, she joined the order.

Nuns then had to choose a saint's name when they took their perpetual vows. Mary Agnes took Aurelius, the name of the bishop of Carthage in the early days of the Church and a friend of Saint Augustine. The order was pleased with Mary Agnes's unusual choice and approved the name.

But Aurelius told Rosaria the real reason she chose the name was because she was an admirer of Marcus Aurelius, the Roman emperor and Stoic philosopher, whose *Meditations* she'd read and appreciated. Her favorite quote had been, *Don't be put off by the criticisms and comments that may follow; if there is something good to be done or said, never renounce your right to it.* Rosaria thought about how much that motto had influenced her own life under Spike's guidance. How much it was guiding her even now in her search for answers.

"Hey, do you have any decent music in here?" Nuncie examined the car sound system controls.

"Turn on Sirius." Soft jazz soon filled the car.

Rosaria turned briefly to Nuncie. "Hey, apropos of nothing, but why do they keep referring to her in the papers as *an elderly nun*? She only had...what? About fifteen, sixteen years on us."

"Well, that would make her old, honey. We're no spring chickens. Besides, she dressed old, wore the old-fashioned habit an all."

"I know."

"Her armor against the world." Nuncie gave Rosaria a wry grin.

Rosaria smiled in return and nodded. "Yeah, maybe so."

Traffic slowed for an accident near the Route 1A exit. As they got closer to the scene of the accident, they could see the red BMW had been taken out by an Ipswich clam truck. The BMW driver was pacing in the grass behind the barrier, gesticulating with his arms and yelling into his cell phone while his car smoked on the side of the road. The clam truck looked unscathed, the driver leaning casually on the cream and blue truck, taking a cigarette break.

"Ah, there is justice in the world." Nuncie smiled and settled comfortably in her seat for the rest of the ride.

———

Years ago, a devoted Catholic dairy farmer had decided that when he got too old to farm, he would not sell his seaside fields, sprawling house, and barn in Maudsley to developers. "They'll just ruin it," he said to himself. Instead, he'd give it all to the Sisters of Jeanne d'Arc to serve as their Motherhouse and retirement home. Under the agreement, he would live in a small cottage on the property under their care until his passing. And so, in 1954, he did.

Now, the long parlor window of the Motherhouse reflected Rosaria and Nuncie as they walked up the circular gravel driveway. Rosaria slowed her steps for Nuncie and stopped once to inhale the rich scent of long harvested hay mixed with damp salt air. "Glorious," she murmured. The two women didn't speak as they approached the heavy wooden doors of the Motherhouse and rang the bell. A young novice came to the door and, after quietly greeting them, ushered them into a front parlor where Sister Katherine James waited.

Rosaria noticed Sister Jamie closing another button on her heavy navy blue cardigan before she rose to greet them. Convents were always kept cold, to save money on heating. Being familiar with the frugal strategies of the Sisters, Rosaria expected that the closed areas of the Motherhouse, where the nuns lived privately, were kept warmer in compassion for the age of the retired nuns like Jamie. These public areas, the parlors and the formal dining room, were, however, left very chilly in the winter months unless guests were expected. Now, she could hear the house's ancient heating system coming noisily into gear. Sister Jamie must have received permission to turn the thermostat up for her guests in this visitor parlor, but Rosaria thought the area was unlikely to warm up until long after she and Nuncie had left the building.

The Motherhouse parlor at Maudsley had the furniture polish smell that the old convent at the Immaculate used to have. The same heavy drapes on the windows, a kind of olive green velvet meant to protect the furniture and rugs from the sunlight. Here, the curtains were tied back to take in the pleasures of the broad view and coastal light, leaving the rugs and furniture to fade as they would.

Pictures from the Immaculate convent hung on the parlor walls. Rosaria faced the familiar Assumption of the Blessed Virgin in a heavy gold frame, with Mary gazing blissfully upward, surrounded by saints and angels, as she ascends on a bright cloud into the heavens. To Mary's right, the Sacred Heart in which Jesus directs, with melancholy reproach, attention to his open chest where a bleeding heart lays encircled with thorns.

"Hello, girls." Jamie rose and hugged each of them. "Please sit." She gestured to the parlor chairs and pulled a small table holding hot tea and ginger cookies closer to them before she resumed her seat. She smiled in apology when neither woman moved to take off her coat in the chilly room.

As she settled in her own chair, Rosaria took a discreet, sidelong glance at the statue of a swooning Saint Maria Goretti, virgin and martyr, dominating one corner of the parlor. In Rosaria's youth, the statue had stood in an alcove at the top of the wide staircase of her school. Jamie didn't look up from the tea table when she said, "Some of the older sisters find the artwork in this parlor comforting. Our young sisters prefer the artwork in the other rooms."

Rosaria laughed. "How do nuns do that? Know what we're up to without even looking at us?"

"One of the first things we learn, dear," Jamie responded, and looked up with a gentle smile after she'd poured them each a cup of tea. "A special class in surveillance. The NSA could learn from us."

Rosaria could see that the nun had dressed carefully today for her visitors with a smart navy skirt, white blouse, and vest. And, of course, the heavy navy winter cardigan. A tiny dab of clear nail polish, used to stop a run, was visible near the heel of the black stockings worn with heavy, orthopedic shoes. From under close-cropped gray curls topped with a short navy veil, Sister Katherine James looked up at her guests now with round, child-like blue eyes behind wire-rimmed glasses. Those eyes, Rosaria knew from experience, disguised the force of the nun's character to the casual observer. Rosaria suspected that Sister had always found this miscalculation helpful.

"I know how hard this is for you both—especially for you, Rosaria. You were so close. The sisters are in shock too. Sister Bernard thinks it's her fault for not minding Sister Aurelius better that day at the Daleys' party."

"No one minded Spike," commented Nuncie. "She couldn't be minded."

"Well, that would be true, I suppose."

Rosaria picked up her tea and took a sip before turning toward the nun. "Jamie, when you and I talked last night I mentioned that Nuncie told the police about Aurelius's last conversations with you."

"Yes, dear, I'm glad to talk with them if they call, but, to be honest, I don't know what else I can tell them." She clasped her hands tightly in her lap, shaking her head slightly. "Sister was just so impassioned when she talked about the task she had before her, something she called her *last mission*, that I was concerned.

"That's why I mentioned it to Nuncie at the McCarthy wake. I wish Sister had told me more, but she kept things close, you know. And stubborn. Holy Mother, was she stubborn. Like a dog on a bone when she had a mind of it. And she was fierce on something, whatever it was." The nun stopped. "I miss her terribly."

Rosaria reached out, touched the nun's hand lightly and said, "It's hard not to, Jamie. She was a special one. And, you know, I'm not sure if stubbornness is such a bad quality sometimes. You could call it by another name—maybe resolve." They all smiled and were momentarily distracted by some whispered chuckle somewhere, perhaps down the hall.

"Light years ahead of the rest of us too," Jamie said. "The Monsignor and the other sisters got so upset when Sister raised the possibility of women priests one day, and another time talked about the rights of gay Catholics, even questioning why they shouldn't be married in the Church." Jamie laughed. "Oh, the roof nearly came down on that last one. I'm embarrassed to think how narrow-minded we could be then.

"Of course, she drove the Monsignor crazy. It seemed to be her favorite pastime to challenge him. I tell you, we all miss that woman." Jamie's blue eyes glittered with something like mischief. The nun paused, fingering the buttons of her navy sweater. "You know, lingering too long in grief, in *selva oscura*, in the dark woods, can lead us into despair. Despair is a mortal sin, a deep bog in the dark woods that will suck us down. I pray against despair every day, but," she sighed, "I'm only a frail human being, old and weak, and this has nearly crushed me." The nun's chin trembled slightly.

"Yes, it's a hard one, Jamie," Rosaria said. She understood Jamie's warning about despair, but she herself couldn't seem to shake the heavy regrets she felt about Aurelius. Then, meeting the nun's eyes after some time, she said, "You know, Aurelius's last mission could have been around some social action. Remember how hard she fought that development they were going to put on the wetlands near the Middlesex Fells?"

Jamie burst into a long, high laugh. "Oh God, I do remember that, Rosaria. She had talked about chaining herself to one of the old swamp maples. She wasn't really serious, but Mother Superior was completely exasperated with her." The nun wiped her eyes. "You know, though, she made such a fuss that people got to talking and that development never happened, did it?"

"No, it never did. She always had impact." Rosaria felt a wave of pride for her old mentor.

"That's true." The nun reached out for Rosaria's arm. "But this mission was different, Rosaria. I knew her. This was different. This was bigger."

Bigger and perhaps more dangerous, thought Rosaria. As the women sat in silence for some moments together, Rosaria gazed through the long parlor windows at rolling brown fields sweeping down to sand dunes and the Atlantic in the distance. "This is beautiful property, Jamie. Heavenly."

Jamie hesitated. "Yes, Malachy Sullivan made the same comment."

"Malachy Sullivan. Was he here?"

"Yes, I was surprised to see him. He talked to Mother Superior, but she won't confide very much except to say that he's a man of faith, committed to the financial future of the order. Mother's a deep one, so I don't know if she really means that or if she's being a little sarcastic. It's always hard to tell." She paused, appearing to reflect before she continued. "Anyway, you know we've had some money issues. Monsignor McDermott apparently recommended that Malachy speak to us about his buying and developing the property here to help us out. I understand Mr. Sullivan may take over the Immaculate property too, by the way."

"I hadn't heard that," said Nuncie.

"No? I guess it's not public yet." Sister Jamie paused again. Rosaria waited as she watched Jamie's face. She could almost hear the whirr of calculation in the nun's mind, and then see her come to a halting decision somewhere in the vicinity of the old saying, *As well be hung for a sheep as for a lamb.*

"I'm not sure Mr. Sullivan wants it public. He plays things pretty close to the vest, if that's the way they say it." The nun gave them a coy smile. "He's certainly charming, though. And very handsome, don't you think, so tall with all that dark hair and that dimple in his cheek?"

Rosaria and Nuncie both laughed. "Jamie, I didn't think you noticed things like Malachy Sullivan's dimple. I'm shocked," Rosaria said.

The nun gave a small laugh herself. "Well, we are only human, dear." Then her face grew more serious. "But there's something about him. I don't know. Aurelius said it was a travesty for the Immaculate to fall into his hands, of all people."

Jamie looked out the window for some time. Rosaria was glad they'd made the trip to the Motherhouse. She could see the nun needed to talk to someone, someone with the history to understand, even at the risk of being indiscreet or sinking further into that deep, boundless bog of despair.

"And, God forgive me, I don't know if Mother Superior really feels Mr. Sullivan has our best interests at heart with our property here, but we do have some financial troubles. We haven't been well served by the advisors we had at one of the big investment houses. Perhaps we were naive, you know. We're thinking now that we should have some of the younger sisters study to become more expert in managing our small endowment ourselves.

"Anyway, we've joined the Benedictines in a suit against this investment firm that both orders used, but that will take years to settle. Those big companies have so many lawyers and they're so cold. I don't know how they sleep at night. Thankfully, the DiCenso firm has taken our case pro bono. Meantime, we have big ongoing expenses—this place, our missions. It's a struggle. I know Mother Superior has to consider every option." She sighed and looked at Rosaria and Nuncie. "It's not easy."

"I wish there was something we could do to help, Jamie," Nuncie said.

"Thank you, dear. We're in good hands with Mr. DiCenso."

"I know him," Nuncie said. "I'll give him a call. And you have a lot of loyal and generous alums, Sister. Perhaps they should know about this situation. I'll connect with a few."

"That would be very kind of you, Annunciata." Rosaria saw her friend flinch slightly at the nun's use of the resplendent name Nuncie had been trying to escape for most of her life.

"My pleasure, Sister."

Rosaria started to button her coat. "Well, we'd probably better get going now, Jamie. I'm glad we came."

"Yes, I'm so glad you did too, dear. Your visit was a great comfort to me." Then, looking from Rosaria to Nuncie, she added, "Would either of you like to use the facilities before you go?"

Rosaria shook her head. "I'm good. Thanks, Jamie."

"I think I will," said Nuncie.

"Right down the hall to the left, dear."

When Nuncie had left and was some distance from the parlor, Jamie turned to Rosaria, her face grave. "I'm sorry about Annunciata, Rosaria. She doesn't look well at all."

"Thank you, Sister. She's not, but she's doing her best."

The nun nodded and then continued, a clear urgency now in her voice. "I wanted to talk to you alone, Rosaria." She put her hand on Rosaria's arm. "If I weren't an old nun tucked away up here, I'd find out why Sister was so upset about the Immaculate's falling into Malachy Sullivan's hands. I'd find out exactly what's happening with that property, and why it would be a travesty for him to get it." The nun stopped. "There's something there. I know there is."

Yes, I know there is too, thought Rosaria. *Yes, something there.*

Jamie continued, all business, looking hard at Rosaria. "But, most importantly, I'd find out what Sister's last mission was. It was so crucial for her. She burned with it, Rosaria. She burned with it."

Putting her head down, the nun smoothed her skirt. "You know," she looked up again with filled eyes, "I'd do that for Spike's sake."

Rosaria leaned back in her chair, her hands on her lap. She looked around the room at the holy pictures briefly before she turned back to the nun with a pensive smile and said, "Are you giving me an assignment, Jamie?"

Just then she thought she heard the clicking of a nun's rosary beads in the hall, but she knew she was mistaken. They didn't carry beads like that anymore. Only with the old black-robed habits. The sound reminded her of Aurelius, and she found herself turning to look, sure she would see her mentor standing there. She felt a pang of loss so sharp she had to force herself to take a slow breath.

"Oh, I wouldn't want to put it that way, Rosaria. But she wouldn't want us to just leave things, you know what I mean? She'd go after it. She'd want us to go after it. No need for the world to know that we are, but whatever is going on has to be addressed." The nun tightened her lips and nodded to herself.

"The police have an investigation, Sister."

"Oh, the police, the police," Jamie said in a testy voice, and waved her hand dismissively. "This needs something different. Someone who understood Aurelius enough to figure out what was driving her on her last mission. They won't give that any weight. It's not concrete enough. You know how they are."

Rosaria did think she knew how they were.

Jamie looked closely at Rosaria. "Aurelius picked up the gauntlet as an old woman." Her gentle blue eyes filled again. "I just hope she didn't pay a price for that. Do you think she did?"

"Oh, no, I don't think so, Jamie. Hard as it is to think about, it looks as if Joey Mucci went into a violent rage—God knows why—and Sister was in the wrong place. And, the secret of her last mission most likely died with her."

"I know the police would say that, Rosaria. But you should have been trained by us not take the first easy answer to a problem." The nun straightened her back. "And I, for one, don't want to believe her last mission died with her. You shouldn't either, of all people."

Rosaria gazed into the nun's eyes, now a little less innocent. "You're a hard woman, Jamie."

"I pride myself on that, dear." Jamie squared her shoulders. "Aurelius always used to tell us that Rosaria was the one to take care of business. Now I'm asking you to take care of business."

Nuncie could barely contain herself until after they said their goodbyes to Sister Jamie and were on the road.

"Son of a bitch," she muttered as they rode along Route 133, so agitated she was barely able to sit still in her seat. "What's Malachy sniffing around there for?

They have enough troubles as it is. And why is the Monsignor pushing him on the nuns?"

"I don't know," said Rosaria. "But let's be fair. Monsignor's probably being realistic, suggesting the nuns face up to their shaky financial situation. Malachy Sullivan would probably love to put acres of seaside townhouses in Maudsley. He'd make a fortune with those views, and a deal like that would solve all the order's financial problems. Ah," she grimaced, "but what a thought, desecrating that beautiful land."

"And getting the Immaculate complex too, probably with some federal funding under urban renewal. He's already in line to pick up the old shoe plant and the land around it. Of course, the Redevelopment Authority is stacked with his pals," said Nuncie, looking out the window as they passed the Maudsley creeks and marshes.

"Well, yeah, but he does nice work, Nunce. Not the worst outcome for those properties."

Nuncie snorted.

"I mean it. Someone has to develop these old complexes and you know he's done good quality projects. So, we don't all love him, but that's not the point."

Nuncie didn't respond.

Rosaria looked over at her friend. "Hey, you up for a little walk on the beach?"

A light winter wind blew on Good Harbor Beach and the tide was low enough to walk out to Salt Island if one were so inclined. Dogs of all sizes and breeds raced around Rosaria and Nuncie as they walked. There was something about a wide expanse of beach like Good Harbor that drove dogs into a happy frenzy. Their indulgent owners, smiles on their faces and collars turned up against the wind, strolled and threw the occasional tennis ball into the low waves. Then they watched as their charges crashed wildly into the icy water, returning triumphantly with the soggy balls and begging for them to be flung again.

"It bothers me to just drop whatever was bothering Aurelius. I'd like to check on a few things." Rosaria dodged a black lab barreling toward a thrown tennis ball.

"Stop it, Ro." Nuncie sighed heavily. Rosaria could see she was getting tired. "Leave something like that to the authorities. You're just going to get in their way and you don't know what the hell you're doing anyway. Always butting in." Then she smiled with the long memory of a childhood friend. "Who do you think you are, missy?"

"Why is everyone always asking me that question?" Rosaria gave a short, deep laugh and landed an affectionate, gentle punch on Nuncie's arm. "I'm a hungry woman, that's what I am. Let's eat."

A fox terrier raced by Rosaria in fruitless pursuit of a seagull. She wished then that Archie were with her on the wide beach instead of curled up in his doggie bed in Boston.

The Halibut Point Tavern was nested in a narrow red brick building near the waterfront. Dark and welcoming, the bar extended the length of the low-ceiled front room, which led to a small back dining area dominated by a stained glass window of swimming fish and the mounted shell of a giant gold lobster.

"To Aurelius." Rosaria raised her glass of Magner's hard cider, her voice almost drowned out by a crowd of locals arriving at the bar in the darkening winter afternoon. She and Nuncie touched their glasses. Nuncie's was filled with a good house red, which seemed to bring her color back. Rosaria watched her friend lean back in a worn wooden captain's chair. She knew Nuncie was only good for a couple of more hours before she should go back to her house and bed.

Rosaria lowered her glass, thought for a moment and then raised it again, looking at Nuncie. "To Aurelius's last mission."

Nuncie did not touch Rosaria's glass this time, but looked over to scan the blackboard menu on the brick wall across from their table. "I think I'll go with the grilled scallops and wasabi mayonnaise. And," she turned her eyes to Rosaria's, "Just for the record, I'm not signing up for any last mission."

CHAPTER 6

 alachy Sullivan extended his arm for a handshake. Then he gestured for Leo to have a seat in a green chair, welcoming him into his office. "What can I do for you, Leo?"

Leo felt a rush of envy as he sat in the deep chair, his palms feeling the softness of the leather. He looked around Malachy's office. A gas fireplace flickered under an antique marble mantel. A large scene of the Cliffs of Moher, deep in the mists of Ireland's Western shore, hung behind Malachy's wide, handsome desk. To the right of the painting hung an award for exemplary service and support from the Malford Boys Club, with a picture of Malachy and the Mayor.

Under the desk a large boxer bitch raised her tan head, on alert as Leo entered the office. Leo had heard Malachy rarely went anywhere without the dog.

An ornate globe stood in a heavy mahogany stand before tall windows over-looking a small park. He had seen the sign near the park's gravel path thanking Claddagh Properties for its upkeep. Leo thought of his own battered city-issued metal desk and grimy window overlooking the Department parking lot. He and Malachy went to school together, but their lives were so different now. Choices. All about choices.

Malachy had always had a certain talent. When Malachy had been named a *Boston Globe* Scholar-Athlete in high school his senior year, Leo had been tempted, as the earnest, envious, and skinny freshman he was, to write an anonymous letter to the *Globe* about Malachy's entrepreneurial initiatives involving pills. In the end, Leo had stifled the urge to write the letter as the sad, spiteful gesture that it would have been.

Over time, Malachy had graduated from selling packets and pills to real estate development, which had done well by him. His work refurbishing old buildings and complexes was well regarded, and Leo had to admit that Malachy brought much-needed energy to the old city of Malford. Hard as it was for Leo to accept, Malachy deserved his success.

"Mal, I'm stopping by to check on a few things. We're talking to everyone at the Irish-American the night Sister Mary Aurelius was murdered. I know you've given a statement to Detective Johnson, but I have a few questions myself. You're probably more familiar than most people with everyone who was there."

Malachy nodded. "I understand, Leo." Malachy sat on the sofa, leaning forward with his elbows on his knees. Malachy seemed a larger man than the sofa was designed to hold. Leo knew he had an inch or more on Malachy's height now but was annoyed to find that, after all this time, being near Malachy still made him feel like a short fifteen-year-old.

Across the room, the boxer rose and walked slowly over to Leo's chair, pressing her flat black nose against Leo's arm in greeting.

"She's just saying hello. Over here, Maisie girl." Malachy gave the dog a rough, affectionate rub as she turned to her master and thumped to the floor at his feet, her cordial brown eyes on Leo.

"Nice dog."

"Yeah, she was supposed to be a watchdog, but she's such a softie, I gave that up as a lost cause a long time ago. Now, she's just my pal. Right, girl?" The dog looked up and smiled at Malachy.

Malachy turned to Leo. "So, what would you like to know, Leo?"

"Well, the party at the Irish-American. Tell me, Mal, did you see Sister Mary Aurelius leave the party, or know of any reason why she might leave the party early?"

"Well, you know, it was pretty packed and, God, it was noisy. Dot and Tom have a crowd of friends and, between the two of them, an army of relatives." A smile crossed Malachy's face and then disappeared as he leaned back and spread his long arms across the length of the sofa back. "I never saw Sister leave and I don't know why she would. Maybe she was getting confused. Old people can wander like that."

"By all accounts, Sister didn't miss a beat and was still sharp."

Malachy raised his eyebrows. "I guess." Without waiting for an answer, he continued, "Imagine, killing an old nun. Then, I suppose he can't be held responsible for his acts. That guy has been gonzo for a long time."

"We haven't charged anyone with this murder, Mal."

"I know you haven't charged him yet, but look how you found him. I don't know what in God's name you're waiting for." Malachy stopped himself. "Well, I suppose you know what you're doing." Malachy's expression didn't look as if he thought Leo knew what he was doing. Leo was irritated to feel a flush of anger on his neck.

"We'd like to think so." Leo let a moment pass before he continued, trying to regain his equilibrium. "Did you happen to leave the party for some time yourself, or notice if any of the other guests did?"

"I never left the Irish-American, and I didn't see anyone else who did."

"Can you think of anyone who'd want to harm Sister for any reason?"

Malachy let out a long, exasperated breath and looked to the ceiling before responding. "Jesus, Leo, no. Who the hell would want to kill an old nun except a crazy person? Look, you already have the whack job in your hands. I don't know why you don't take care of him before he goes off again and hurts someone else." Malachy sank back into the sofa. "I heard you have him up at Saint Jude's. He should be locked up, not at some loosey-goosey halfway house. He's a danger to the community. What in God's name are you waiting for?"

"We'll make that call, but not right now." Leo rose from his chair. "Thanks for your time, Malachy."

The two men looked at each other for a moment, the tension palpable. Leo stood taller and widened his stance. Malachy's jaw tightened. He shook his head slightly. Leo could see how frustrating the pace of the investigation must be for Malachy. As a power broker in the community, he was used to taking the lead, calling the shots, making decisions quickly. He would have made short work of this case and had Mucci done yesterday.

"Anytime, Leo."

Leo stared at Malachy a beat longer than necessary, and walked to the outer office area. As he did so, he found Malachy's office manager, Dorothy Murdoch, sitting close to the door. Now, she looked down and fussed with two file folders as he passed.

All along the corridor to the elevator were paintings of sailing ships and ducks—mergansers. Not for the first time, Leo wondered about the relationship between the well-appointed offices of successful men and paintings of ducks. He could see the sailing ships, but he never got the part about the ducks. Maybe that explained why he was still sitting at a battered city-issued desk looking out a grimy window at a parking lot, and Sullivan had a soft green leather chair and a fireplace.

Leo saw Father Hanrahan exiting the crowded Dunkin' Donuts on Salem Street. The old priest wore a knitted, navy Red Sox cap with an improbable white pom-pom that bobbed as he negotiated the dirty, frozen snow and tried to balance his coffee and doughnut.

He pulled his car in front of a break in the snow bank and opened the passenger side window. "Want a ride, Father?"

Father Hanrahan raised one gloved hand holding a jelly doughnut and nodded. Leo leaned over to open the door of the car. The priest slipped his big frame into the front seat, deftly balancing his coffee with the doughnut in waxed paper on top.

"Give me a minute, Father. Have to get rid of this junk on the windshield," Leo said. Hopping out, Leo walked around the car and picked up a chunk of snow from the banking. After he'd rubbed both sides of the windshield with the snow, he stepped away from the cruiser to inspect his work. Then, he climbed back in and turned on the windshield wipers until the windows were clean. Satisfied, he took off his wet gloves, placed them on the floor of the back seat, and put on a dry pair of gloves from the side pocket. He turned to see the priest smiling at him as he sipped his coffee.

"You're a fastidious man, Leo."

"Just don't want glare coming off that coating of gunk. Besides, it looks grubby. Where're you coming from, Father?" Leo started the cruiser, and checked his side view mirror before pulling into traffic.

"Saint Jude's. Try to get there once a week." The priest took a dainty bite of his jelly doughnut and another sip of his coffee.

"Where do you find the time? Seems to me, you're doing everything at the Immaculate."

Leo couldn't remember the last time he'd heard of Monsignor McDermott leading a parish activity, at least since Father Hanrahan had showed up. It was as if he had gratefully dropped his responsibilities onto the back of an affable old donkey that had wandered into his yard. Then the Monsignor went off to do other, more interesting things than everyday pastoral work, which was apparently not to his taste. Now, the affable old donkey sat in Leo's cruiser, enjoying the simple pleasures of a sugared jelly doughnut with a hot cup of coffee.

"The Monsignor has a number of important commitments outside the parish, Leo," the old priest said. With his thumb, he skillfully turned the wax paper further down the side of his doughnut to take another bite of the pastry.

"Like what?"

The priest chewed thoughtfully for a moment before responding. "Well, he works with the staff at the Chancery on various archdiocesan matters. And he's active with the Mayor and the city council on a few committees and advisory boards. And, of course, there's his personal mission around academics and college admissions at the Catholic. I couldn't give you all the details, but it keeps him very busy." Father Hanrahan gulped his coffee and then, with obvious pleasure, hit the sweet jelly at the center of the doughnut with his next bite.

Leo kept his eyes on the road. "I guess." He knew that most people in the parish had decided the old priest was worth three of his boss, and Leo agreed.

Father Hanrahan lowered his coffee and doughnut to look at Leo. After some time, he said, "You probably know I lost my last parish, Leo."

Stopped at the light at the intersection of Salem and Main, Leo glanced over at the priest before turning his eyes back to the road. "Yeah, I heard."

"And you probably know why."

Leo nodded again.

"Yes, it's an open secret." The priest inhaled deeply, his shoulders slumping as he exhaled a long breath. "I've had my own struggles. Mine were—are—with the bottle. The priesthood can be very lonely, Leo, and there are a great many demands. Some of us are not always equal to it. That's why I understand the men at Saint Jude's so well. There but for the grace of God and all that."

His rheumy blue eyes met Leo's. "As for the parish duties, don't pity me, Leo. I know the score. How could I not? But it's a chance to run a parish again, to attend to the pastoral needs of these hard-working people. It's all I ever wanted to do. I'll take it all."

The light changed and Leo pulled across the intersection toward the Immaculate rectory. "Got it, Father." Leo stopped the car and touched the priest's arm. "And, you know, we're lucky to have you."

Father Hanrahan smiled softly. "Thank you, Leo. That means a great deal to me."

After a moment, Leo asked, "See Mucci at the House?"

"Yes, I did." The priest pursed his lips and looked down. "Wouldn't say he's doing great, but he's getting help from the counseling staff affiliated with Saint Jude's."

"I don't know, Father. Maybe he should be someplace more secure. He's not right. We're taking a chance here." Leo rotated his neck, still working out the stiffness that wouldn't seem to go away the last few days.

"Maybe so. None of us are totally right, Leo—but I'll give you that he's deeply troubled."

"Mentally unbalanced."

Father Hanrahan frowned. "I'm not a therapist—professionally anyway, but I'd say that man went through something that knocked him off kilter. It concerns me."

"Like what? He talk about it?" Leo leaned back against the door, waiting.

The priest shook his head and gave Leo a sharp look. "Normally, I wouldn't tell you if he did, Leo, even if he talked to me outside the bonds of confession. I'm a priest. People talk to me assuming I'm not going to be blabbing their business all around. That is, of course, unless there's a danger involved."

"Certainly is here," Leo commented.

"Yes, I'll give you that. There is. Well, in any case, I can tell you that I haven't had that conversation with him. Yet." He paused. "I'd like to think I have some modest amount of wisdom to offer after all these years in my profession, but if my guess on his past is correct, he probably would need more professional help than I could offer him."

The priest paused as he finished his doughnut and tucked the wrapper into his empty coffee cup. "Of course, though some feel he's not capable of it, I have to say it's very possible that Joey went into some terrible, dark fury and killed poor Sister Aurelius. I can sense that there's a good deal of rage bottled up in that man."

CHAPTER 7

eo knocked at the door, then removed his gloves and stuffed them in his coat pocket and waited for the door to open. "Appreciate your making time for this, Mrs. Rafferty."

"Oh, please. Call me Pearl, Leo. Mrs. Rafferty makes me feel ninety years old, for Chrissakes." She reached over to squeeze his arm lightly and stood back to let Leo in the door. Her lithe body still dressed in workout gear, Pearl pushed a yoga mat to the side of the hall.

Leo smiled. "Okay, Pearl."

"What do you want to know? Whatever any of us can do to help, we will. I never heard of such a thing—killing an old nun. I'll tell you, I'll never get over us finding her and Joey like that. I still wake up in a cold sweat at night." She rubbed her arms and shivered.

"I can imagine."

Pearl sat on the couch and gestured toward a nearby chair. "Sit down, Leo. You want a cup of tea or coffee? I have some of those Girl Scout cookies left. Too many. They snagged me as the cookie mother for Jeanine's troop again. It's the death of me. They're all stacked in the dining room. I try to be a good mom with volunteering with the fifth graders and all, but Jack and I don't need a houseful of Thin Mints calling our names." She laughed.

With her artless, open face and blond hair in a kind of bowl cut that Leo thought used to be called a Dorothy Hamill, Pearl Rafferty looked a little like a Girl Scout herself. "I'm good. Thanks."

"I don't know what else I can tell you about that night, other than what I've told Detective Johnson."

"People usually know more than they think they do, Pearl. That's why we go over things again and again. So, just bear with us. It's what we have to do."

Pearl nodded, sat up straighter, and closed her eyes as she spoke. "Okay, this is what happened. We were walking home from the Daleys' party and cutting through the Immaculate from Lloyd Street, when I heard someone singing in kind of a funny, high voice. You know that old hymn 'Immaculate Mary'?" She opened her eyes and Leo nodded. She closed them again. "I thought I was hearing things and so did Jack. But we went over to the girls' school where the sound was coming from and that's where we found Joey and Aurelius." She opened her eyes again. "And that's it. Aurelius was already dead. I saw no one, heard no one, except, like I said, Joey Mucci singing." She paused, and then asked, "Want me to talk about Joey more?"

"No thanks, Pearl. This time, I'd like to concentrate on the party a little more."

"Oh yes. I heard you were interviewing everyone about that. A long list at that party, Leo, and everybody was having a really good time, believe you me." Pearl winked at Leo.

"So I hear. Let's start with Sister again. Did you notice when she was gone or can you think of any reason she'd leave to go to the Immaculate grounds?"

"God, no. I can't for the life of me think of why she'd leave. I heard someone was saying maybe she was getting a little off, like a little demented, wandering off like that. But don't you believe those people, Leo. If they say that, they didn't know her. She was always sharper than most and still was." Pearl paused. "I'm not saying she was a saint. Not as bad as some of the other ones—she never knocked anybody's head on the blackboard or anything like that."

"That's true. She was okay." Leo smiled.

"I'll give you that she was quick with the ruler on the knuckles. You remember that when we had her." Pearl waved her hand in the air. "But, so what? You know, Leo, some people, they get their knuckles rapped when they're ten, and they whine the rest of their lives about some overworked nun with a class of fifty kids. I think they make half of it up just to entertain people or get some attention." Then, she softened a little. "Well, maybe there were some bad apples, that's the truth, but most of them were good women."

"Did you happen to notice when Sister Aurelius left the Irish-American, Pearl?"

Pearl shook her head. "Sorry, it was packed. Everyone was having a good time with the music and the dancing, catching up with old friends. I couldn't see where Jack was half the time."

Leo smirked. He wasn't sure, given Jack's girth, how anyone could lose him.

She looked at Leo sharply and grinned. "I know what you're thinking, Gelenian. Cut it out. The man's a mountain of goodness. Anyway, you could hardly see across the floor. It's like Francie Sullivan said, we should have had one of those new GPS tracking things for each other. She couldn't find Malachy anywhere."

Leo bit his lip. *Interesting.* "Is that so? I see. Well, it sounds like quite a party." He spent a few more minutes chatting with her about the party and then stood to leave. "Thanks for your time, Pearl. Have to go now. We'll be talking."

"Glad to help, Leo. Anything I can do." The woman paused. "I know there are those who would say you should put Joey Mucci away right now, but, like I said about Spike, it's people who don't know him, poor soul. I know him. He was in my class. He couldn't do this, Leo."

"We'll see, Pearl. Thanks for your time." Leo left the house with two boxes each of Thin Mints and Caramel deLites under his arm for the squad room. He put the boxes of cookies in the back seat, and cursed himself as he headed for the Sullivan's expansive house overlooking the reservoir. Should have questioned the wife *before* he talked to Malachy. What was he thinking? Long shot if it mattered anyway, but still.

Francie Dooley Sullivan met him at the door as if expecting him. Malachy must have given her a call after Leo's visit.

"This way, Leo. I'm glad you came." Francie moved with a certain doe-like elegance as she gestured for him to follow her and started down the hall.

"Thanks, Francie." Leo followed her slim, graceful figure into a stunningly appointed parlor that had no apparent signs of life or use. No, he didn't care for a cup of tea or coffee, thanks.

Francie's soft brown hair caught the winter sunlight through the living room window, and her dark blue eyes were mild and flat. No, she hadn't seen Aurelius leave the party, and she couldn't imagine why she would. Oh, and Malachy, he was out of her sight for just a few minutes when they'd gotten separated in the crowd. They'd enjoyed the entire party together and never left the building until the party was almost over.

Leo sat in silence for a moment, feeling a great wave of sadness. He looked at the distant woman sitting serenely before him, the woman who used to be Francie Dooley before she was Francie Sullivan. Francie Dooley, who would share her lunch with anyone, who tap-danced in patent leather shoes to "Tiptoe Through the Tulips" in the spring vaudeville, and who would collapse into sweet giggles before she could finish telling her lame jokes. He wondered where a joyous spirit like that went, and if it was still secreted somewhere deep inside Francie, locked tight, a faint glimmer in a small, windowless room.

A part of Leo still felt abandoned when he saw Francie Sullivan. He and Francie, even then "beautiful inside and out" as the nuns used to say, were in the same grade and close from elementary school into high school. Somehow, his young, adolescent self thought it would always be that way. But all that was lost freshman year, when senior Malachy Sullivan walked into the Winter Gala at the Immaculate Girls High School.

Francie had never looked back at sweet, nerdy Leo Gelenian, who didn't have his impressive growth spurt until junior year. As a freshman, he still only came up to Francie's shoulder. Malachy Sullivan, *The Globe* Scholar-Athlete, was a good six feet. And then there was that mess of black hair, that goddamned dimple, and that wide smarmy smile. Leo was toast.

"Francie?"

For just a whisper of a moment, Leo saw a flicker somewhere behind those impossible navy blue eyes. Somewhere in there was a tiny pilot light that hadn't gone out yet. And then it vanished.

"Can I get you anything, Leo?" she repeated.

"No, no, Francie. I'm okay. I'll be going now. Thanks again for your time."

Francie walked Leo to the front door. When he turned his head after getting back into his car, Leo saw her, still watching him, before she quickly closed the door.

There had been a baby, or the beginnings of a baby, before the accident on the stairs. Malachy didn't mean to push her. It just happened. He said she was being dramatic. She could have grabbed the railing. It was only a little jostle. If she hadn't fallen back like some drama queen, she wouldn't have gone down the stairs.

Dr. Duggan had looked at Francie closely. She'd been so ashamed when he saw the bruises. "Is there something you want to tell me about, Francie?" he'd asked.

She'd just shaken her head, looking down at the floor in her grief and shock. "No, it was a fall, doctor, just a bad fall. Clumsy of me. My own fault. My own awful fault."

The baby was lost, a little girl. The fall had damaged something in Francie's insides. It was unlikely—not impossible, but unlikely—there would be any more babies. There were days even now when Francie felt she was still carrying a child. A small, sad, weeping child inside her.

Francie averted her eyes when she saw babies on the street, and some part of her mind turned off as people talked about their children. She saw their mouths moving, but she heard only a low, distant murmur. Her heart ached in private grief for the children she'd never have. She'd learned to smile pleasantly and utter banalities like "Isn't that wonderful?" when she took a cue from their faces that she was supposed to respond in admiration.

A family friend had suggested she and Malachy consider adopting a child. Malachy had dismissed the prospect out of hand when Francie brought the subject up. As time went on, she thought perhaps that was for the best. If she couldn't protect herself, she didn't know how she could protect a child.

Some years after Francie lost the baby, Malachy bought a dog. Francie loved Maisie too. Who wouldn't? But she was envious of the affection Malachy showered on the big boxer. She'd watch them head off together to Malachy's office or to inspect his properties, Maisie in the passenger seat looking squarely forward, Malachy chatting to her as if she were a person. He would occasionally laugh and call Maisie's name, at which point the dog would turn to him with a loving boxer smile and lolling tongue. Such a pair, thought Francie.

Francie was glad of the dog many days. Maisie brought an energy and animal affection into the house, which was usually very quiet, even when Malachy was home. Especially when Malachy was home—dinners particularly so.

Malachy liked to have the television news on during the meal, to stay abreast of events. So, they didn't talk when they ate in the evenings, except during commercial breaks.

"Francie."

Francie looked up quickly to see a car commercial on the television screen. "Oh, sorry." She reached for the remote and pressed the mute button.

"Just hate listening to that shit. I have to go to the bank tomorrow. You get my gray suit and that yellow tie from the cleaners?"

"They're in the upstairs hall closet. I got your white shirts while I was there too."

"Good. I hope they didn't put too much starch in them this time."

"No, no. I spoke to them before and the shirts look good."

The television screen went blank for a moment, as it does when the news is about to resume. "Francie."

"Oh, right." Francie disabled the mute button. "Oh, it's that pipeline business. Representative Markey—"

"Don't talk, Francie. I can't hear what they're saying when you talk."

CHAPTER 8

eo unlocked the back door. He took off his jacket, hung it carefully in the back hall, and removed his winter shoes, putting them on a rubber tray by the radiator. Next to the tray, a pair of leather slippers waited for him in the same place every night.

Taking a quart of Ipswich clam chowder from the Quarterdeck Diner out of its brown paper bag, Leo put it in the microwave to warm while he cut some thick slices of scali bread from Sevi's bakery. He took down one of his mother's Baccarat wine glasses from the darkened dining room china cabinet, as he did every night, and poured himself a glass of good wine—tonight a nice chardonnay to go with the chowder. He knew most people liked beer with their chowder, but Leo preferred wine.

Leo Gelenian still lived in the family home, a handsome Victorian on Hancock Street in Malford, one of the sturdy neighborhoods that continued to anchor the changing city. Originally, coming home after college, he had intended for this to be a brief stop. But, as will happen, one thing led to another. Sometimes, we just slide into life's major decisions without knowing it until much later.

It was convenient to live in the house on Hancock Street while he was getting his masters in Boston, a streetcar's ride away. Then, after he joined the Malford Police Department, he was grateful to come home to find the meals his mother Mary left for him in the warmer after late nights and busy, disjointed days.

Leo was a late-in-life baby. As his parents aged, he stayed on Hancock Street. Not because he had to, but because he wanted to stay close. Now, they had both been gone for some years, but Aran and Mary still felt very present in the house to him.

The spacious house remained the center of Leo's extended family. His sister Virginia continued to cook big meals for the holidays in the Hancock Street house. For the Armenian Christmas in early January, Easter, and Thanksgiving, the kitchen was crowded and noisy with talented Armenian cooks. Mary's good china came out of the cabinet and the long dining room table would be full. A more somber dinner with prayers and readings was held on April 24th. Martyrs'

Day marked the 1915 Armenian genocide, which Leo's great-grandparents barely survived, though most of their families had not.

On at least two or three Sundays in the summer, Leo would barbecue a leg of lamb, praying he didn't get a call from the station that would pull him away, and there would be a family feast. He usually had a date at these barbecues, often quite an attractive one.

Yes, there had been women he'd enjoyed, but somehow none ever took root. His job didn't have an easy schedule and, as time went on, police work became a deeper and deeper focus of his life. Something he was good at. Something he was meant to do. Leo learned to live with the inevitable ambiguities as well as the sadness and frustration. He had often thought that the grittier aspects of his job made him incapable of staying in a relationship. He was more comfortable with people at the station than anywhere else.

Leo wasn't sure what it was about the job that suited him so well. Some were attracted by the camaraderie, the uniform, and the hunt, or the law enforcement fairy tales they'd seen on television. He got that, but there was more. An old detective once said that it was the prospect of bringing something like a temporary order, or the chance of it, to disorder. Leo thought it was often more than disorder they faced on some days, maybe a kind of anarchy. A kind of anarchy brought to brief equilibrium. Even if just for now, because anarchy was always waiting around the corner.

Over time, he was so absorbed in his work that there was no room for much else in his life. Now, there were new challenges as the population of the city had changed—from predominantly Irish and Italian with a smattering of French and Maritime Canadians, Jews, and Portuguese to a new immigrant profile. South Asians, Chinese, and Vietnamese, along with a heavy influx of Haitians and Brazilians, were increasingly buying up the city's inventory of two-family houses. The department had just ordered a new device that accessed an on-call translating service to handle the frequent language gaps that occurred when police officers were on site.

Now, the house was quiet. Virginia's boys didn't come over like they used to when they were younger, to spend the weekend or a long day with their Uncle Leo. The closets in one of the upstairs bedrooms, the one with the tall twin beds, still held their tracksuits and soccer balls. He hated the idea of cleaning the closets out even though Steven was in grad school in Chicago, and Brian had moved to New York after college.

Later that evening, after washing up and leaving only the small stove light on in the kitchen, Leo walked into the dining room with a cup of strong Armenian coffee and his briefcase. Taking the dining room table pads out of the buffet, he placed them carefully on the long table and brought up Yo-Yo Ma playing the Bach cello suites on the sound system. Only then did he set up his workplace.

He took out his handwritten notes from conversations and interviews that day, along with his own observations, from a battered leather briefcase. The lights in the dining room stayed on until the early hours of the morning as Leo organized, pondered, and studied the case of the Immaculate nun murder.

Why was Sister Aurelius in the Immaculate schoolyard late that winter afternoon when she was supposed to be at an anniversary celebration at the Irish-American?

Perhaps the old nun had just wanted to slip away to visit the school where she had taught for fifty years. And maybe it was just a coincidence that a violent person, apparently Joey Mucci, was at the schoolyard at the same time, turning a brief, sentimental stop for the old nun into a brutal horror and the end of her.

Or perhaps he had followed her there, seeing the nun walking alone in that long black habit down Lloyd Street from the club. Leo wished one of the neighbors had caught a glimpse of her on that quiet Sunday afternoon. He couldn't understand how she could have been missed.

Leo just couldn't figure out the motivation. The why. Joey was unbalanced, but no one ever figured him for this. The nun had been good to him. "He's just a little odd," she used to say when they were kids at the Immaculate, "but aren't we all odd in our own way?" Now, Leo was struggling with the fact that something seemed off here.

He was tired. Stretching his long arms overhead and yawning, Leo turned to making a list of immediate action steps for himself and his team to wrap this ugly case up tight. About three in the morning, the light in the dining room went out and there was a brief flicker of light in one of the upstairs bedrooms. Leo crawled into bed for a few hours' sleep before beginning the day again.

CHAPTER 9

reddie, proprietor and chief cook at the Strand Diner, eyed Maisie as he wiped down the counter. "You know, the Department of Health is going to cite me for her one of these days. Dogs aren't supposed to be in here, except for those blind people dogs or maybe those therapy ones for vets with PTSD."

"You just tell me who bothers you about it, Freddie, and I'll take care of it." Malachy Sullivan slipped into his usual booth at the back of the Strand Diner on Western Avenue, a booth he'd claimed almost every morning for over a decade. He patted Maisie as she settled in at his feet and placed his newspaper and iPad on the table.

"Everyone will want to bring in their dogs, and it'll just be a zoo." The stark pre-dawn lights of the diner reflected off Freddie's bald head and glasses as he lined up filter baskets with coffee grounds behind the counter, ready for the morning rush.

"Shut up, Freddie. Get me a cuppa and a full Irish. Where's Becca?"

"That shitcan car of hers gave out yesterday. She left it over at Foster's place, taking the bus in." Freddie put Malachy's first cup of coffee in front of him. "Foster's good, but he's not a miracle-worker. That car's crap."

"Maybe if you paid her more, she could afford to get another one."

"Hey, this ain't the Four Seasons here. Wish I could pay us both more." Freddie stopped and looked up. "You could take care of it for her from your loose change, big shot. She has a rough time trying to hold it together. Lady needs a break."

"Where's the guy?" Malachy leaned against the back of the booth.

"No guy—dirt bag left years ago. You wouldn't mind, but she's from one of those old families that came over on the *Flowerpot* or some damned thing. Didn't have a penny and she grew up dirt poor, but her family thought they were something special. Dropped her cold when she hooked up with Linsky, small time crook. So, she's just on her own with the kid."

Freddie collected the sugar dispensers and arranged them for refill. "Linsky took a walk when the baby came. Long time ago. She doesn't even know where he is anymore. Josiah's probably sixteen or seventeen now. Becca's always hooking up with losers, one worse than the other." Freddie unscrewed the tops of the glasses, and concentrated on filling the sugar containers. "You give all that money to the Catholic and the Boys Club. Why don't you throw a little Becca's way?"

"I can't run around paying everybody's bills, Freddie." Malachy snapped his paper open.

Freddie gave a sidelong glance as he put Malachy's sausages and black pudding on the grill and cracked three eggs with a practiced hand. "Just saying maybe you could do a thing or two private-like that don't get covered on the front page of the *News* with the Mayor and all."

Malachy didn't respond as he lowered the paper and gave Freddie a cold, dead stare.

Oops. Too far. "Okay, okay." Freddie raised the spatula and his arms overhead in a gesture of surrender, a Navy tattoo showing beneath the black hair on his arms.

The door to the diner banged open, and a well-built, fortyish woman with a cascade of straight blond hair hurried inside, bringing a burst of cold morning air.

"Sorry, Freddie. Damned busses are supposed to start running at five. The guy didn't show up till half past. God, it was cold out there. Hi, Malachy." Becca Linsky leaned down to take off her boots. Still standing, she took a pair of sneakers from a plastic Ocean State Job Lot bag and slipped them onto her long, slim feet. Then, taking an elastic from her pocket, she started to pull her hair back into a long ponytail. "What a day."

"Hi Becca. Bad week?" Malachy asked, watching Becca bend her head and lean forward to catch hold of her long, sandy hair.

Becca threw her hair back and looked at Malachy. "I guess. Damned car punked out again. Piece of junk. Josiah can take the bus to and from school, and to Dunkie's downtown for his shift, but he'll have to walk home afterward." Her eyes watered slightly. Then, Becca shook her head quickly and looked away.

The diner door opened again and two FedEx uniforms arrived for breakfast, bringing a blast of cold air with them.

"Hey, guys." Becca put her black parka on the wall hook near the restroom, her boots on the floor below. She picked up a light blue Strand Diner apron and, tying it on, found her order pad under the counter. Then, Becca straightened up and smiled at her first customers of the day. "What'll it be? Coffee to start?"

On his way to the office that morning, Malachy stopped by Foster's Repair. Becca's old gray Honda sat to the side of the garage.

"Want to buy it? I know someone who'd sell it cheap. Maybe even pay you to take it. Hi, Mal."

"Hi, Fos. What's the story?"

"What isn't? Transmission, brakes, everything. I'm dreading when she calls this morning. What can I tell her? I can't afford to give her a freebie. A few bucks off, but this is too much."

"Fix it."

"You're kidding. You can buy a pretty good used car for the same price." Fos looked closely at Malachy with a quizzical frown.

"Fix it. Send me the bill. Give her one too, a small one. Make something up. Spark plugs? I don't know. Something. She won't know the difference."

"Okay. It's your pocket."

Malachy started to walk away when he turned. "Don't screw me over with the bill, and keep quiet about it. She doesn't know. No one knows. Got it?"

"Yeah, yeah. Okay." He watched Malachy climb into his SUV, with Maisie in the passenger seat, and drive away. Fos wiped his hands with a greasy rag, "Well. Well."

Later that week, the diner had just opened, smelling of coffee and Malachy's full Irish breakfast cooking. Becca filled his coffee cup, her mood much lighter than a few days earlier.

Freddie called out to Malachy, "Our girl finally caught a break. Fifty bucks for spark plugs. Fos gave her a pass on the labor."

Becca sighed happily. "That was close."

"Lucky break," murmured Malachy as he scanned the morning paper.

Becca started to move to the next table when she turned to give Malachy a long look. Then, she glanced over at Freddie who had turned his back and was engrossed in his work at the grill.

"How's Josiah?" Malachy asked as he turned a page of his paper.

"He's good. No real trouble so far, just trying to get him through school and keep him clean. Then maybe the army. Projects aren't a great place to raise a kid by yourself." Becca went to pick up Malachy's order from Freddie. "These days, we're like ships passing in the night. He works the late shift at Dunkie's downtown and I'm on the early shift here."

"Yeah, it's a tough road, but I hear you're doing a good job. Make sure you keep him clean. A lot of junk floating around these days."

"All you can do is try, Malachy, but nothing's ever guaranteed. So much out of your control."

"That's the truth."

CHAPTER 10

he day after her visit to the Motherhouse with Nuncie, Rosaria threw herself into a flurry of phone calls. She worked the phones from well before dawn to catch the distributors and dealers in her region during working hours. Checking on progress, settling disputes over territorial infractions, and absorbing the endless, ritual whines about how the price points were killing their business. She walked about the apartment as she listened to her assistant rattle off a list of updates, checked email on her cell, and watched boats on the harbor and planes from Logan. Finally, she closed the conversations. "Have a good week, Stash. We'll talk soon."

"Okay, Madam. We love you, you know."

"Ah yes, and well you should."

Later that morning, Rosaria visited Malford City Hall. She entered the faded grandeur of the Hall's lobby through a side door, since the tall wooden doors with their heavy brass handles at the front of the building were locked against the winter cold. The elevator was broken, but Rosaria didn't mind walking up the wide marble staircase to the offices of the Malford Redevelopment Authority. The office was quiet with two clerks working on ancient computers and a young manager in a windowed office talking on the phone. Rosaria stood at the worn, wooden counter and asked if there were minutes available for the Redevelopment Authority meetings, specifically about the Immaculate Conception property.

"Are you from the *Malford News*?" A middle-aged woman with a baroque mass of carefully structured dark brown curls approached the counter. The scent of Avon Eternal Magic hung in the air, and an Avon catalog sat on one of the nearby desks.

"No, just a citizen. Do I have to get some Public Records Request paperwork? If I have to, I can do that," replied Rosaria, hoping that the clerk wouldn't ask if she were a citizen of Malford.

"No," said the clerk. "Let me ask my manager." Rosaria watched the manager hold the phone away and frown as he listened to the clerk. He hung up and came out of the office, approaching Rosaria with a fixed smile. Young, slight, and well-dressed, with gelled, spiked hair.

"Hello, ma'am. I'm Dennis Scanlan, the manager here. Can I help you?"

"Thank you, Mr. Scanlan. I'm here to take a look at the Redevelopment Authority minutes for the last year or so. Would there be a problem with that?"

"Not at all. May I ask why? Maybe we can help you find specifically what you're looking for."

"No, that's okay. Just an interested citizen. I can handle it by myself." Rosaria smiled.

A brief hesitation, but then: "Okay. Just a minute," and he went into another room. Mr. Scanlan took his time and returned in ten minutes with a set of binders as well as a form for her to fill out.

The clerk ushered Rosaria into a small, overheated conference room with windows to the larger office. The scent of the clerk's *Eternal Magic* perfume was noticeable, though not unpleasant. As she sat down, Rosaria glanced over to see young Mr. Scanlan in his office, picking up the phone while glancing in her direction, that frown still on his boyish face.

Rosaria settled down to read. Boring stuff. Same names. Some she knew—Councilman Murray, Danny Hartnett from the funeral home and the Chamber, a clergyman from that little church over in the Oakwood neighborhood that no one ever seemed to go to. Other names were not familiar, but the agenda topics were expected for these kinds of agencies—lead paint abatement, parking garages, housing rehabilitation, etc. Occasional guests, identified after the first mention by initials.

She checked her watch. Rosaria always wore a man's watch with a big face. She'd picked up the habit early when she was in business. So much easier to check the time discreetly in a meeting with this kind of watch face than trying to squint at the dainty little watches her mother used to buy her, in a fruitless effort to make her look more traditionally feminine.

Only people her age seemed to wear watches these days, if you didn't count the trophy watches advertised in the Times supplement. Most everyone younger seemed to check the time on smartphones openly with the same casual rudeness with which they checked their emails in the middle of a conversation with a friend or even during a client meeting. Well, times change and, for crying out loud, had she really been here for two hours already?

Her eyes were starting to glaze over in the stuffy heat. The old radiators were clanking and the florescent lights buzzed lightly, blinking and crackling occasionally. This was a fool's errand, and boring to boot. She wasn't even sure what she was looking for. Then, something odd. For three or four months, pages would be missing. Just one or two. Perhaps the first page with the agenda and the attendees, then a page or two later. She did, however, notice the initials of an outside guest in the body of the text on page six of last September's meeting. *Msgnr. McD.* The discussion was the Highland Avenue property—otherwise known as the Immaculate school complex. The text read:

> A blighted property. In line with the master plan for the city, the Redevelopment Authority recommends to the Archdiocese through Monsignor Owen McDermott, pastor of the Immaculate Conception parish, a timely sale to Claddagh Properties, prime bidder, at the suitably distressed price on offer. Monsignor McDermott is in support of this initiative.

A blighted property? thought Rosaria, suddenly alert. That wasn't right. Those buildings would stand until the next millennium. They were not blighted properties. And sold at a suitably depressed price. Ridiculous. Malford was twenty minutes from Boston, close to Route 93. Condos here would get a good price, sell in a flash.

The next page of the minutes was missing. *No accident,* thought Rosaria. "Missing pages, me eye." She smirked a little after she whispered the old expression *me eye.* Where had she heard that expression so often? Aurelius, of course. Rosaria chuckled softly and whispered again, this time addressing the spirit of Aurelius, wherever she was. "Is this what you wanted me to find?"

Rosaria thought she heard a rustle, felt a warm breeze, but it must have been her imagination. She looked up, suddenly sure someone was watching her. No one in the hall. *Calm down, O'Reilly. You're losing it.*

Rosaria walked back to the office. "Is there a reason some pages are missing?"

"Oh, I don't know," replied the clerk. "Maybe someone borrowed them and forgot to put them back." She fidgeted with a gold-colored angel pendant. Rosaria wondered if it came from the Avon catalog, too.

"I want someone to locate the pages and have the borrower return them. No one should be removing material from official records."

More energetic fidgeting of the gold-colored angel. "I'll have to talk to my manager," said the clerk as she turned to the now empty office. "Can you leave your number, and I'll call you after I talk to him?" As Rosaria was writing down her cell number, the manager himself came down the hall. The clerk turned to him. "Mr. Scanlan, this lady has noticed that some of the pages of the Redevelopment Authority meeting notes are missing."

"Really?" He turned to Rosaria. "We'll look into that—which pages do you think are missing?"

Rosaria had, for a short time, been a seventh grade teacher early in her career. It had taught her more about human dynamics than she'd learned anywhere else. Now, she gazed thoughtfully at the practiced innocence on the young man's face. *Oh, please.*

"What's happening to the old Immaculate property on Highland Avenue?" she asked.

"I really couldn't say. I think it's been under discussion."

"What's your role with the Authority, Mr. Scanlan?" Rosaria gazed levelly at the younger man.

"I'm the business manager for redevelopment activities." Galled, lips pressed together.

"Is the Authority really recommending that the Immaculate be sold at a distressed price to Claddagh Properties as a derelict property? That's crazy."

"I really couldn't say."

"Why, in heaven's name, not?"

"The conversation's incomplete. I suggest you formally submit any questions to the Authority in writing." She saw an angry flush beginning to creep up Scanlan's neck.

"That sounds like obstruction to me, Mr. Scanlan." Rosaria could feel her height in relation to the smaller man and so could he. She could see he was standing as tall as he could and pressing on the balls of his feet to lift his heels another tiny fraction of an inch of height. Despite these efforts, Scanlan still had to raise his eyes to hers as he spoke, a fact that clearly infuriated him.

"I'm sorry, that's our process. Write your questions out and submit them, Ms. O'Reilly." He emphasized and drew out the Miz.

"It sounds to me as if your process is to obstruct. What are you trying to hide?" Rosaria knew her tone was turning harsh, but she was past caring.

"We're not hiding anything. Just send us your questions like everyone else, Ms. O'Reilly." His voice was the soul of reasoned patience, as she was losing her temper.

"Okay, I'll do that, Scanlan, and you can bet I'll be back looking for the missing minutes." Rosaria felt her hands gripping the pages of the minutes tightly. She suppressed an impulse to smack Scanlan's gelled hair spikes with the pages.

"Yes, you do that, Ms. O'Reilly. Thanks for coming by." The man turned his back to her to go into his office.

"You'll see me again, Mr. Scanlan," she called after him. "Plenty of other people would be interested in those missing pages. The *Malford News,* for one."

Scanlan's back stiffened at this, but he kept walking.

Rosaria strode to the copier with pages of the minutes that showed the Monsignor McDermott's initials and references to the Immaculate. Afterward, she left her cell phone number with the clerk, who stood uncomfortably beside her desk. As Rosaria walked to the small conference room where she'd been working to pick up her coat, she passed Scanlan's office. He looked up at her briefly and pointedly while he made a phone call.

Rosaria's face was flushed and her heart was racing in fury and frustration as she descended the stairs to the lobby of the City Hall. When she reached the bottom of the stairs, she was still so angry that she decided to go right back to the second floor and have it out with young Mr. Scanlan again.

But as Rosaria turned back to the stairs, her jaw set for a good confrontation, she caught sight of a very old and bent man standing in the lobby. She felt she'd entered a time warp. Bill Kenneally, long retired supervisor of the packing room at the now defunct shoe plant... and her first boss. Benevolent, ever smiling—even now as he walked painfully with not one, but two canes. Same flat tweed cap, same rosy cheeks, and same bright blue eyes, though now his nose and his chin almost touched as he smiled.

She hugged Bill, perhaps too hard and too long. He smelled like her dad. Wool and cigar smoke. She felt years fall from her, like a small girl in her father's embrace.

"How are you, sweetheart? And what are you doing here?"

"Just checking on a few things. You?"

"Ah, those assessors. They think my little house is a castle. But let's not talk about that," Bill chuckled.

He was just what she needed right now, a little normalcy and good conversation with an old friend. She couldn't let Bill go. The hell with that jerk Scanlan. "Like a cup of coffee, Bill?"

"Well, what a nice surprise. I'd like nothing better, Rosie. We have some time. Terry's picking me up in an hour," Bill said, referring to his youngest daughter. "Though you know, we've gotten very fancy lately. The City Diner isn't here anymore. In its place, we've been blessed with a French and cheese shop. Can you fathom it, now? All that gourmet, organic-y stuff that costs a fortune. Thank God, though, they do make a good cup of coffee and have a place you can sit and watch these swells throw their money away."

"Oh, yes. I know how it is," said Rosaria, as they slowly made their way to The French Connection. Rosaria held Bill's arm tightly, skirting patches of ice on the sidewalk and navigating the crowd around them. Waiting to cross the street, she stopped briefly with Bill to smile and absorb the new faces of Malford and the sounds of other accents, the languages of recent immigrants on the streets of the city. A rich mixture, breathing new life into the old city. Rosaria thought she heard Vietnamese and Cantonese, mixed with an odd Boston-accented American English, and the rhythms gave her a rush of pleasing energy.

Rosaria and Bill came through the front door of The French Connection into the warmth of the shop, bustling with customers, smelling of good cheese and coffee. Rosaria went to the counter and came back with two cups of strong coffee and fresh croissants, while Bill located a free table and leaned his canes against a chair.

They settled in for a few minutes, removing coats and scarves. Bill took a sip of the coffee, declared it excellent, and then started to rearrange his flat hat on the table, looking closely at Rosaria. "If you don't mind my saying, Rosie, your face looks drawn. Is it that business with your friend, that poor nun up at the Immaculate? Sad business. Sad business." He shook his head slowly, closing his eyes.

"Can't get the images out of my head, Bill. You just couldn't imagine such a thing happening, could you?"

"No, you couldn't, darlin'."

"And there's something else going on that I can't figure out, but I'm trying."

Bill opened his eyes and looked across the table with interest. "And what would that be, Rosie? Maybe I can help"

"Not sure, but it would help me just to talk it through." Rosaria settled back into her chair and went on to tell Bill about Aurelius's comments on the disposition of the Immaculate property and the missing Redevelopment Authority minutes. She decided not to touch on the larger subject of Aurelius's mysterious "last mission" because she didn't know what that was all about herself. "I tried to get more information but, good gravy, it's like running into a stone wall in that place. Like the Kremlin."

"To tell you the truth, I'm not sure you'd want to get into all that mess now, sweetheart. You'd be wading into pretty deep water. People around the Hall these days have short tempers. Be careful where you step." He laughed softly. "Of course, I shouldn't say that to you. If I remember, being told to be careful where you step is like a red flag you can't resist."

Rosaria was grateful for the release as they both laughed. "Some things don't change, Bill."

"I suppose not." Then Bill thought for a moment and ran his fingers along his tweed hat. "Anyway, I still have a few friends left at the Hall. Let me ask a couple of questions—quiet-like. You know," Bill looked across the table at her, "you don't always have to go at everything head on, Rosie. Sometimes, it's better to have at things more low key and maybe from the side. Now, I'm not promising anything, mind you, but I may be able to help. Better for me to do that. It's no problem."

Rosaria didn't respond for a moment. *What a gallant old man.* So little of his life left and so frail, but still wanting to ride to the rescue. "Bill, that's too kind. I appreciate just talking things out with you. Please, please, don't go to that trouble. If there are some short-tempered people around, I don't want you to be in their way either. I'd feel terrible if it caused you some difficulty with the wrong people."

"Ah, who's going to bother with an old man, now? What harm can I do?" he asked, holding up his two canes.

"Oh, I remember you. Plenty, plenty." Rosaria grinned and then looked over Bill's shoulder to catch a glimpse of Francie Sullivan walking through the food aisles with one of the shop's wicker baskets.

"Hey, Francie."

Startled, Francie looked up sharply when Rosaria called her name. She hesitated, as if she'd been lost in thought, and raised her hand in a distracted wave. After she had turned back to her shopping, Bill commented. "World's a funny place. I can remember when Malachy Sullivan was a kid. That family couldn't afford meat but once a week. It would be oatmeal for dinner. And now here's Malachy's wife shopping for him in the fancy cheese section. Life's a wonder, Rosie. Life's a wonder."

"I used to babysit for Francie when she was little. Adorable kid."

"I bet she was. She's still a very pretty woman."

"She is. Haven't seen her around much. Of course, I'm always traveling."

"Oh, you mightn't, even if you were here all the time. Francie and Malachy move in different circles now. Of course, you're such a big shot, you'd be welcome, I suppose."

Rosaria rolled her eyes and Bill chuckled. She looked over to see Francie slip to the back of the store to change aisles. If she didn't know better, Rosaria would have thought Francie was trying to avoid them.

"Malachy's quite the man now, you know, with his picture in the papers all the time. Quite the climber," Bill said. "Never got over where he came from, always running from the projects. I'd say the rest of us are just the old shoes now."

Rosaria laughed. "There's a lot to be said for old shoes, Bill."

Francie would have liked to walk over to chat when Rosaria called her name. Rosaria was one of her favorite people, her old babysitter. Francie had adored Rosaria when she was a little girl. So pretty, so much fun. And who didn't love old Bill Kenneally? Her father used to say that Bill Kenneally could talk to a telephone pole.

But no, it had been too long. She didn't know if she had the energy and time to start rebuilding those bridges right now. No, it would be better to leave it with a wave and a hello. She saw Rosaria and Bill glance in her direction and was hurt to think they might be talking about her. She slipped to the back of the store and entered the next aisle out of their line of sight.

She reproached herself for avoiding Rosaria O'Reilly and Bill Kenneally, two people she'd always loved. But she just couldn't handle all that today. Francie was startled to find her eyes were tearing up and a sudden sense of desolation washed over her.

She'd never felt anything near that same ease with the people Malachy invited to their house now. With their bright smiles and high chatter, and that superficial way of looking at you, while always being aware of whoever else of more importance might be circulating. At the last party, when Francie walked among the guests in a royal blue dress Malachy had told her to wear, she had her own bright smile on. A glass of sparkling water in her hand to greet these people, knowing she could never call on a one of them if she needed help.

Who *could* she call on if she ever needed help?

Francie moved into the aisle of dried fruits and nuts. Malachy liked organic specialty foods, so she shopped carefully for him to help him watch his health. At the same time, she knew that first thing in the morning before work he went to that greasy spoon on Western Avenue for a full Irish with eggs, sausages, black pudding, and brown bread. When she'd teased him about it a while ago, he'd gotten that dangerous, cold look. So, she'd dropped it quickly. He was a hard man to tease.

Francie wasn't sure when those cold looks had started. When she was younger, even before they were married, she'd tried not to think too much about those looks. Inexperienced, enveloped in Malachy's easy charm, Francie was confident that over time she could love those cold looks away. But then she'd learned that some things you just can't love away.

Before Francie and Malachy had married, she'd had one hesitant conversation with her mother about him. She didn't want her parents to be alarmed, and she didn't want them not to like Malachy. She had fallen so in love with him. Francie could barely eat or sleep sometimes, she was so caught up in thoughts of him. She had wasted pads of paper practicing her married name in different scripts and variations.

That was why the comment she'd made about Malachy's "going off" now and then to her mother as they were preparing dinner together one weekend was so low key and casual. Busy with cooking and not seeing the mute appeal in her daughter's eyes as she waited for her mother's response, Mrs. Dooley didn't stop in her rhythmic carrot peeling, but only continued the conversation in a chatty way.

"Well, some men are just high-strung, dear," she had said as she arranged the carrots around the roast. "He's a good man, very ambitious, and he'll go far. I know he really loves you." Mrs. Dooley wiped her hands on her apron and gave Francie an encouraging smile. Francie smiled back.

She could forgive Malachy all that. Not forget, but forgive. She just couldn't forgive what had happened with the baby. It was so hard for her to think about the baby. No, she couldn't forgive about the baby.

Shaking her head, Francie pushed away her thoughts as she always did, tucking them deep within a part of herself she could never share with anyone. She checked her wicker shopping basket. She already had the goat's milk cheese Malachy liked from that artisan place in Vermont, and she'd taken a chance on a different cheese for him to try, one from Indiana called Arabella. They liked the flatbread crackers with their soft cheeses, so she stopped by the cracker aisle for those before heading to the condiments, where she scanned the shelves and, after some time, found the special treat for Malachy she'd come for. How fortunate. There was one left. A jar of specialty olives, accidentally hidden in with the Greek black olives. Francie read the label carefully before she put the jar in her basket.

Out of the corner of her eye, she saw Rosaria escorting Bill to his daughter's waiting car, double-parked outside the shop. Francie was approaching the cashier when Rosaria came back to pick up her bag and papers. Francie raised her hand in greeting again, glad that Rosaria responded with her own raised hand and didn't stop by to chat.

"Having company, Mrs. Sullivan?" the clerk asked Francie.

"No, no, Sam—just us. Special treats for Malachy. He deserves something special for all he does."

"Now, there's an appreciative woman," the clerk laughed.

"Oh, yes. Very appreciative."

Rosaria smiled again as she passed by to leave the shop. It was a few moments later, as the clerk was bagging Francie's groceries, that they heard a loud, sickening thud and a scream from the street outside.

CHAPTER 11

onfused when she first opened her eyes, Rosaria realized she was in a double hospital room with wide windows looking over the city. The other bed in the room was empty.

"You okay, hotshot?"

Rosaria worked hard to focus on Nuncie's face. "I think so," she mumbled, though she ached all over.

"Good. Just checking before I lay into you. Now—what the hell were you doing? Don't you know that you're supposed to look both ways when you cross the street?"

Rosaria winced. Her head ached. The sound of Nuncie's voice hurt. "Stop yelling," she moaned. "What happened?"

"What happened?" Nuncie lowered her voice and tried briefly to sound consoling. She failed and pressed on. "A van hit you while you were just waltzing out on the street without looking." Rosaria was touched to see Nuncie's red-rimmed eyes. "Could have flattened you, but some nice Haitian lady happened to be on the sidewalk near you and pulled you back. So, now you're just beat up instead of being flat as a pancake. They're keeping you here for observation overnight. I'll tell you...."

"Give her a break, Nunce." Leo walked into the room, his brown leather jacket open, one hand holding a black wool scarf and the other rubbing the back of his neck. "Besides, she wasn't at fault. For some reason, the guy swerved toward the sidewalk. How are you, Ro?"

"I'm okay," Rosaria winced with pain as she shrugged her shoulders. She could remember the dark van suddenly swerving toward her and, just for an instant, she could see the man's face. There had been something strange about the man's face. Something off...

"Detective Johnson's been here to get the details, right?" Leo asked. "Good. Leaving the scene of an accident with personal injury is a criminal offense." Leo cocked his head to the side. "What were you doing in the Square anyway? Since when are you hanging out here?"

"She's been meddling where she shouldn't be, that's what. Nosy Nellie looking for trouble," said Nuncie.

"She can talk for herself, Nuncie." Leo raised his chin at Nuncie, shoving one hand into his pocket.

"Thank you, Leo." Rosaria shot an irritated glance at an unrepentant Nuncie. Then, grimacing from the effort, she slowly hitched herself up to a sitting position. "I was just checking on a few things up at city hall in public records. We went up to the Motherhouse the other day and talked to one of the nuns who told us that Aurelius was very upset about the Immaculate property going to Malachy Sullivan. So, I thought I'd take a look, to see what was going on."

Leo's jaw tightened and he looked out the window, shaking his head, before turning back to Rosaria. "Listen, let's get this straight, Ro. You should be doing nothing up there with the nuns but offering your condolences right now," he snapped. "You shouldn't be talking to them about Aurelius's comments before she was murdered. That's not your job. I told you we'd follow up and we will. We don't need an amateur sleuth here."

Nuncie raised her eyebrows and let out a long, low whistle. Rosaria narrowed her eyes and restrained herself for a few moments. Nuncie rolled her eyes, waiting.

"Listen, Detective, you guys didn't seem to be in any big goddamned hurry to talk to the nuns, and somebody should have." Rosaria's voice was low and furious. She paused for a breath. "And, Leo, I'll talk to whoever the hell I want."

"Not if you impede our investigation, you won't. I'm telling you right now, leave this to us."

Rosaria turned away without answering, but not before Leo gave her a warning look.

He straightened his jacket. "Anyway, gotta go. I wanted to stop in while I was in the building. They're bringing a kid from Gardens to the ER downstairs." Leo was referring to the Bishop Riley Gardens public housing project, which might have looked like a garden sometime in the distant past, but now could only be described as a public housing slum. "Kid OD'ed. Heroin laced with some kind of opiate. Don't know what's going on over there, we had something like this a few weeks ago from the Gardens."

He shook his head. "I talked to Roger O'Toole, the Authority Director, about it. He hasn't a clue what's going on." Leo put his scarf on and rubbed his neck again. "But he's clueless to begin with, a political appointee—somebody's pal. Why did I even try?" He let out a long breath. "Anyway, I'll see you later."

Before leaving, Leo walked in front of Rosaria and looked her squarely in the face with his dark eyes. "Stay out of trouble, Ro."

Rosaria stared past him out the window and didn't respond, though she did turn to scowl at Leo's back as he left the room. In the hall outside, Leo stopped to answer his cell. Rosaria and Nuncie could hear his side of the conversation in bits and pieces.

"Yeah, okay... interview with the staff at Martin de Porres shelter near the Common? Good... follow up on the Immaculate site... matchbooks... the ones in town first... that dive in Chelsea. The Creek, or whatever it's called. Yeah, Chelsea... cigarettes... Canada... mail order?" And then Leo was out the door and down the hall.

Nuncie shook her head after Leo walked away, down the hospital corridor. "Poor kids. Enough trouble growing up in those projects without pushers hanging around every corner. I heard someone got beat up within an inch of his life two weeks ago—think it was one of the Fortunatos—the youngest one, the black sheep. Forget his name. The one who's always getting into trouble. Probably drug-related. Poor Ida Fortunato—what a worry." Nuncie paused. "Anyway, I really hope this kid makes it."

Rosaria remained motionless, still nursing a cold fury. The police were taking the easy answer. Joey was the easy answer. This was more complicated. She could scream from frustration.

Nuncie watched her. "Just leave it, Ro. Leo's right."

"Where's my bag? Did anyone get it?"

"Yeah, some guy picked it up for you."

"Give me the bag."

"Okay, sunshine." Nuncie turned to retrieve Rosaria's satchel from a small closet. "By the way, Jamie called to say you're excused from your assignment. What's that mean?" Nuncie stood with Rosaria's bag to her chest. "You've been holding something back, O'Reilly?"

Oh, Nuncie was going to have a fit about Jamie. Rosaria stalled, inspecting the bruises on her arm. Colorful, but nothing broken. She'd be fine.

Nuncie tapped her foot impatiently. "Well?"

"Jamie wanted me to find out what was happening at the Immaculate and what Aurelius's last mission was. Aurelius's talk these past few weeks really bothered Jamie. Me too." Rosaria gave Nuncie a defiant look. "Now give me my bag."

"Jesus, I think you're all crazy." Nuncie flung Rosaria's bag onto the bed and shook her head before she collapsed with a groan into the room's visitor chair. "Well, she just released you from whatever promise you made. So, let it go. For Chrissakes, let it go." She gave her friend a weary look.

"Too late. I'm in."

Nuncie closed her eyes and emitted a loud sigh. "You just look for trouble. That's it. You just look for it."

Rosaria's bag was badly damaged and scuffed from the accident. She rummaged through the satchel twice, emptying work papers onto the bed and shaking the bag upside down, scattering Life Savers, Kleenex tissue packets, duty-free receipts, and spare pens onto the floor. The copies she'd made from the Redevelopment Authority were gone.

She felt a flutter in her chest. She didn't know if it was rage, fear, curiosity, or all three. And excitement. She had to admit there was excitement. *Game on.*

"Okay?" Nuncie asked.

"Yep, okay." No need to get Nuncie all worked up again. She kept her poker face on and put everything back in her bag.

After Nuncie had left, Rosaria checked her cell phone. There were two increasingly frantic calls—one from Dimitri and one from the New York office looking to know if the big Central Asian order was going to come in before the end of the quarter.

And a voicemail from Genghis Khan. "You're killing me, Madam. You have no trust in us after all these years. Why do you disrespect me by sending a young boy to do business? He offers me a territory where half the population is living in yurts. They are not going to buy my athletic shoes."

Then, Rosaria checked the last voicemail from an unknown number. A few moments of silence on the other end, though Rosaria could feel the palpable presence of a person, not a nice person, on the line. Light breathing and the sounds of traffic in the background. Then, a click as the person hung up.

Wesley Johnson's big black hand placed the desk phone back onto the receiver with such an exaggerated gentle touch that Leo knew he was deeply annoyed. Only a long practiced habit of emotional restraint prevented Johnson from slamming the phone down. If he did slam it down, he would have shattered it. "Goddamn, he's a pushy son of a bitch. No wonder he's loaded."

"Who was that?" Leo was putting on his jacket as he walked down the hall toward the outside doors, pulling keys out of his pocket.

"Malachy Sullivan. Hate to be on the other side of the negotiating table with him. But, I guess I just was. I told him not to call me here. We were too busy to tie the phone up for anything but urgent police business. But he could not care less." Johnson shook his head in annoyance. "Rules are for other people. Just does what he wants."

Leo stopped. "What's Sullivan negotiating with you for?"

"Basketball camp. And he didn't negotiate with me. He just told me what was going to happen. Jesus." Officer Johnson dropped back in his chair with an exasperated sigh.

"Come again?"

"You know I help with this basketball camp the Celtics run for kids in the summer? We're already filled up. Signed up more than we should have early on, and gave away all the scholarships we had money for. So, enter the great Mr. Sullivan. He has a kid he wants to get in."

"Who?" Leo asked, a curious frown on his face.

Johnson checked the name he'd written on a notepad. "Josiah Linsky. Know him?"

"Yeah, I think I know his mom. She's a waitress over at the Strand Diner. Hear he's a good kid." Leo leaned against a nearby desk, put his keys in his pocket and faced Johnson.

"Sullivan says he's a good ballplayer, too. But I told him we just couldn't fit another kid into the program." Johnson shrugged.

"Too bad."

"Too bad, but don't worry about Josiah. We took him. First, Sullivan offers double tuition. I say I can't make that kind of decision, and I go to the Camp Director who says, no, we're already overbooked. Maybe next year.

"Then, Sullivan gets the name of the director. Calls him directly and says he'll make a donation. Cover one-half the cost of the *whole program,*" Johnson dragged out the words *whole program* and extended his sizable arms wide to the side, "if they take the Linsky kid."

"And the Director changes his mind, pronto."

"Well, what'd you expect? I'd do the same thing. Money buys." Wesley Johnson leaned forward on his elbows to ask, "Is the Linsky kid like a nephew or something?"

"I don't think so. Sullivan has a lot of money. He does things like this once in a while. He didn't have such a great life as a kid himself." Leo stood and straightened his jacket to leave again.

"Just the luck of the draw for Josiah, I guess. Wish I'd had a sugar daddy like that when I was growing up in Dorchester. Maybe I would have made it big." Johnson stretched his long legs in front of him. "That's what I was missing. A sugar daddy."

"You're missing more than that on the court, Johnson. How about steam?" someone called from across the squad room.

"Shut up. I'm quick, man," Johnson replied with a grin. "Faster than a speeding...."

"Molasses."

"Okay, okay," said Leo. "Well, until your own sugar daddy comes along, Johnson, see if you can mail order those Du Maurier cigarettes, the ones we found at the Immaculate site."

"Got it."

CHAPTER 12

 osaria waited at the top of the steps to the Immaculate Conception
church for Nuncie. She could see her friend call up some hidden store
of energy to climb the stairs of the big brick church for Aurelius's funeral
Mass without holding on to the iron railing. Rosaria knew enough not to offer her
arm, having had it slapped away more than once. The two women slipped into a
middle pew, and knelt for a moment before sitting back. Beside her, Rosaria could
hear Nuncie trying to measure her breath and mask her gasps from the effort of
climbing the stairs.

It was hard to believe that only four days had passed since Aurelius's murder.
To Rosaria, it felt like weeks. She was bruised from the hit-and-run in Malford
Square, though nothing had been broken. Mostly she was tired. A nervous tired.
She hadn't slept well since the murder.

Images and memories of Aurelius flashed through her mind. Someone had
given Aurelius tickets to a Red Sox game one year, and she'd invited Rosaria and
Sister Jamie as her guests. Rosaria's father had driven them into town and dropped
them off at Fenway Park on a perfect summer night. The Sox played the Yankees
and won during extra innings. Aurelius bought Rosaria a Fenway frank and a
Sox pennant, and the crowd sang "Take Me Out to the Ballgame" and "Sweet
Caroline." Rosaria was not sure that she would ever be as purely happy as she was
that summer night with Aurelius at Fenway Park.

But then each cherished memory quickly gave way to the horror of Aurelius's
being bludgeoned to death in her own schoolyard. A fierce, moaning black wind
swept everything good and bright in Rosaria's memory away, leaving only desolation.

Rosaria closed her eyes and shook her head to release these images before
scanning the large crowd in the church. The first three pews were filled with
Aurelius's family and her fellow nuns. Many of the nuns were old and leaned on
each other as they walked down the aisle, genuflecting shakily beside the pews.
Rosaria exchanged a discreet nod with Sister Jamie as the nun settled into her seat.

Generations of former students packed the church. Most long gone from the
Immaculate and Malford, spun out into the larger world, living lives their parents

and grandparents could only have dreamed of. Standing in the back of the church, she saw Leo Gelenian and Wesley Johnson. Leo's hands were stuck deeply into his jacket pockets, and Johnson's arms were crossed in front of his substantial frame, his feet wide. No disguising what these two did for a living.

Father Hanrahan said the Mass. In a firm, resonant voice with its comforting Boston accent, he spoke from the heart about steadfastness in the face of evil, and faith in times of pain and confusion. Afterward, he walked in front of the altar, his heavyset body flanked by the tall candle pillars. He and the congregation sent Aurelius, Aurelius the Pugnacious, off with her favorite prayer of peace.

Oh Lord, make me an instrument of Thy peace.
Where there is hatred, let me sow love.
Where there is injury, pardon,
Where there is doubt, faith,
Where there is despair, hope.
Grant that I may not so much seek to be consoled as to console,
To be understood as to understand,
To be loved as to love.
For it is in giving that we receive,
It is in pardoning that we are pardoned,
And it is in dying that we are born into eternal life.

Rosaria watched Aurelius's family, always theoretical in her mind, but here in flesh and blood. She'd never expected to actually see these people. Variations and echoes of Aurelius in the set of the jaw, or green eyes in strong-boned faces. And the steely, upright posture.

Flown far away, years ago, from an old mill town, flown on the winds like the white flossy seeds of milkweeds growing on the banks of the tainted Merrimac River running through Lowell. Now, brought back to lay to rest the eldest sister who'd mothered them long ago when the mother they hardly remembered had been lost. Old children, they stood close together, touching each other, arm-in-arm or holding hands lightly. Hands now wrinkled and age-spotted. They were still a handsome tribe, tall and long-limbed. Though their faces were no longer young and their steps were no longer as sure, in Rosaria's eyes, they still had a life force.

Rosaria could feel Nuncie preparing herself to stand and line up for Communion toward the end of the Mass. When the time came, Nuncie rose with as much vigor as she could muster and stood patiently in line with everyone else. Though Rosaria hadn't been to Mass in years, she followed Nuncie, noting how the shoulders of her friend's black coat drooped and how her thin neck was now lost in the coat's collar. Rosaria chilled with the profound, impending loss of another anchor in her life. She was seized with a grief for what hadn't happened yet, but loomed on the horizon.

After Mass, the mourners walked out of the church to a pearly gray sky and the beginnings of snow. In Rosaria's car, she and Nuncie joined the line of funeral cars processing up to the nuns' cemetery at the Motherhouse in Maudsley and arrived an hour later at a small plot of simple headstones surrounded by a plain iron fence and gate. In the center stood a tall, gray concrete Blessed Mother, eyes cast down. Her left hand gently touching her heart, forefinger extended from curled fingers, her right hand palm up, reaching out in supplication or consolation.

The mourners who'd come to the interment left Aurelius's family some privacy at the grave after the ceremony. Sitting back in the warmth of her car, snow starting to stick on the windshield, Rosaria could see the family stand for a long time at the grave without speaking. Great, silent, soft flakes of snow fell more heavily as, after some unspoken signal, Aurelius's brothers and sisters moved toward their cars.

"Ro?"

"Yeah?" Rosaria turned to Nuncie, resting with her eyes closed after the exertions of the day. She looked even smaller, lost in the black cashmere coat, like a child wearing her mother's clothes.

"Remember our deal?"

Rosaria inhaled deeply and shivered in the warmth of the car. "I remember."

"Pretty soon."

Rosaria reached for Nuncie's hand and covered it with her own. "Okay."

"You promised, remember?"

"I know that, honey."

Nuncie nodded, eyes still closed, and seemed to fall asleep.

Rosaria patted Nuncie's hand and said, "I'll be right back." Nuncie, now deeply asleep, didn't respond.

Rosaria opened the door of her car and approached the grave. The Blessed Mother had the beginnings of a snowy mantle, and a fresh white blanket began to cover the recently shoveled earth and wilting funeral flowers.

Rosaria closed her eyes, swaying as a slight dizziness hit her. So many tears in her that wouldn't come. She didn't know if they ever would. For now, wet flakes of snow struck her face and melted in comforting, cold tears of their own. Rosaria was grateful for the afternoon snowstorm, holding her in its sweet, frosty embrace.

CHAPTER 13

 few days after Aurelius's funeral, Joey Mucci sat staring into space. His big frame filled one of the maple chairs that surrounded the heavy kitchen table at Saint Jude's Halfway House in Malford. Outside, more snow was falling, muffling the noise of traffic and leaving only the gentle ticking of the regulator clock on the side wall.

Leo contemplated the sturdy maple kitchen set for a moment. It must have represented an alert staffer's triumphant find, perhaps at the Salvation Army store on Route 1 in Saugus. A family, maybe from Melrose or Stoneham, had sat at this table for dinners on winter evenings like this one. Now, perhaps, the heavy pieces held some echoes, some vestigial warmth and strength of that history for the lost souls at the House, all trying to claw back, reaching for just some fraction of that world.

This particular lost soul and resident of the House stared into the distance, holding a gauze pad with blank disinterest against the side of his split and still bleeding mouth. Joey's right eye had been also beaten closed, the swollen red color now deepening to a bluish black.

"Just after breakfast." A slight young woman named Carmella with lank blond hair leaned against the spotless kitchen counter. "We'd only just finished cleaning up. Joseph had kitchen duty in here. People were getting ready for appointments or jobs. And then, just like that, doesn't that other one come through the door and fly across the room at Joseph?"

An Irish accent. What was this young woman doing here in such a job, wondered Leo. Did her parents in some suburb of Dublin or a small town in West Cork know she was handling a houseful of men like Joey Mucci and the man who had pulverized his face this morning? This woman who couldn't weigh more than 110 pounds.

"That other guy's been nothing but trouble since the day he came. We should have tossed him out two weeks ago," Leo heard someone say. He turned to see a wide-shouldered, older black man with a clipboard eyeing Joey's swollen eye from the doorway.

The man walked into the kitchen and extended his hand to Leo. "Hello, Detective. I'm the house manager. Henry Thornton."

"Good to meet you, Mr. Thornton. So, do we know the guy that did this downtown?" Leo pulled for a moment on the slacks below his knee where the fabric, wet with melted snow, clung damply to his legs.

"Doubt it, but you probably would have gotten to know him soon. Real trouble-maker. Shouldn't have given him a pass. We always hope, you know. Sometimes it just doesn't work out." Thornton grimaced. "We gave the other officer all the details we had. We won't see the guy again. He'll take off, but he might make a stop at the Pine Street Inn downtown before he does."

"Yeah. We're following up with them now." Leo's eyes moved to the large-type glassine-sleeved list of House Rules hanging from the broad refrigerator door. *You are required to attend at least three 12-step meetings per week.* And below the Rules, the grounds for immediate dismissal. *Being under the influence, threats or acts of violence, lies, weapons, property destruction, failure to submit U/A.* Rules to cage the beast within. The red-eyed beast, barely held in check, caged and tethered, but always waiting, with the occasional low growl. Waiting with tooth and claw in these men.

Next to the list of House Rules, magnets from the CVS Pharmacy and Johnny's Foodmaster held a prayer to Saint Jude, patron saint of hopeless cases, to the front of the refrigerator. *Saint Jude, glorious apostle, faithful servant and friend of Jesus, patron of the hopeless, pray for me, who am so miserable...*

Leo leaned down to get a closer look at Joey, who hadn't moved. "The officer get a good picture of this?" He inspected Joey's battered face.

"He did," said the young woman. "And told us to come down to the station when Joseph is ready to file a complaint."

Leo nodded. "Say again, Joey, why do you think he did this?" Joey winced as he pursed his lips and shrugged, and then mumbled a response. Leo moved closer. "Say it again, Joey?"

"Nun-killer. Said I was a nun-killer. Killed the old nun." He avoided Leo's gaze.

"Guy said he's a devout Catholic. Old style. Whatever that means," observed Thornton, leaning on the counter with arms crossed. "Saints talk to him directly. He's got one nasty crew of saints there, best as I can see."

"I didn't do her. I didn't do her. I told you that, Leo. I just found her." Joey's beseeching eyes looked into Leo's.

"I know what you told me, Joey. I just wish you could remember more of what you say you saw that night, about the shadows and everything."

"Just shadows. Just shadows and her lying there."

"You hear anything?"

Joey didn't respond. Leo was about to ask another question when Joey said, "Two shadows."

"Two shadows?" Leo watched Joey closely. "You're sure there were two shadows?"

Joey nodded and looked at Leo. "A smell, maybe." A flicker of hope on Joey's face. Maybe he'd be believed this time.

"Like what kind of smell?"

"I don't know, like somebody smoking, but different. Sweet."

"Sweet like a ladies perfume or a man's cologne?"

"No, Leo. No. Don't be stupid. Not *perfume*." Joey's mouth turned down in sarcasm as he drew out the word perfume. He waved his hand impatiently in the air. "Smoke. Like a sweet smoke. Just a little." He twisted his mouth. "Perfume," he said, shaking his head in disbelief. "Not perfume."

"Smoke. Okay, Joey." Leo wrote a note to himself on the pad he kept in his shirt pocket. "Joey—"

Joey turned his head to the side and looked up at Leo. His voice rose. "Leave me alone now." A sharp intake of breath. "Leave me alone now, Leo." Articulating every word.

"All right then," Leo said, putting his notepad away. "You just did a real good job there with information. It'll help us. Thanks." Joey looked out the window, not meeting Leo's eyes.

Leo contemplated Joey. Two shadows and a sweet, smoky smell that night with the nun. And Joey Mucci showing up in a darkened corner of the schoolyard to take the wrap, a stroke of luck for two shadows. Leo considered the possibility that he'd been tying this case up all wrong.

But then, everyone knew Joey was a whack job—seeing, feeling things other people didn't see or feel. Who knew what he saw or was thinking that night. All the same, Leo was glad he hadn't locked it in with Joey yet, though his chief was getting impatient with him.

Leo's thoughts were interrupted by Henry Thornton's voice as he asked Joey again, "Sure you don't want to go to the ER?"

Joey shook his head, now staring into space.

Thornton looked at Leo. "We have a volunteer nurse that comes in once a week. She's due this afternoon. I think we'll be okay."

"Would you like something to eat, Joseph?" Carmella asked. "I think we still have some chocolate ice cream."

Leo thought he heard Joey moan. He couldn't be sure, but there was no mistaking the force behind Joey's response. "Hate chocolate ice cream."

"Now, who hates chocolate ice cream?" Carmella raised her eyebrows.

"I do. I hate it." Dark rage. Staring at Carmella directly as he spoke. Joey rarely faced anyone head-on. "Hate it."

Henry Thornton gave Joey a long look before meeting Leo's eyes. The older man raised his eyebrows and cocked his head as if to say, "*Who hates chocolate ice cream?*"

Carmella glanced at Henry Thornton with a worried expression. "Well then, would it be a nice cup of tea and a biscuit, a cookie then?" she asked Joey in a careful tone. "I've been hiding some oatmeal ones with raisins, but I might share them with a nice guy like you." A whisper of a smile touched Joey Mucci's face, and Carmella went to fill the teakettle.

A two-foot statue of Saint Jude himself stood on a wide shelf on one kitchen wall. A plaster Pentecostal flame rose from the saint's head and an ax, symbol of his martyrdom, rested in his hand. In Leo's childhood, he had seen images of the resolute Saint Jude, credited with traveling to Armenia in the early days of the Church and now considered one of the patrons of the Armenian Catholic Church. The few images Leo remembered from his childhood had been more benign than this statue in the kitchen of the halfway house. Of course, given the demons the residents of this house were battling, a fiercer Jude Thaddeus—this one with the bushy eyebrows and glowering stare across the kitchen table, ax in hand—needed to be on call.

Rosaria's CEO needed more revenue from her and he wanted her in the field. What the hell was she doing in Boston now? Shouldn't she be in Pretoria finishing the deal with that new distributor? That guy was a guaranteed big start-up order. And what about that Central Asian order? Just get that done and wrap it up. But she'd damned well better make sure nothing leaked into the Moscow gray market. There'd be hell to pay.

When the conversations ended, her boss had somewhat gracelessly agreed that Rosaria was better in Boston working the phones. She had a good team in the field. On that last point, Rosaria tried not to think of the vast and bleak desert mountain territory, populated by sustenance level nomadic herders, that Dimitri had offered Genghis Kahn to mollify the distributor on pricing. Rosaria was still cleaning that conversation up.

She wasn't leaving. She was staying here until she found some answers for Aurelius. And that was that. Besides, she was experienced enough to manage the business from here for now, and it was more efficient anyway than flying all over the globe.

Rosaria had just picked up the phone for more calls when her vision began to alter. Spinning kaleidoscopes, sparkling wheels of color now wherever she looked. Migraine auras. *Oh great.* Why didn't New York just leave her alone and let her do her job? And then laying more revenue numbers on her. Jesus.

Rosaria was taking aspirins for her swiftly developing migraine when the cell rang again. She almost didn't answer. She needed to get to her bedroom, close the shades and lie down with the pain until this thing passed in its own time. Then, she saw through her disturbed visual patterns that it was the Motherhouse calling. Closing her eyes and covering them with one hand, she accepted the call. A young nun was on the line. Would Rosaria come up to Maudsley for a short visit the next day? Mother Superior had something to discuss with her.

Rosaria had no time. She'd lose hours with this migraine and New York would be calling again. She wished she could block those calls from New York. *Oh, what the hell.* She could do business while she drove, using the speaker feature in the car. She could use a little Maudsley right now, so yes, of course she'd be there tomorrow.

Rosaria hung up the phone, melancholy thoughts of Aurelius gliding through her mind again like a flock of wide-winged and graceful dark birds. Her head was throbbing as she drew the blinds in her bedroom and lay on the bed with a glass of water beside her, Archie at her feet.

The next day was cold, dry, and sunny. As she drove, Rosaria was on the phone to Germany, arranging the transfer of last year's shoe models from the German market to her distributor in Central Asia. Russian consumers wouldn't pay full price for last year's product, so there would be no danger of transshipment and, with the discount she negotiated, she could sell the shoes to the Central Asian distributor at his price range. She wished she could unsnarl everything else in her life so easily.

Rosaria pulled into the driveway of the Motherhouse and parked. She was glad to shut off her phone. A novice greeted her at the front door of the Motherhouse and ushered her into Mother Marguerite Fontaine's office.

The nun's office area and its furnishings were simple. A plain cross hung on the cream-colored wall, and neat folders of paperwork sat beside a slim MacBook Pro on an old wooden teacher's classroom desk. In the corner of the room, an antique table of Quebec country pine held a small statue of Saint Kateri Tekakwitha, the Seventeenth Century Mohawk-Algonquin saint from the time of the French Jesuit missions in the New World. Rosaria had heard that early in her career Mother Superior, half Mohawk herself, had been posted to the Kahawake reserve in southern Quebec.

"Rosaria, so good to see you." Mother Superior's face was lined with the cares of administering a large organization with endless demands and never enough money, but she radiated some mysterious nunny cheerfulness that Rosaria had never fully understood. The nun wore a trim navy suit and white blouse, and the cut of her short, dark hair was, Rosaria thought, considerably more stylish than her own. Now, Mother Superior rose and took both of Rosaria's hands. Her slim brown fingers were dark against Rosaria's larger, pale hands. "You are looking well, Rosaria, considering. What a terrible incident with the hit and run, on top of everything else."

"Yes, Mother, I'd say so, but I'm okay now. Just a little shaken up."

"Oh, you can't keep a good woman down." The nun smiled as she took Rosaria by the arm. "We can take a little walk around the pond now. The weather's so fine. A little chilly, but so fine." The nun's small, elegant face was gracious and her soft voice calmly authoritative.

With that, Mother Marguerite put on a dark coat with a matching navy and gold patterned wool scarf. She picked up a small gray velvet bag from her desk as she guided Rosaria out the French doors in the office to a narrow stone path leading through a garden. Rosaria knew from her visits with Aurelius that the garden was lovely in the spring and summer, but now the plants were dormant, cut back and brown in the winter cold.

Mother Superior put her arm through Rosaria's as they walked along a shoveled path around the frozen pond, circled with tall brown grasses and cat o'nine tails. A couple of intrepid ducks paddled in the few patches of open water.

As they walked, the nun began, "Rosaria, I know you're aware that the Sisters have few earthly possessions."

Rosaria nodded, remembering Aurelius's spartan life. "Of course, Mother."

"For all of Sister Aurelius's years of service, she leaves behind only this small bag of her own personal items. Funny, isn't it?" Mother Superior smiled as she held the bag up. "A long life and all that remains to hold in your hand are a simple cross and a couple of books of prayer and philosophy." She looked into Rosaria's eyes. "But she left more, so much more, didn't she?"

"Oh yes."

"She'd want you to have these few things, Rosaria."

The bag was so small. It was nothing, yet all that remained of Aurelius to hold. A sudden surge of grief seized Rosaria like a vise. She stood very still, breathing deeply, while the nun held her arm before she said, "Thank you, Mother."

Rosaria held the small gray bag tightly in her hands when the two women entered the Motherhouse again. As she made her goodbyes, Mother Marguerite said, "After the investigation, we'll send you Sister's wooden rosaries. We think you should have them." Mother touched her arm, "And, Rosaria, please stay in touch."

"I will, Mother. Thank you."

Later, at her dining room table on Trinity Wharf, Rosaria sat with a glass of cabernet and examined the final worldly possessions of Mary Aurelius, Sister of Jeanne d'Arc. A small green Connemara marble cross, a well-worn prayer book with the daily Divine Office, and a heavily used, compact, leather-bound copy of *The Meditations of Marcus Aurelius*. Rosaria smiled to see a brown and gold Bruins bookmark in the book.

Sipping her wine, she flipped through the *Meditations* to find the book opened easily to certain sections and pages that seem to be often read. In Book Five:

> Do not be distressed, do not despond or give up in despair, if now and again, practice falls short of precept. Return to the attack after each failure.

In Book Seven:

> Take it that you have died today, and your life's story ended; and thenceforward regard what further time may be given you and live it out in harmony with your nature.

Rosaria caressed these pages knowing they had spoken with special meaning to Aurelius. After some time, she started to close the little book, and then paused. There, on the inside front cover was a neatly taped small brown envelope. Carefully lifting the dried tape, she removed the envelope and held it up. An old safe deposit key envelope with no identification or markings. Rosaria shook her head and removed a small brass key from the envelope. The key bore the number 33, so faint it was barely readable and, again, nothing else in the form of identification. Rosaria took a sip of her wine and let out a long breath. How to figure this out? Maybe start at one of the banks downtown for advice.

She looked at the key. "I wish you could talk."

Rosaria slipped the envelope and key into her bag. The *Mediations,* she put aside to go on her bedside table.

CHAPTER 14

ecca didn't mind that they had to meet in her apartment or away from Malford. She understood why she and Malachy couldn't be seen together. He had a big position in the community and a lovely wife whom everyone adored.

Yes, he had a lovely wife—but he needed Becca. She knew he did. She and Malachy were alike in many ways. Living in the projects left a certain mark of hard reality on a person that Francie would never understand. Becca and Malachy spoke the same language, as they say, and Becca could appreciate Malachy in ways Francie could not. Malachy never said anything about Francie, but Becca knew the score.

Those evenings when Malachy would come over, he would tell Francie he had a meeting in Boston. Then, he would stop over to Becca's apartment after her boy Josiah had taken her car to his late shift at Dunkin's. They would sit at her small kitchen table and talk over a roast chicken dinner from Boston Market and a couple of cans of Budweiser.

Oh, how they would talk. About people. About politics. About Malachy's business. Everything. Becca loved when they talked like that. Malachy listened like what she said really mattered. She wished they could be together every night... and sometimes—lately—she felt Malachy wished that, too.

Once or twice, they drove up to the shore. Becca would drive her car up Route One as far as the Costco parking lot where Malachy would pick her up. They'd gone as far as Portsmouth one time and had dinner on the harbor. Malachy had ordered a bottle of wine, and they'd watched the sunset off the restaurant deck.

When they were walking hand and hand along the harbor, Becca felt *they* were the real couple. Francie was just for show.

"For pity's sake, why did you wait so long to come, Mrs. Linsky? I hope I can save the tooth." The dentist looked at Becca Linsky uncomprehendingly. "If you'd been here ten days ago, I could be sure, but now we'll just have to do our best."

"Oh, you know how busy it gets, Doctor. Just so much going on." Becca gave an apologetic smile and a shrug. The dentist didn't reply.

Becca wondered what was the matter with this man. She didn't come earlier because she had no goddamned money to come earlier. You needed prior authorization for the Mass Health Dental plan for low-income citizens, and they covered extractions, not root canals. She had been trying to save some money over the last few weeks to keep the tooth. Josiah needed basketball shoes and a winter jacket. The kid didn't ask for much, God knows. Thank God Malachy had covered his athletic fees.

The dental hygienist smiled at Becca with some sympathy while the dentist prepared his tools. At least somebody around here had a heart and a brain in her head, Becca thought.

Josiah hadn't noticed his mother popping ibuprofens every few hours over the last week for the pain, but Malachy Sullivan did when he came in for breakfast that morning. After she told him what was wrong, he called his dentist and got Becca a same day appointment after her shift at the Strand. And told her he'd cover the cost.

Becca felt a sudden surge of happiness to be sitting in this dentist's chair getting her tooth fixed. Getting her tooth fixed like other people did when they had a bad toothache—not just popping pills, living with the goddamned thing until it had to be yanked out because they couldn't afford to go to the goddamned dentist.

She took a long breath. What a difference Malachy had made in her life. This appointment, even the comfortable Crocs he'd bought her last week. Just left them in a box on the table with the cash for his breakfast bill and tip. Nurses' shoes, he said, for people that had to be on their feet all day. It was bliss to wear the Crocs after her Keds, light shoes with no support, bought from a remainder bin at the Ocean State Job Lot store some months ago. She'd been soaking and rubbing her feet every night after wearing the Keds all day, praying she didn't get a stress fracture. Being a waitress, her feet were, in many ways, her livelihood.

Malachy got Josiah into the Celtics summer camp in Waltham. Oh, God! The kid was so excited. He never got a break. He floated around the apartment these days just thinking about Malachy's getting him that chance.

The dentist had big hands that were uncomfortable in her small mouth, and the pressure from the drill hurt her jaw. But she was hesitant to say anything to him. She was so grateful to have this work done. *Just suck it up and concentrate on more pleasant things,* she thought.

Becca didn't dare linger on Malachy's talk the other day about buying one of the new townhouses over in Edgewood as an investment. Maybe she and Josiah could stay in it for awhile, while the property appreciated for Malachy—whatever that meant. She'd seen the ones with the garage underneath, a deck out back and a little yard, three bedrooms and a modern kitchen. Jesus, she could weep at the possibility of moving out of the projects.

Becca's thoughts had wandered so much that she only came back to the present as the hygienist was taking cotton rolls out of her mouth and giving her prescriptions for pain medication. Becca would have to see how much of that was covered under the Mass Health. If they weren't covered, she'd deal with it. More over-the-counter ibuprofens.

Becca walked to the reception area and was taking her coat from a rack when she heard someone entering the dentist's reception area.

"Hi, Helen. I'm a little early."

Becca felt a thump in her chest as Francie Sullivan walked in the door. She wondered if Francie knew who she was, but Francie gave her such a warm smile before turning to the receptionist, she figured not.

The receptionist took a quick look at Becca, and then at Francie before responding. "Not at all, Francie. We're ready for you."

"I saw they put more time on the parking meters outside—two hours. I'll bet the merchants like that." Francie turned to Becca and smiled. "Hi."

"Hi." Becca knew her voice had quavered, but Francie didn't seem to notice. The receptionist looked down at her appointment book.

Francie's sweet energy seemed to fill the office. In spite of Becca's knowing how much Malachy loved her—she was sure he loved her more than Francie—in her darker moments, she did wonder why he was bothering with her—a still pretty, but worn waitress from the Strand Diner, a single mother without a dime to her name.

After thinking about the question for a long time, Becca had finally decided it was his mother. Malachy would sometimes talk about his mother after a few drinks at Becca's place. He'd get a little teary and sentimental as he talked "God, how she worked, Becca," he'd say. "Double shifts at Johnny's Foodmaster to supplement the old man's disability from the T."

Only once did Malachy talk about his father. "Pretty clear that all he was disabled by was the booze. Drank himself to death." Malachy gave a short bitter laugh. "An Irish suicide."

He did for Becca what he was unable to do as a kid for his mother, now gone. He was taking care of another mother who needed help. Becca was grateful and would take the situation as it was, but that part felt a little weird.

Francie wasn't the mother figure, Becca could see that. She was the lovely, picture book wife of the successful man, the high school sweetheart. But then, behind the warm smile on that lovely face, Becca thought she saw just a tinge of something else. Becca was too familiar herself with that screen of warm cheer and good humor to the world, hiding a deep despair, a dark melancholy. God knows Becca had spent many a hard day with that kind of smile on her face. Maybe Francie knew that Malachy's heart was elsewhere now.

But now, Becca acutely felt her Costco down coat, the CVS hair elastic holding her ponytail in place, and her waitress Crocs. She watched Francie take off her fur-lined coat to reveal a sweet blue cashmere twin set over a black pencil skirt and high, black leather boots. A gust of bleak reality swept through Becca. She knew where she stood now. A temporary woman on the side with no claim. *Not yet anyway.*

Becca had a track record. She knew that husbands usually made up various complaints about their wives to justify their wandering. Becca used to wait to see if there was anything unique coming, and there seldom was. Malachy never did that. Never said a bad word about Francie. Never talked about her at all. Becca used to wonder about that. Francie seemed like a nice person, a good person. Malachy must have known that, too.

Well, Becca thought, *I'm a good person, too.* She felt a sudden wave of resentment. It was her turn. Francie had had her turn. Now, it was Becca's turn to have something. To have the good-looking, successful husband, the cashmere twin set, and the tall leather boots. Her turn not to be on her feet all day. It was Josiah's turn, too.

Malachy would take care of Francie. She'd do all right. But this was Becca's last shot. She had to take it. She wasn't going to lose it.

CHAPTER 15

ut of his kitchen window, Bill Kenneally watched his friend Patrick Cronin maneuver his blue Ford Focus through the snow and parked cars in the short dead end of Sherman Court. Finally, Patrick turned the little car around and parked it on the corner of the street, halfway onto the sidewalk near a mailbox and a telephone pole. Gathering his papers from the passenger seat, he worked his ample frame, made larger by his winter weight parka, out of the car and onto the sanded street.

Good of Patrick to stop by on his way home from City Hall, thought Bill. Patrick had agreed to bring Bill copies of the Redevelopment Authority notes from the last year.

Patrick knocked on the back door. "When did you start knocking at my back door, Cronin? Come in, come in." Leaning on just one cane, Bill was pouring hot water into the old green teapot.

"Thanks, Bill. Didn't want to startle you." Patrick's jacket rustled and swished against the other coats and umbrellas on hooks as he passed through the cramped back hall.

"I'm too old to be startled," Bill responded with a snort. "Go on, go on. Lead the way." He gestured toward the small living room, and then followed Patrick to the sitting area. A plastic dish of Cheez-It crackers sat beside two mugs and a small sugar and creamer. The dish pattern, nineteenth-century villages with stagecoaches and hoop-skirted women, was part of the set Bill's wife Lizzie got at the supermarket years ago with the green stamps.

Bill shuffled to the kitchen and brought a bottle of Jameson for the tea.

"Here you are, old son. To celebrate the end of the workday. I hear working at City Hall is no walk in the park these days." With some ceremony, Bill placed the whiskey bottle on the small table.

"Thanks, Bill. That's the truth, but you don't have to go to all this trouble."

"No trouble. No trouble." Bill sat heavily into the worn comforter-covered lounger. His large black cat Genevieve leapt into his lap, circling several times until she found the best spot to lie down.

"We'll let that tea steep a little longer. Hate weak tea. My mother used to say tea should be strong enough to stand up and declare itself." Bill stopped talking and looked at Patrick's face. "What's that face about, Cronin? Something happen?"

"Sort of."

"God, I hope it doesn't have anything to do with those missing minutes from the Redevelopment Authority I asked you to get for me."

"I don't think so. There, I got lucky and was ahead of the game for once. Had a great intern. Very quick kid, and he had all those notes scanned before some of them went missing. I have it all here." Patrick fished in his pocket and pulled out a small black plastic rectangle.

"What would that be?" Bill squinted.

"Thumb drive. Can hold hundreds of pages. You just plug it into the computer and you transfer all the documents to the drive and then another computer."

"Isn't that a wonder, now? Such a wonder."

Patrick pulled a padded, stamped envelope out of his parka and set it beside him on the couch.

"Thank you, Patrick. That is very good of you. I hope it wasn't too much to ask. I know there are new people at the Hall and things are different now."

"Oh, that they are, that they are, Bill." Patrick shifted in his seat. "And you're welcome. Citizens are supposed to be able to request these things. I'll tell you, it's not just the Redevelopment notes and the Immaculate in there. The old Malford Shoe site is another dicey deal. There's some stuff there that would make anyone ask hard questions about deals being made. I can't believe some reporter from *The Malford News* hasn't been around yet on those. But there's something else. Something bigger."

Patrick looked down and ran his fingers through the few remaining strands of his thinning dark hair. Bill noticed Patrick's hand was trembling and there was a slight sheen of sweat on his brow. Patrick was silent for a few moments, and seemed to wrestle with some internal conflict.

Bill waited, giving him time, and then Patrick looked up at Bill. "Just between us, okay?"

"Deep as a well, Patrick. Deep as a well." Bill's furrowed his brow. *Trouble on the horizon.*

"The other day, young Nellie Vespucci walks into my office. Nice girl, just graduated from Bentley in accounting and came on board a few months ago. She works for Roger O'Toole's nephew." Patrick smirked. "You know O'Toole. He's the useless, overdressed windbag who's supposed to run the Housing Authority."

Bill smiled and nodded.

"So, O'Toole puts his nephew in to run finance and administration at the Housing Authority," Patrick continued, wrinkling his nose as if against a bad smell. "What a joke. Do-nothing fat-ass. Must be genetic. Anyway, I suppose they thought they'd put this sharp kid in to make it look as if the nephew knew what he was doing. As if. She's just a kid, tiny little thing. So, they figured they could handle her."

Bill smiled. "But they underestimated the kid."

"Oh, I guess they did. She even knew enough not to go to O'Toole's nephew. She came to me for advice." Patrick rubbed his cheek with his big hand. "Nellie found some parallel records. Stuff you'd expect from these lowlifes. Padded, no-bid contracts on everything. The bill for trash was huge, as big as the whole city. Maintenance, repairs, and upgrades that were funded, but never happened. Only did any work when they got a tip from some guy they paid off that an inspection in certain apartments was on the Fed schedule."

Patrick inhaled deeply and exhaled a long breath through pursed lips. Bill clucked his tongue, shook his head and took another sip of his drink.

"Friends and relatives on the payroll. Cronies and Housing Authority managers living in the better Authority apartments for a pittance, while the list of people who really need them is as long as your arm. Big cars bought for Roger O'Toole and his pals."

Patrick threw up his hands. "Oh, I could go on and on. But the cherry on top could be O'Toole's salary. Reported to the state and Feds as $120 thousand, but he's really taking in $350 thousand a year."

"You've got to be kidding me. Doesn't anybody watch over these guys?" Bill set his drink on the coffee table and shook his head.

"Nope, independent. City's not responsible. When the program was set up, they were afraid that the Mayor and city council would put their own guys in and corrupt the system. Ha. The Mayor won't touch it. Okay guy, but he's afraid. Just looks the other way. State audited them a while ago and someone got paid off or spoken to. O'Toole goes out and raises a shitload of money for some powerful people, you know. So, they got a clean bill of health."

Patrick shifted in his seat, reaching beside him. "I took the info," he held up the padded envelope and drive, "and decided to think about it overnight. I told Nellie to take a trip somewhere far away for a while, borrow the money and do it fast. Maybe Italy. Say her grandmother's dying. Anything. Quit if they won't give her the time. If they find out what she knows, something could happen. It's that bad, Bill. These guys can be rough."

"Rough like how?" asked Bill.

"Oh, a guy in another department talked to a reporter without permission a few months ago about the likely schedule for the shoe factory land and who was interested. Next day, someone takes a bat to his windshield in the parking lot, and suddenly his vacation is yanked for an urgent project that nobody ever heard of." Patrick stopped before turning to Bill again. His hands trembled as he reached into his pocket and took out two white pills which he washed down with the Jameson-laced tea.

"Careful, fella."

"I know, I know. My nerves are shot. I never used to need anything like this until the new crew at City Hall came in."

Patrick rubbed his thigh with his big hand. "The payback with the baseball bat and all was for that guy—for being too chatty, you know, but it was a message for the rest of us too. And I'm telling you right now, Bill, I'm giving you this development stuff because you're a taxpayer and you have every legal right to ask for it. But I'm telling you as a friend that you shouldn't go near this cesspool. It looks all of a piece. A damned shoddy piece."

They were both quiet. Bill's cat Genevieve turned and settled herself on his lap.

"They pay you back fast if you step out of line. Job, pension. I'm fifty-eight now. They can do you in. Hate to say it, but a guy could get kicked around bad if they feel like it."

"That's terrible, terrible. Not for me to say, Patrick, but something should be done."

"I know, I know." Patrick sighed. "But I can't think about it right now. Bill, I can't put myself and my family out there. I could really pay a price. I'm not going to be a martyr." He gulped his tea and leaned forward in his chair. "I need to sleep on it." He stood and started to button his jacket. "Have to take off now. I'm meeting Sean, my youngest, at The Point for a couple of beers before we go to the Garden for the Canadiens game."

Bill walked Patrick to the door after tea and then worked his way back to the living room. As he picked up the tea mugs, he turned to see the brown padded envelope still on the couch. Addressed to the Attorney General's office. Perhaps left by mistake. Perhaps not. Poor Patrick. Bill worked his way to the window to see if he could catch Patrick, but the blue Focus was already halfway down the street.

Bill ventured outside his house later in the evening. By the light of the street lamps, he walked slowly up the middle of the sanded, narrow street, pushing his aluminum canes before him. Tucked under his arm was the small padded mailing envelope. He stopped to secure it several times as he headed step by painstaking step toward the big mailbox on the corner.

Bill had known Patrick long enough to recognize that he wanted Bill to do this for him. Patrick didn't need to say anything. The addressed and stamped envelope propped on the couch plain as day was a message, a plea for Bill to take over this hard decision and do the right thing. Patrick, in an agony of indecision, couldn't take the step himself. He knew his friend could and would. As Bill had said, something should be done.

_____

Rosaria walked from her condo on the waterfront over to Massachusetts General Hospital where she was going to keep Nuncie company on one of her chemo infusion days. This morning, in particular, Rosaria had so much to talk about.

Her mind alternated between business issues and events in Malford as she walked up Cambridge Street toward the hospital. She was waiting at the intersection of Cambridge and Blossom Streets when a thought flashed briefly through her mind. Something important. She tried to catch whatever that firefly of a thought was, blinking briefly before closing into darkness, but she was not fast enough and it eluded her.

Long experience had taught Rosaria not to chase a thought that blazed for only an instant. Just leave it be until it decided it was ready to land. Whatever it was that flashed across her mind would present itself fully formed sooner or later, if she let it come in its own time. And so it did a short time later as she entered the lobby of MGH. Slipping into a quiet corner of the lobby, Rosaria took out her cell and made a call.

"Good morning. French Connection," a young, energetic voice answered.

"Yes, I'm calling for Bridie Callahan. Could she come to the phone for a moment?"

"Bridie's with some customers. Can you call her back in about ten minutes?"

"I won't be but a second. Please, it's important. Tell her it's Rosaria."

Some reluctance and then, "Okay. Just a minute."

Shortly afterward, Bridie's bright voice came onto the phone. "Hey, Ro. How're you doing? What's up?"

"Doing great, Bridie. I have a quick question for you."

When Rosaria asked her question, Bridie responded, "Well. I don't know why you'd want to know that, Ro, but my cousin lives on John Stark Road."

"Too long a story, but thanks, Bridie. That's all I needed."

"Okay, Ro. See you soon."

Rosaria's next call was to a long ago school friend from The Immaculate who'd settled in Chelsea. The tough old city of Chelsea on Chelsea Creek. The city where Bridie Callahan's cousin had complained about Malachy Sullivan's SUV blocking

John Stark Road. The city with a bar called The Creek, with matchbooks like the one found at the site of Aurelius's murder. A matchbook Rosaria had overheard Leo talking about at the hospital after her hit and run. Perhaps two random, unrelated pieces of data. Perhaps not, but still worth exploring. Worth a bus ride.

"John Stark Road?" Rosaria's friend answered her question. "Not much around there, just houses and, oh, a little bar. Let's see. What's it called? The Creek. That's it."

"I thought that might be what it's called."

"How come you thought that?"

"Never mind. A place I could go into without sticking out too much?"

"You'd stick out anywhere, Ro. You're a looker."

"Yeah, well, you know what I mean."

"If you're talking about The Creek, you'd stick out like a sore thumb. Why would you be going to a place like that?" She laughed. "They'd be in shellshock with you walking through the door."

"I'm just checking on something for a friend."

"Oh, I know how that goes. The wandering boy?"

"Something like that." Rosaria felt a twinge of guilt—but not too much—in how she presented this visit to her old friend. "Okay place for me to go then?"

"Well, depends. They're not used to outsiders. Couldn't your friend find some-one else, like maybe a man, to check this out?"

"It's hard to explain, but I'm really the only one who can do this."

Then, as Rosaria had hoped, her friend said. "Well, if you feel you have to go there, let me send my Pauly with you. He's off this afternoon—fixing my storm window, and Sheila's with the kids at her mother's. My window can wait."

"Oh, that would be great. Thanks so much."

Rosaria put her cell back in her bag and, her mind racing, rode the elevator to the eighth floor of the Yawkey Building. She thought about calling Leo to tell him where she was going after MGH, but he'd just complicate things. He'd tell her she couldn't go. She'd be furious and it all would just end up in a mess, because she'd go anyway. Better to just go do it.

On the infusion unit floor, Rosaria saw Nuncie near the far corner, beside the windows. She walked over and gave her a quick hug before she dropped into the visitor's chair. She could have told Nuncie about her plan too, but she nixed that quickly. Nuncie was as bad as Leo.

Nuncie's blond wig peeked from her large red purse beside the recliner. She was already hooked up and had a Scrabble game ready for them on her tray. Outside the broad windows of the eighth floor, the Charles River was a brilliant blue under a cloudless New England winter sky. The Longfellow Bridge stretched across the river to Cambridge and MIT with trolleys, cars, bikes, and pedestrians sharing the old gray stone bridge, called the "Salt and Pepper" Bridge for its distinctive round towers.

The infusion unit was filled with people in recliners. People with tubes in their arms, some wearing wigs, hats, or scarves, some comfortable with their baldness. Watching videos, playing cards, talking softly as the life-saving poison entered their bloodstream. Nurses with just the right level of efficient upbeat kindness, blessedly devoid of false cheer, moved from patient to patient as volunteers brought soup and sandwiches.

With her tiny stature and favorite big, red-framed eyeglasses, Nuncie had a certain Yoda look to her today, thought Rosaria. The cancer had been slow-growing for almost a year, but these past months, it was advancing aggressively. The yellow cast to Nuncie's skin was pronounced. Even a few weeks ago, it could have passed for the remains of a golden tan, but not anymore. Before it had been an uncertain whisper. Now, it was bold, and it spoke of mortality.

"That's not a word," Nuncie objected, as Rosaria spelled out the word *zax* with her tiles. "And don't bring out that screwy dictionary with all those made-up words," she added, while Rosaria was pulling out her Scrabble dictionary to explain that a zax is a slater's tool.

They quickly lost track of Scrabble words as they started to discuss what Rosaria had read in the minutes of the Malford Development Authority meetings from several months ago.

"Shit," said Nuncie, "Let me get this straight. They're recommending that the Archdiocese sell the Immaculate as a distressed property, which it's not, to Claddagh Properties at a below-market price?" Nuncie shifted angrily in her chair and had to readjust the tubing at her side in the process. "Wouldn't that frost you? Jesus."

"That's what it looks like. We all know it's not a distressed property," Rosaria said. "But why in God's name would Monsignor McDermott be pushing this? The Archdiocese could make three or four times that profit on the open market. They're no dummies."

"Well, I can see why they want to keep this hush-hush."

"I'll bet the Chancery isn't fully on board, and Malachy doesn't want any negative publicity before he locks this all up. That would make sense."

Rosaria paused to take a cup of soup for Nuncie from a volunteer. "You know it would take nerve for the Monsignor to talk like this to the Development Authority unless he had the full backing of the Archdiocese. If Malachy charms the nuns into selling him the Motherhouse up in Essex on top of it, Malachy's really in the money. But the big question for me is—what about the Monsignor? Is he in the money, too? What's in it for him?"

Rosaria and Nuncie gazed at each other, each contemplating the question.

"Everybody's got a price." Nuncie cautiously tasted the soup. "You know, this is probably pretty good, but I just have that metallic taste in my mouth all the time."

"I know, honey."

"Never mind," Nuncie said, putting the soup aside. "What do you think about the Monsignor?"

"Well, he's not my favorite guy and maybe I'm wrong, but I think he's above doing something for personal gain. Must be something else motivating him." For a few moments, Rosaria took in the view outside the hospital window of the broad Charles River wending its way through the city. "I think there's something bigger going on than a garden variety sweetheart real estate deal."

"Don't let your imagination run away with you, O'Reilly."

"Hello, ladies. Who's winning?" Richard, Nuncie's favorite nurse, came over to change the infusion bag. "This is the stinky stuff, Nuncie. And it's going to feel cold."

Nuncie grimaced. These procedures had become a fact of her life. She kept going and planned her best activities for the third week after chemo, when she could function reasonably well again. But then, like a bad joke or Groundhog Day, she would have to be back to get another jolt.

"Gave up the game, Richard. Nuncie's such a poor loser. Anyway, we're trying to figure something out. Church business," said Rosaria. "It's complicated."

"I bet it is," commented Richard as he packed up the empty infusion bag and wound some surplus tubing around his muscular arm. Rosaria could see a Red Sox tattoo under the short sleeve of his uniform. "Everything they touch is complicated, starting with the abuses. Didn't come up smelling like roses. How can you have trust after that?" A melancholy fatalism came over the nurse's full, kind face as he attached the new infusion bag.

"Of course, on that one, some of the guys that came forward as victims were all messed up with drugs and alcohol. At first, the Church said they were just looking for money. But, for me, they're telling the truth, and the settlements are justified. Something like that could totally screw you up forever, you know? I'd be self-medicating too if that happened to me."

"Me too, "said Rosaria. "How could anyone cover up preying on innocents like that?"

Rosaria thought about how the clerical abuse stories had gripped the city, and how complete strangers would talk about it together—on buses, in the grocery store, and now in an infusion room at Mass General Hospital. To try to understand—to comprehend as a society—how they all could have been so blind, so trusting...?

Later, Rosaria helped Nuncie pack up and walked with her to the pickup area in front of the hospital where Nuncie's brother Sevi waited. Rosaria waved goodbye and stood briefly on the sidewalk, surrounded by a bustling stream of patients, some in wheelchairs pushed by volunteers, before she started out for Chelsea and The Creek.

CHAPTER 16

osaria was relieved to be accompanied to the bar by her friend's husky son, Paul, assistant football coach for Chelsea High. She felt something else too. Maybe the excitement, the energy of the hunt. Maybe onto something now, whatever that something was. Rosaria's pace was animated as she walked over to the Blue Line on the T where she picked up the subway to Maverick Square in East Boston. Better to take public transport. Parking was hard in East Boston and Chelsea.

The 111 bus from Maverick Square to Bellingham Square in Chelsea carried a full load of passengers—mostly Hispanic workers, with a smattering of students headed for the Chelsea Annex of Bunker Hill Community College. The bus, overheated in the winter cold, traveled through dense neighborhoods of well-cared-for aluminum sided houses sprouting dozens of satellite dishes on each street. Rosaria sat in the middle of the bus, next to a woman whose uniform for the housekeeping staff of a major Boston hotel was visible under her winter coat. She and Rosaria exchanged smiles, but Rosaria felt out of place, as if she were in another country.

And she was.

Rosaria breathed in the faint smell of oil from the terminal and tankers on the Chelsea River when she got off the bus. Just a few blocks past Bellingham Square, looking down near the next intersection, she saw a small lighted and chipped plastic sign advertising The Battle of Chelsea Creek Tavern. She passed the sign for John Stark Road, which also displayed a plaque commemorating John Stark, leader of the Battle of Chelsea Creek during the Revolution.

Just two narrow horizontal windows graced the brick front of The Creek, and they were high up on the wall, giving the building the look of a hostile squint, daring her to enter. Rosaria stood on the sidewalk for a few moments, feeling a shiver of trepidation, which she quickly smothered. She took a deep breath, pushed the battered red metal door open and entered the bar. Cold air from the outside surged in behind her, and the patrons of The Creek turned to assess this sudden oddity blown in from the street.

When her eyes adjusted fully to the light inside, Rosaria could see men in work clothes seated at the bar and in the row of booths to the side. Truckers, workers from the terminal, delivery and mailmen, and a couple of firefighters were clustered around one end of the bar and the front booths. On a large, flat screen TV, the Bruins were playing the Montreal Canadiens. The bartender, a man about Rosaria's age with a buzz cut and a broken nose on an impassive Irish face, efficiently cleared and replaced empty bottles.

In the suburbs, men were creating "man caves" for themselves. *Weak imitations,* thought Rosaria. *This is a man cave.*

A few minutes later, Rosaria, sitting at the bar in her gray turtleneck sweater, smiled and waved to her friend's son Pauly as he entered The Creek during a commercial break in the Bruins game. The men at the far side of the bar continued to stare at Rosaria, as they had since the break started. Now, they turned their eyes to Pauly. Rosaria caught a glimpse of a vaguely familiar big man, who'd moved to the rear of the crowd when she'd first come in, slip out the side door of the bar. She craned her neck to see the man, but lost him. There was something about his face, the way he moved his big body that brought back a memory. She just couldn't place it.

At the other end of the bar, a tall man, still in a winter weight Noonan Oil jacket, looked at Rosaria and took the lead for the group. "You lost, sweetheart?" A few of the men laughed, not unkindly. Most continued to eye her with a stolid, flat animosity.

"No. I'm okay. Thanks, dear," Rosaria responded directly to Noonan Oil. She met him straight on with a smile that told him she knew how incongruous it was for her to be sitting at the bar in The Creek and to hell with them all. The pack exchanged glances.

Pauly slid onto the stool beside Rosaria. "Couldn't find parking. Everything okay, Ro?" he asked, fixing Mr. Noonan Oil with a tight smile.

"Never better, Pauly." Rosaria gave him a quick hug and patted his back. "You know, it's funny. For a minute, I was sure I saw someone I knew over there, but I guess he's gone or maybe I was mistaken."

"Would be a real long shot for you to know anybody that hangs around here."

"Hey, Pauly," a trucker with the build of an aging athlete called across the bar.

"Hey, Knocko," Pauly acknowledged with a nod and the same tight smile.

The Bruins game recommenced, and all eyes turned to the screen as, shortly after, Marchand, "the little ball of hate," drove the puck down to the Canadiens' net. "Jesus, he's golden today," murmured one of the men, with something akin to love.

"What'll ya have?" the bartender asked flatly, wiping the counter.

"I'll have a Sam on draft," Ro replied, leaning both elbows on the bar. Pauly smiled at her and then turned to the bartender. "I'll have the same, Tommy."

"Coming up," said the bartender. "Who's your pal?" he asked Pauly, nodding his chin toward Rosaria and pulling the blue-flame tap handle for two glasses of Sam Adams lager.

"This is my Aunt Ro. Be nice to her."

"You're a real classy guy, McLaughlin. Bring your Aunt Ro to The Creek. Jesus," commented Noonan Oil with a slow smile, his eyes not leaving the screen where Chara was flying down the ice like a pterodactyl with his enormously long arms and legs.

"Screw you," responded Pauly with a friendly grin.

Rosaria and Pauly watched the game for a few minutes, as the bartender moved to the end of the bar away from them. After some time, he came to their end of the bar for some clean glasses. Rosaria smiled at him. "Do you pretty much get the same crowd here all the time, Tommy?"

"Yeah, pretty much," Tommy responded cautiously, wiping a glass as he watched her.

"Get people that stop in from out of town now and again?"

Tommy looked at Pauly. Pauly hesitated, shrugged and nodded at the bartender.

"Somebody not from the neighborhood or the trucking, I mean," said Rosaria.

"Like you?" Tommy challenged. Rosaria suspected that the undertone would have been more hostile if she hadn't been Pauly's ostensible Aunt Ro, and if Tommy didn't seem to like her. From his amused eyes and smile, she could tell he was entertained with the idea of her being at The Creek.

Maybe it was because she had just breezed in here, totally clueless or totally gutsy. Maybe a little of both. Well, that was okay.

That would do.

"Yeah, like me," she replied.

She could see Tommy considering whether to answer her question or just do an Irish goodbye by giving her his back and walking to the other end of the bar without a word. He dried a few more glasses with a spotless towel, not looking up. Then, a key seemed to turn in the old lock. He smiled and leaned forward on the bar. "And what can I do for you, Aunt Ro?"

"Tall guy. Athletic build. Really dark hair, almost black. Kind of a hockey dad look. Wears a barn jacket."

"Dimples."

"Dimples." Ro repeated, remembering Malachy Sullivan's single deep dimple in his right cheek.

"Yeah, hates it when we call him Dimples," the bartender looked at her with a crooked grin. "So, naturally, that's what we call him. Doesn't mix when he comes in. Usually meets with Gus-Gus over in the last booth."

"Gus-Gus?"

"Mother of God," Rosaria heard Pauly breathe in the seat beside her. He moved closer and spoke in a low voice. "Fat rat in Cinderella."

Rosaria nodded with a confused look on her face.

"Augustus McPhail. Looks like Gus-Gus. Not as nice as Gus-Gus." Pauly paused. "Tommy can call him Gus-Gus. Nobody else can." He took a quick swallow of his beer and picked his jacket up from the back of the barstool.

Rosaria looked at Tommy and could see he was enjoying this. "Going somewhere, McLaughlin?"

Onto something, thought Rosaria. She didn't know what, but she could feel her adrenaline building.

Pauly put his hand on Rosaria's arm. "Look, Ro, we'd better get going. This is not a good idea."

"Okay, Pauly. Just a minute." Rosaria turned to Tommy. "So, Sullivan meets with Gus-Gus. How often?' asked Ro.

"Maybe once a month," responded Tommy, grinning at Pauly. "Over at the corner booth."

"Were they here recently?" asked Rosaria.

"Come on, Ro. We need to leave now." Pauly took Ro's coat from a nearby hook. She heard him mutter, "Jesus, do I have to drag you out of here?"

"Just last week." Tommy paused. "Maybe doing a little business."

Rosaria nodded and started to ask another question.

"That's it. No more," said the bartender, pulling back from the bar and looking at Pauly with a sly smile. "You've got enough from me for now, sweetheart. I think your nephew," Tommy emphasized the word *nephew* and paused for a moment, "really wants to get out of here, and he should."

"Thanks, Tommy," said Pauly, shaking his head slightly as he looked at the bartender. "Son of a bitch."

"Yes, thank you, Tommy." Rosaria took a slow sip of her beer before she slid down from the barstool, almost bumping into a small ferret of a man exiting the bar. "Sorry," Rosaria called after him. The man responded by raising his hand without turning.

"See you later, Pauly. Bye, Aunt Ro." Noonan Oil smiled, turning to look at her across the bar as they left. Deep in thought, Rosaria managed only a half-smile this time.

As Rosaria and Pauly were approaching the door to exit The Creek, Rosaria caught a bulletin on the television screen. A passenger car had apparently been forced into a barrier on the Zakim Bridge by an unidentified dark van. The driver of the passenger car, Patrick Cronin, fifty-eight, a manager at Malford City Hall, father of four and grandfather of three, had died instantly.

"Poor bastard," one of the men at the bar commented. "Wonder who he ticked off? Hey, Tommy, another Bud down here?"

Pauly was impatiently holding the door open for Rosaria and a winter chill blew into the bar, but she remained still—staring into the distance with a perplexed and thoughtful frown on her face.

None of the men at the bar had moved their eyes from the TV screen. Moments later, the room exploded in joy as Patrice Bergeron scored a beauty on the Canadiens goalie Carey Price.

Without speaking, Rosaria walked out of the bar with Pauly.

Pauly let the door to The Creek close. "Drop you at Maverick, Ro?"

"Thanks, Pauly."

Rosaria climbed into Pauly's Jeep with the Saint Rose's School sticker on the bumper and the Baby on Board sign on the rear window.

They rode without speaking through the neighborhoods, streetlights coming on in the darkness of an early winter evening. When they pulled up in front of the stop at Maverick Square, Pauly turned toward her.

"Don't know what you're up to here, Ro. My mother didn't tell me. I guess she didn't know herself, did she?"

Rosaria shrugged her shoulders. "I think she thought I was helping a friend with a wandering husband."

"My mother watches too much daytime TV."

Pauly looked in the rearview mirror. "I didn't feel good in there, Ro. The guy your friend has been visiting? McPhail? McPhail's a drug lord, a big one, and he's ugly. You see that little creep that slipped out of The Creek just before we did? McPhail knew ten minutes ago that we were in there asking questions. Before we even got two blocks. I'll pay. Tommy will pay too. Maybe not too much. He's related somehow."

A wave of remorse and self-reproach flowed through Rosaria. She felt as if she'd been hit in the gut. So focused on her own agenda, not thinking of what could happen to other people. Involving Pauly without thinking, putting her friend's son in danger. She was sick to think of it. *Stupid. Stupid.*

"I'm so sorry, Pauly."

He went on as if he hadn't heard her. "These guys aren't people you fool around with, Ro. McPhail is dangerous—a cold, fat bastard. He's capable. You know what that means here? He's capable of killing you at the drop of a hat or having one of his jobbers do it. Leave it. Drop whatever you're doing here. You could get hurt bad. This isn't a fucking—sorry, Ro—this isn't a fucking movie. This is real. People get hurt."

"I'm sorry I asked you to come, Pauly."

"You should go home," Pauly said flatly and looked out the front window, his normally rosy face drained of color.

"They may have killed a nun, Pauly."

He shook his head, shaking away her comment. "That's too bad, Ro, but I'm not going to say it again. Get out of here. They don't waste any time. I'll get a warning from some ugly son of a bitch, maybe even before I get home. Tommy'll get hit somehow. I don't know what they'll do about you. Be careful."

Rosaria's hand shook slightly as she reached for the door handle and got out of the car. She leaned back down before she closed the door. "Thank you, Pauly. I shouldn't have gotten you involved. I didn't think."

Pauly didn't answer. He just pulled away from the curb before the door was completely closed.

Dazed and sick to her stomach, Rosaria walked toward the Maverick T station. A shabby, unshaven man stood at the entrance, holding a barely legible brown cardboard sign with the words *homeless* and *veteran* on it. Rosaria felt in her pocket for one of the single dollars she carried for the purpose and handed the man one. "Good luck," she said.

"Good luck to you too, lady," mumbled the man without meeting her eyes.

She started down the escalator, everything blurred with the shock of regret for the danger she'd put her friend's son in. When she reached the subway platform, Rosaria turned and saw the panhandler from the entrance of the T running down the escalator, staring at her. He wasn't holding a sign anymore and was ripping his hat and gloves off as he ran. Rosaria moved further up the platform where there were groups of young people. The man continued to head toward her, working his way quickly through the congested platform, clearly keeping her in his field of view. Her heart started to pound and she dropped back further into the crowd. He'd never do anything with so many people in the area, surely.

But the man seemed to quicken his step, his dark eyes fierce on her face. Panicked, she looked around to see if anyone else could see this man racing toward her. When a young man in a dark jacket who'd come down the escalator with her came to stand beside her, she gratefully stepped closer to him. Far away down the track, she could see the red light of the train. Everything would be fine once she got on the train with a crowd of other passengers.

The young man threw her so quickly, grabbing her by the shoulders and shoving her off the platform, she had no time to react. Rosaria screamed and felt herself falling sideward onto the tracks. Out of the corner of her eye as she fell, she caught a fleeting glimpse of the young man in the dark jacket sprinting away—and the homeless man still running toward her across the platform.

People were yelling. She was still screaming as she hit the tracks. She saw the details of the gravel, the long tail of a scurrying rat and, as she turned her head, the red light of the train, screeching metal on metal as it turned the corner on the tracks.

Terrified, Rosaria tried to stand. Her legs were shaking and the first time she fell. The second time, stumbling, she managed to get to her feet just as the pan-handler jumped into the well of the tracks and reached her. Lifting from under her arms, the man dragged her quickly over to the platform. In a swift, forceful motion, he hoisted Rosaria up to the arms of a bystander who pulled her to safety. Then, he swung himself up to the platform in one fluid movement with a gymnast's easy grace.

She heard loud screeching as the train ground to an emergency stop just beside them, and then, a blessed quiet. So quiet, just for an instant, that she could hear only her own heavy breathing and that of the panhandler. Around them, low murmurs eddied through the crowd of stunned passengers on the platform.

"We've got her, Belkin. Great job." An MBTA police officer raced toward Rosaria and the panhandler. Another was bounding up the steps after the young man who had thrown her onto the tracks. As Rosaria looked at the panhandler, she now saw a dark, fit, balding man in shabby clothes, who carried himself like a soldier or a cop.

"Blew my cover, but it was worth it. What would a lady like you be doing to get these guys going?"

"I don't know. God." She thought she was crying.

"That guy doesn't run with a good crowd. What were you up to, sweetheart?"

Sweetheart? Did he call her sweetheart? Really? In a blur of shock and pain, she was in no position to be huffy, and he did just save her life. Rosaria closed her eyes before she answered. "Nothing. Just visiting an old friend in Chelsea." She wiped her nose with the arm of her soiled coat, annoyed to find herself unable to stop her tears.

He shifted his stance, looked at her skeptically and cocked his head. "Right. If you say so, honey."

This time she couldn't handle it. Between weepy gulps, she muttered, "Don't call me, honey, Officer."

He grinned and held up two hands in apology. "Detective Belkin. Saul Belkin. Sorry, sorry."

Two MBTA officers started to usher Rosaria toward a nearby office when Belkin touched her back lightly. "Take care of yourself."

In her foggy state, Rosaria waited for some smarmy appellation—what would it be? Honeybun, princess, lovey? Her shoulder was starting to hurt and she thought she might have broken a rib, but she swore to herself she'd slug him. "Take care of yourself, soldier."

He gave her a level gaze.

She turned to him, wiped her dirty cheek with a dirtier hand and managed a small smile. "Thank you, Detective Belkin."

Rosaria declined medical assistance, though now that the shock was wearing off and no longer working as an anesthetic, she ached all over. Her shoulder throbbed and her rib hurt when she breathed. If she could just get home, pour a cup of hot tea with Jameson and crawl into bed, Archie at her feet, she knew she would be fine. In body, if not in spirit.

Instead, Rosaria sat for what might have been forty minutes, but felt like hours, on an uncomfortable plastic chair in a small windowless office, holding a Styrofoam cup filled with a tasteless, lukewarm brown liquid purported to be coffee. She gave her statement on the incident to both the MBTA and Boston Police. Belkin would be writing up his own report. Rosaria did not mention her visit to The Creek. No need to complicate things.

Yes, she told the police, she would be willing to file a complaint and testify against this young man in court. Rosaria was disappointed in herself to find that, although she had agreed to do so, she now was filled with fear at the thought of testifying against this man, who almost certainly worked for Augustus McPhail.

And McPhail himself—to her a faceless drug lord. The thought of that terrified her. Rosaria was beginning to understand that she'd followed a path into another world, only to see just how violent and brutal that world was. Nothing had prepared her for this reality. She wasn't equal to it. She felt small and foolish and old.

The police asked if Rosaria wanted to call someone to pick her up. She gave it some thought before she called Leo to come—and then regretted it all the way home.

When Leo arrived, he spoke to his Boston law enforcement colleagues, got the details of the event, and then opened the car door for Rosaria without speaking. His jaw was tightly clenched and she thought she saw a slight tremor in it.

When he had regained some composure, Leo asked. "Okay, what *really* happened, Ro?"

Then, she had to tell him that she'd overheard his conversation in the hospital about a matchbook from The Creek and that made her remember a snatch of a conversation at the coffee shop about Malachy's frequenting that Chelsea neighborhood. Thinking it all led to The Creek, she had decided to check it out. Rosaria knew this last part would drive Leo to distraction.

Leo was quiet for a long time, a murderous quiet. He started the car and began to drive down Meridian Street to pick up the tunnel to the North End and Rosaria's apartment. After some time, Leo spoke again.

In a dangerous, low tone, still facing squarely forward, Leo said. "You are totally out of your league here, Ro. What a goddamned stupid thing to do. And you endangered other people. Think of someone other than yourself, people who could get hurt. Your friend's son, for one. And us, for God's sake, the people whose job it is to work on these things. Me, coming to talk to those guys at Boston as if it was just some creep who threw you on the tracks. Nothing about just coming from one of their biggest target's hangouts. They knew something was up. They knew the guy that threw you. Jesus. What am I going to do with all that now?"

Rosaria stared forlornly out the side window, rubbing her shoulder. She had a pounding headache, a drumbeat right in the center of her forehead. "I know, Leo. I didn't think things through. I'm sorry." Then, in a stubborn defiance, "But good information, right?"

"You let *us* get the information." Leo's voice rose. "You are not—let me repeat, not—a member of the police force. I told you before. You are not on this case, Ro. Who do you think you are?"

That question again. Leo was shouting now. Rosaria winced. She could feel the pain in her shoulder and her rib. Maybe she should have gone to the hospital after all. She just wanted to be home in her own bed. And she wanted Leo to shut up.

"And this—waking up a nest of city rats, putting yourself and other people in harm's way. I thought you were a smart woman. This isn't smart, doing something half-ass like you did here. Did you think? Did you think at all?" Leo hit the steering wheel with his hand before raising his hand to acknowledge the toll collector as he entered the Sumner Tunnel.

They rode for some time in silence, Rosaria deep in misery and physical pain.

As Leo approached the North End, she heard him say quietly, "Prime info. Jesus." Then, his voice rose again. "But a goddamned stupid thing to do. Completely," and then even more loudly, "*completely* out of line." Then, quietly again, "It's big. I don't know where we go from here, but it's big."

They pulled in front of the heavy granite mass of Trinity Wharf. Leo turned to her. "I'd like to arrange police protection for you, Ro. "

Rosaria lifted her chin. "No."

"Be reasonable. This is a tough outfit. I don't think you're safe. You need protection."

"No, thanks, Leo. I don't want anybody following me around."

"That's not how it would be. Just somebody nearby." Leo's voice rose again. "Look, I'm not going to get down on my knees. Be reasonable."

"No." She looked out the side window.

Leo shook his head. "Jesus, you are so annoying." He threw up his hands before slapping them back onto the steering wheel. "Want me to come in or call anybody now?"

Rosaria opened the car door. "No, I'll be fine." She stepped onto the sidewalk feeling a sharp pain in her shoulder when she moved. Then, she leaned down, facing Leo before she closed the door. "And, Leo," she said in a stone-cold voice, "you're welcome."

CHAPTER 17

ill Kenneally and his wife Lizzie had raised five children in the small Sherman Court house. These days, Bill's range of activity in the house was defined on one side by a kitchen table covered with a blue checked oilcloth, a collection of plastic CVS prescription bottles, and a brown plastic radio. On the other side, a small living room, where he slept or dozed on an old recliner facing a large, flat panel television given to him by his children. A thumbtack on the wall above the television held a small palm leaf cross from last year's Palm Sunday Mass, and another held the new calendar from the Maryknoll Missions.

The radio in the kitchen was always on, the volume deafening to his children and grandchildren, but just right for Bill. He liked the Sox and Bruins games better on the radio than the television. Closing his eyes, with his cat Genevieve on his lap, he could see the game better in his mind than he could on the screen. He only turned the television on to watch Catholic TV for the Mass or the rosary.

The radio was tuned now to a rerun of Saturday's Celtic Sojourn, three hours of Irish music. Brian O'Donovan always started the show with an air. So sweet. It brought Bill back to when he and Lizzie were young.

Today, though, his heart was heavy with grief. Patrick. What a thing, driven to his death on the Zakim right after he'd left Bill's house. Some witnesses said they were sure it was on purpose. It was hard for Bill to contemplate that there really were people who would do such a thing. And Rosaria struck down in Malford Square, just after they'd had their coffee and he was riding off with Terry. All following this terrible business about the nun being murdered.

It was almost too much for an old man to bear. Jesus, he was mad about it. He was smoldering angry. He wished he were a young man. If he were the man he used to be, Bill thought, he would do something. He would find the bastards and do something, by God.

The phone rang in the kitchen. Bill sat heavily in a chair beside the phone and, leaning his canes against the wall, started to unravel the twisted phone cord as he answered the call.

"Hi, sweetheart. Wait a minute, this cord is all wound up again."

Bill held the cord up and let the receiver dangle, allowing it to rotate several times until the cord was unraveled to his satisfaction. He placed the phone to his ear again, "Okay, all set."

He listened to his daughter. "Now, don't start, Terry. I don't need another phone. Those wireless ones are always buzzing in my ear. This phone is perfectly good. It just gets tangled sometimes. So what?"

Bill leaned back in his chair and stroked Genevieve as she came up to him. "Yeah, I'm doing okay, honey. I just feel god-awful about Patrick. Such a good friend. Do anything for you."

Bill and his daughter talked for some time. He always felt better after he talked to Terry. So much like her mother.

After he'd hung up the phone, Bill picked up his canes and walked to a table near the stove to pour the tea he'd left steeping there. He'd leaned his canes against the front of the stove and poured his cup of tea, with its little whiskey nip, when he heard a noise behind him. Bill turned, almost knocking one of his canes to the floor.

A man stood in the open door to the back hall. A big-framed man with rough black hair, high, pitiless cheekbones, and a crushed nose. A wide mouth that might have been generous on a different man.

"Come for me now, have you? Am I next?" asked Bill with a steady stare. Genevieve ran behind Bill.

"What have you been up to, old man? What did Cronin give you?"

"What're you talking about?" Bill picked up his tea and took a sip, willing his voice and hands not to shake.

"Don't fool around, pops. Don't give me that shit. Just tell me what you got from Cronin." The man moved closer.

"Don't know what you're talking about," Bill said, taking a large gulp, tasting the sweet whiskey in his tea, and eyeing the big man. God, this man's eyes were dead.

He knew he should be afraid but, Jesus, he was mad. *And what a way it would be to go,* he thought. In a tussle with this apparition who looked like evil incarnate. This great cold brute who probably did Patrick in and clipped Rosaria. Maybe even did the nun. Oh, to be fifty years younger. Bill took another gulp of his tea before the big man knocked the cup out of his hand. Thank God, it was almost empty. Waste of good whiskey.

The man was in his face, pushing Bill against the stove. "What's going on, you pathetic old bastard? What are you all up to?" He held Bill's face in one large, rough hand and brought his own face close to Bill's. A fierce and angry brute, breathing heavily in his face, Bill should have been weak with terror. But he wasn't. He was furious.

Searching, Bill's arthritic fingers somehow found one of his canes leaning against the stove. He lifted it and shoved it into the man's arm with all the force he could muster and a primeval yell from somewhere deep inside. He felt young again, as if he were playing the football.

Startled, the man stopped and looked down at the red area on his forearm. "Jesus." Enraged, he lifted Bill and threw the old man across the kitchen in one powerful arc. Bill landed against the table, bringing all the medicines and the still-playing radio down with him. He lay there unmoving, groaning and cursing quietly before finally falling silent.

Not a bad way to go, thought Bill dimly as he was fading. Better than in a hospital bed with tubes stuck in everywhere. Going out in a just fight. In spite of the pain, he managed a weak smile. *And I gave the colossal bastard something to remember me by.*

Genevieve came and sniffed Bill's face gently before curling on his chest. Increasingly angry sounds came from the other room—drawers furiously opened and closed, closet doors slammed. *Must have thought I'd be Mickey the dunce, keeping the finger drive, or whatever the devil it is, here for you to find,* Bill thought *The old man's smarter than that, you dumb son of a bitch.*

Then, with Genevieve's yellow eyes looking steadily at him and with the tiny smile on his face, Bill's eyes slipped closed. Only the sounds of fruitless searching in the other rooms and the fiddle of Martin Hayes broke the afternoon stillness.

Rosaria watched Leo shovel three spoonfuls of brown sugar into his coffee as they talked some days later at The French Connection. "They put him in a medically induced coma. Touch and go. He might just pull through. Kenneally's a tough old bird," he said.

On the other side of the table, Rosaria, still aching from a bruised shoulder and rib but reasonably mobile, stirred her own coffee absently. She noticed the ashes on Leo's forehead. Ash Wednesday. How fitting. Ash Wednesday—that's what it felt like. Ashes in her mouth. Ashes in her heart.

"I'm just sick about this, Leo. I haven't slept since it happened. I keep seeing what must have happened to Bill in that kitchen and to Patrick Cronin on the Zakim." She looked up. She had a bitch of a cold. Outside, she could hear mournful late winter winds blowing stray brown leaves and the occasional slips of paper debris down the sidewalk.

"They never would have gone after Bill and Patrick if I hadn't told Bill about those stupid Redevelopment Authority notes. I don't even care about them—what the hell is it to me? What did I think I was doing?"

"You all certainly tipped into something ugly. That young accountant stumbled onto a big game at the Housing Authority, and Cronin paid the price. Something tells me that the shoes may not have finished dropping there. Maybe there's a third set of books at the Authority." Leo shook his head in disbelief. "Rotten through and through."

"I should have left it alone."

"Stop it, Ro. How were you to know what a pit it's turning out to be? Now, just leave the rest to us and the DA's office." He gulped the rest of his coffee down and stood. "Gotta go. Saw you in here and just wanted to let you know about Bill. I'm leaving them short-handed today. Have to make a trip to Cambridge to check something out there, and later I have to talk to a guy from the DA's office. They've set up a regional task force for this heroin and opiate problem. Right now, they're looking at the housing authorities. This story's not over by a long shot. One big ugly mess."

"Sure seems that way. Okay, Leo. Good luck." She hesitated. "They know about Malachy and The Creek and that man McPhail, right?"

Leo's face darkened in an instant, angry to be reminded of Rosaria's foray to Chelsea. "Jesus. Of course, they know. Gus McPhail is a dangerous crime boss with high connections. He's not just *that man McPhail*. Those wharf rats have a big business going. You stay out of this from now on. Don't get in their way anymore." He closed his eyes. "Christ. You are so out of your depth and you just have no idea."

Rosaria did not reply.

Some moments passed. Rosaria could see Leo trying to calm himself. He partially succeeded and raised his forefinger to the side of his head before continuing. "By the way, forgot to tell you about your Chelsea pals. Your friend's son Pauly McLaughlin got off with a black eye and a couple of broken fingers."

Rosaria's heart sank. "Oh, no." She put her hand to her forehead. She was such a fool, bringing trouble to all these good people.

"No, he's lucky," Leo continued," I guess he's got some standing because of the football team and they gave him a break. Could have been much worse. Tommy, the bartender, got his windows and sign broken, and a talking to. Probably rolled off his back. He's no angel himself. Somebody said he's McPhail's first cousin. McPhail's mother would kill him if anything happened to her sister's boy." Leo shook his head and laughed. "Hard to imagine, that goon McPhail afraid of Ma. Never understand the Irish."

Rosaria rubbed her forehead, shutting her eyes. If she could have shut her ears, she would have done that too. But she couldn't do that and Leo was on a roll. He leaned down close to Rosaria's face. She opened her eyes and stared at him steadily. "But you. You're nobody's first cousin," Leo said. "You just got lucky Belkin was around and recognized the guy that followed you into Maverick station or they would have done you then without a second thought. This isn't your game. The right law enforcement authorities are on it now. That's the way it's supposed to work."

"Shut up, Leo," Rosaria whispered. She closed her eyes again, pressing them with her fingers, willing Leo to go away.

He stood and shoved his hands in his pockets. "Christ, get a grip, Ro." He took a deep breath. "There are ruthless, violent SOBs in this world. You've had enough experience to know that. This mess was there before you asked any questions at City Hall or this kid from Bentley found the second set of books at the Authority. The whole thing was just waiting for a tipping point. You and that kid happened to be those tipping points—asking inconvenient questions that started to bring the whole, sorry greed machine down."

"And I think Aurelius did the same thing."

Leo looked out the windows. "Yeah, we don't have anything clearly connecting Aurelius's murder to all this yet."

Rosaria noticed the *yet* in Leo's response. This was new. "You know it's all connected, and we just don't know how yet."

"And maybe it was just Joey Mucci going off the rails."

"You *know* it's more." Her eyes challenged him.

"Yeah, it's probably more," Leo held his hand up as Rosaria started to interrupt. "But just stay away from all this now. One of these times they're going to get you if you don't cut it out. And we can't help you if you keep putting yourself in harm's way."

Rosaria didn't respond, but nodded reluctantly.

"The offer's still out to have some protection."

"No, thanks."

"You're a real piece of work, O'Reilly. What're you doing here, anyway? It's been three weeks since Spike died. You need to move on with your life and stay far away from all this."

"I've been stopping by the Immaculate a few Wednesdays now—good day for me to get away for a little while. I just need to see where it happened again, put a red rose on the spot. Aurelius loved red roses. I'm glad they cleared away the rest of the candles and things. Gets messy. Selfish of me, but I like just a rose or two there." Rosaria stopped and gave a low laugh. "Mostly, I like just mine there. But, you know the way they scrubbed the wall and the pavement?"

Leo nodded.

"It looks more terrible in some way. The walls are sort of bleached. The pavement there is cleaner than anywhere else in the schoolyard. I keep seeing her lying here."

"Yeah, no way to make it easier, Ro," Leo said softly.

"By the way, I'm not the only one who still brings a rose. Someone else brings a white rose with a blue ribbon. I think it's probably on the Tuesday, because it's still fresh when I come by each Wednesday morning."

"No kidding? That's nice. Good to see Spike remembered." He zipped his jacket up. "Really got to go now. See you around."

Rosaria nodded again sadly. "Yeah. See you later, Leo." Cheek resting on her hand, she watched as he hurried out the door of the shop.

Rosaria sat at the table afterward, her coffee and croissant going cold. Somehow, she found herself thinking about systems. This was all part of a functioning, if foul, system—the Immaculate, the Housing Authority, a fat man at The Creek known improbably as Gus-Gus. But she couldn't see the whole yet. She remembered a long ago corporate seminar on systems thinking. Even now, in her mind, she could see the facilitator writing on the white board in a blue dry marker.

One system nested inside a larger system. Small catalytic events causing large changes in complex systems, unintended consequences. She'd asked a question at City Hall and visited The Creek. A young new accountant had stumbled on a hidden set of books and in the aftermath had fled to relatives in Italy for safety. Maybe Aurelius also found something out or was going to do something destabilizing to the system. Maybe all three women had disturbed a dark universe, a well-functioning system of corruption, greed, and violence. Now that system was in disequilibrium—spinning out of control.

She'd picked up a cold and it was getting worse, as she moved through the hours in some watery fog. Other customers looked at her with reproach when she coughed into her arm—a heavy cough deep in her chest. They were right. She shouldn't be out and about with this cold. There were lots of things she shouldn't be doing, she thought miserably.

Rosaria took out another lozenge. There was new printing on the wrappers. *Oh dear.* The manufacturer had started putting little pep talks on the lozenge wrappers. "The show must go on," or "March forward," the wrappers encouraged her through her sick haze.

Something so Yankee about this cheerful vitality and determination. Did these people ever just say, "Oh, to hell with it," or "We'll never make it"? Probably not. For her part, she was tired and sick to her very soul. She could have wept, but she was too sad for tears.

New York was calling every day looking for updates on her sales numbers. She wanted to care, but she was starting to find the calls annoying. She wasn't sure she really cared about the sales figures for athletic shoes in South Africa. People in the townships were chronically unemployed and still without adequate housing. What the hell was she doing selling high-end, fashion statement sneakers in a market where, for most people, the price of those sneakers would have fed a family of four for months? A dark flower of dissatisfaction with the business, with her life, had started to take root, blossoming more fully with each passing day, as each day she fruitlessly searched for answers to Aurelius's murder.

Rosaria unwrapped another lozenge as she could feel a coughing spasm coming on. "What's your battle cry?" asked the wrapper. She crumbled the wrapper and put her face in her hands.

CHAPTER 18

ater that day, Rosaria stood in a CVS drugstore aisle reviewing her options for cold medicine. She leaned down to check the Contac® alternatives when the blues riff on her cellphone told her she had a call. Rosaria hesitated, not recognizing the number. Things had gotten so crazy and creepy lately that she was cautious. However, now she was too tired and sick to think it through and answered the call.

"O'Reilly here."

"Hi, O'Reilly. Belkin here, BPD."

The cop at the Maverick Square subway station. The cop who pulled her from the tracks. "Yes, Detective Belkin, what can I do for you?" she asked warily. Yes, she was grateful, but what did he want now? God, she'd rather forget that whole awful experience...

"Just checking on you, Ms. O'Reilly. You had a pretty bad run-in there with a nasty character."

I guess. "You catch him?" Rosaria's shoulder where she'd hit the tracks at Maverick Square started to throb.

"Got away, but he'll turn up. We'll get him. I'll give you a call when we do."

Rosaria was surprised to find herself hoping that they didn't find this guy—that he'd taken off for Florida or Nevada. The truth was that she was afraid to testify against him and his vicious boss. *How did I get into this? Hubris. That's how. I think I can handle everything. Well, I can't handle* this *bunch.*

"Right now," Detective Belkin continued, "I'm just checking up on you—to see how you're doing."

"I've been better, but I'm doing okay right now. I'm good." *I'm not good. I'm in awful shape. I want to break down and cry right here in the aisle of CVS.* "Yeah, I'm good."

"Want to have a cup of coffee and talk about it?"

Yes, I need a broad shoulder. "Look, Detective Belkin, no offense, but right now I just really want to forget that whole day."

"How about a cup of coffee or a drink and we talk about something else?"

"Like what?" Rosaria picked up a box of night-time cold medicine and squinted to read the tiny print directions on the side of the package.

"I don't know. The weather, your job, the Bruins lineup, what you were doing at The Creek bar in Chelsea that day. No, wait, I didn't mean that last part."

Rosaria snapped her head up. "Okay, that's enough."

"Hey, I couldn't resist it. I'm interested."

"Goodbye, Detective Belkin."

She was about to press the End Call button when she heard him say, "No, wait."

"Yes?"

"I'd like to see you again, Rosaria. We can talk about whatever you want." A pause. "Or nothing at all."

Rosaria leaned heavily against the shelving next to her and closed her eyes. *What's going on here?* "Look, Detective Belkin—"

"Solly."

"Look, Solly, I have to go. I can't handle any of this right now."

"Yeah, sorry," Solly responded, a softer tone to his voice. "Listen, call me anytime. I can help. Right?"

Rosaria straightened herself up and headed to the cash register at the front of the store with her cold medicine. "Right. Thanks for calling."

Without waiting for Solly Belkin's response, she pressed the End Call button. *Too many complications.*

God, her head was pounding. She hoped this cold medicine knocked her out tonight.

———

Detective Tim Skerry of the Cambridge Police Department caught the drip of a Belgian chocolate ice cream cone with his tongue before commenting, "Sullivan's got good crews. Don't know if you'd want to look at their papers, but good workers. Young people over from Ireland, like a pipeline from some towns in Cork and Kerry, Castletownbere, Tralee areas. A few Polish kids by way of Dublin."

The detective turned the cone and took a large bite. Sitting back in his chair with a sigh of satisfaction, Skerry continued, "Ah—nice. The best. Anyway, he pays for their tickets over, boards them cheap in some of his apartments. I hear he pays very well. Some just come for a summer or a year or two to make some money, spread their wild oats before going back to settle down. Others meet someone and stay forever."

After meeting with Rosaria, Leo sat now with Detective Skerry, his counterpart in the Cambridge Police Department, enjoying an ice cream at Toscanini's in Central Square. *The New York Times* had declared Toscanini's ice cream the "best in the whole world." It seemed an exaggeration at the time, but Leo had no argument as he savored his Burnt Caramel cone this afternoon.

"Did you know the community paid the back taxes on this place? Can't live without their Tosci's." Skerry laughed. "You know, Sullivan mentioned to one guy that he was planning to cash it in pretty soon and settle in Ireland. I guess he's already bought a big spread in Kinsale, overlooking the harbor. He was asking how long he had to quarantine his dog when they moved over there. You know, that boxer he's crazy about that's always with him." Leo remembered the big tan dog at Malachy's feet in his office.

Skerry gestured out the plate glass window onto Central Square. "Sullivan picked up early that the area around here was getting hot again. The overflow from Harvard and Kendall Squares, the biotech companies moving in, MIT building some beautiful properties. The Square's looking attractive to people. Sullivan bought quite a few multi-families early on—period pieces and he did a beautiful job renovating them. Have to give him that."

Skerry took another bite of his Belgian chocolate cone. "But cash. All cash. Guys are paid in cash. Uses only certain building supply companies. All cash. Bought some of the multi-families with cash. Now, where would a guy get all that cash, Gelenian? He on your radar?"

"Yeah, and not just for that," Leo replied. "Anyway, in Malford, he does mostly public urban renewal. Union guys, all checks, all legit and very profitable. I know he's got his eye on a couple of properties now—a closed parochial school complex and an old plant. He'll go straight and legit on those once he gets them—not saying the getting of them from his cronies is going to stand much scrutiny."

"No spotlight on him here yet," Skerry said, "but all that cash is starting to look interesting. I think he may be getting careless. Or may just have too much cash floating around. Has to clean it."

"Washing the cash? Drugs?"

"Looks like it." Then he smiled and added, "Tosci's makes a nice cup of coffee. I think you should buy me one since I just gave you Sullivan."

CHAPTER 19

 few days later, after completing a round of early morning calls and submitting status reports to New York, Rosaria attached Archie's leash and rode the elevator to the lobby. Exchanging greetings with the concierge, she exited the building into a blast of raw ocean air. She inhaled it in great greedy breaths.

Rosaria desperately wanted to have a normal day. She had been feeling like one of Archie's old tennis balls lately. No bounce, no spring, no energy. Now, she was a woman of a certain age, walking her dog to the park through her own neighborhood. Rosaria drew energy from the people around her rushing to work, to Starbucks, to the gym. Joggers calling "behind you" as they pounded by, exhaling clouds of wintry breath. Cars zipping in and out of lanes, boats knocking against the wooden piers, metal gear clanking against the masts. She could feel herself grasping at the normality of the day like a drowning person clinging to a life preserver.

Archie pulled on his leash to chase away seagulls fighting over the remains of someone's breakfast muffin on the sidewalk. The gulls briefly departed at Archie's barking, but Rosaria had no doubt who would win the battle if any of the hungry gulls had stood his ground. Graceful and lyrical as they glided over the harbor, gulls were strutting thugs up close on the land, with alert and greedy yellow eyes. A noisy little white dog would be no match for an angry gull with big white wings spread wide, a long, lowered head, and a cruel mouth opened in a screeching war cry.

After the muffin confrontation, a satisfied Archie trotted down the sidewalk, tail held high and head moving from side to side, searching for any other intruders he should put in their place. Rosaria's usual route to the park in front of American Joe's restaurant was blocked by a number of work vans. It looked like a security system installation. As Rosaria was assessing whether to wend her way through the vans and the workmen, or venture out onto the busy street to get to the park, one of the workmen reached out to Archie.

The man's big hand cupped Archie's entire head. Usually, Archie would wiggle with delight, but now he was uncharacteristically still, perhaps confused by the vehicles, equipment, and workmen. The man had a hard-working, rough face. A cigarette hung from the side of his mouth. He smiled steadily at Rosaria, his large hand lingering on Archie's still head. Rosaria noticed a yellowing bruise on his forearm where the sweatshirt was pulled back. She felt a prickle on the back of her neck.

"Morning." The man stood slowly, with that smile, and gave Archie one last pat before he turned to his van. "Cute dog. Bet he's good company." He took the cigarette from his mouth. "Tough watchdog, too?

"Oh yeah, he's ferocious." Rosaria didn't smile.

"Yeah, thought so. Have a good day now."

Rosaria and Archie walked away from the work vans. Her heart was pounding, and, once or twice, she thought she heard some movement behind her, but there was no one there when she turned around. She jogged along the waterfront until she was at the other end of Columbus Park, out of view of the work trucks. It was a short jog, but she found herself breathless.

The relative warmth of the February morning had given way to a gray, chilly stillness that portended the sleety snowstorm the Weather Channel had predicted for the evening. Rosaria walked faster and longer than she'd planned, over to South Station, up to the Common, and back through Government Center and Fanueil Hall. She needed to move her body and to immerse herself in the energy of the city. To take the edge off the panic she was feeling. Finally, tired and with a measure of equilibrium restored, Rosaria walked back to her apartment through the North End, where she picked up a loaf of bread at Modern Pastry on Hanover and a pasta putanesca for dinner at Al Dente on Salem Street.

She'd thought about calling Leo, but she wasn't sure what she would say. A nearby workman gave off bad vibes and asked if her dog was a good watchdog? She didn't know what Leo could do with that.

Rosaria thought she would sleep well that night with several miles of city walking, followed by a good Italian dinner and a glass of Chianti. But she didn't sleep. Her nights had been sleepless and fitful since her visit to The Creek Tavern in Chelsea and the assault in the Maverick T station. She was feeling like one of those impossibly wide-eyed, jittery little nocturnal animals you see on nature shows, constantly wired with nervous tics. If she fell off to sleep at night, she often had bad dreams about falling into a bog, a bog sucking her down into an endless darkness with the red light of a subway train steaming toward her. She couldn't stop the malignant dreams from leaching into her days.

That night, as had been predicted, there was a high wind with sleety rain and snow. The storm assaulted the waterfront, pummeling the boats and the buildings relentlessly. In Rosaria's apartment, wind pounded the floor to ceiling windows with rhythmic, Angelus bell thuds.

Archie was restless and wouldn't settle. His paws tapped on the wood floor as he paced the bedroom. Once, during a lull in the wind gusts, with only the sound of turbulent, choppy water around the wharf, Archie suddenly leaped from the foot of the bed and threw his small body crashing down the hall, barking wildly.

"You big baby. It's just the wind. Honestly, what a racket. Stop it," she called.

Finally, Rosaria slipped out of her bed. She thought she heard a noise, a soft scrape. There was so much noise tonight, it was hard to tell. It was wild out there. She walked to the front window in the bedroom and cupped her face in her hands as she tried to get a better view out the glass. Black and rough under the harbor lights, the ocean changed personalities during a storm. The familiar and comfortable working waterway could turn surly and dangerous within minutes.

Rosaria walked down the hall. Archie was still barking and fussing. She might have heard a tiny creak from the door to the apartment. For just a moment, hand to her mouth in fear, she debated whether to continue. Rosaria turned back down the hall toward her bedroom. She could lock herself in the bathroom. Dumb idea. That lock on the bathroom door probably didn't even work. She couldn't remember ever using it. And her damned cell phone was charging on the kitchen counter.

Rosaria took a heavy flashlight from the drawer of a small chest near the bedroom door and walked slowly back toward the hall and the living room. The rooms were empty. Archie circled her in nervous little rounds, though he wasn't barking anymore. Rosaria checked the apartment door. Unlocked. She took a deep breath, trying to calm the pounding of her heart. She locked and tested the door, and then noticed something on the mail table by the door.

An MBTA schedule she hadn't remembered being there, with the Maverick Square T stop circled.

Jesus Christ. Rosaria's hand was shaking as she put the schedule back on the table. Holding the heavy flashlight, she started to check the other rooms in the condo, including the closets. Nothing. It was the middle of the night. She could call the police, but to what purpose? A lot of fuss to no effect. No one was here. But she wasn't a fool. *A warning.* Trouble. Yes, trouble, but nothing she believed the police could help her with.

Rosaria put the flashlight back in its drawer, surprised to see her hand still shaking. She closed her eyes and breathed deeply as she stood in the hall. After some time, she opened her eyes and walked to the kitchen. She picked up her cell phone and started to call the police twice, but put the phone back on the counter each time.

She shivered and held herself, rubbing her arms, before she reached for a fleece jacket on a hook in the kitchen. Rosaria sometimes wished she was a different kind of woman. Now, she wished she could just call the police, and have Leo or that Detective Belkin—whom she couldn't get out of her mind—fussing over her, worrying about her, asking questions, handling things, creating a cocoon of safety and comfort.

In the end, however, Rosaria decided just to put the kettle on for tea. She rummaged through the tea caddy for ginger tea, wondering if she might put a drop of something stronger in the tea. She headed toward the dining room cabinet for the bottle of Jameson, but then thought better of it. She'd be fine. She could handle this.

CHAPTER 20

f Leo didn't anticipate the tone of the meeting when he'd gotten the message to get himself to Chief Nicolo Cullen's office immediately, it was soon quite apparent to him, from the bulging vein at the side of the Chief's forehead, near where his unruly gray curls began and the angry red rash was creeping up his neck. *Oh, this is going to be ugly.*

"Bring him in, Leo. Enough's enough. I'm not taking another goddamned call from the Cardinal or the Mayor."

"Can't."

The vein looked like it was throbbing dangerously.

"You don't need any more time to build a case, Gelenian. You don't need any more time. The case is goddamned built. The guy's crazy and he whacked the nun. That's it. You're making this too way complicated."

"Mucci's gone." Leo almost stopped breathing after he finished this sentence.

The Chief stopped cold. Staring at Leo, he lowered his voice and spoke with a slow, lethal courtesy. "What are you telling me, Leo? What do you mean he's gone? Where did he go?"

"Just took off in the middle of the night from Saint Jude's."

Chief Cullen turned his burly body toward the window behind his desk overlooking the Square. For a moment, he seemed to be lost in meditation, gazing at the cars and the pedestrians below. "I see. Just took off in the middle of the night from Saint Jude's," he said, using a soft singsong.

Then, as he turned, his voice rose. "Just frigging took off in the frigging middle of the night from frigging Saint Judas's or whatever the hell it is. Sweet Jesus Christ, Gelenian," he ended in a crescendo.

He leaned forward, flattening his hands on his desk, speaking softly again. "Why the hell I let you and that old priest talk me into keeping that lunatic there, I'll never know. You find him, Leo."

Then, he stood back and jabbed his thick fingers at Leo. "You goddamned find him and bring him in—today. You hear me? *Today.* Does anybody else know he's gone yet?"

Leo shook his head.

"Good, let's keep it that way as long as we can. The media will have a field day and people will be terrified. Psycho on the loose. I can see it now. They'll say we showed a lack of judgment in not locking him up right away. And you know what, Leo? They'll be right. Get the hell out of here and find Mucci."

"We're all over it, Chief," Leo replied stoically.

As he left the office, Leo heard Cullen kick a metal wastebasket across the floor. Leo did not feel stoic. He had never experienced a freefall, but he could almost hear the wind whistling in his ears now as he left the office. He should have locked Mucci up.

And he knew he should have told the chief the minute he found out that Mucci had taken off, but he kept thinking they'd pick him up right away. Leo and his officers had been looking and calling all day. The hours had just flown by, the Chief was in Boston at a meeting for most of the day, and now the chief was back. Shit. They'd been in touch with Joey's brother Vinnie, the extended family, the neighbors, all the shelters, asking each if they had seen Joey Mucci and to please keep the search confidential for now. All dead ends. It would be only a matter of time before someone tipped off *The Globe* or *The Herald*. It would be a massacre by media. Only dumb luck that no one had found out so far.

Leo had also called a short list of people, including Rosaria, who might have an idea where Joey would go. He left a voicemail for Rosaria when there was no answer. Now, as evening approached, she returned his call.

"Hi, Leo. Just got your message. I was on calls and I'm only picking up voicemails now."

"Joey Mucci's missing, Just walked off in the middle of the night from Saint Jude's."

"Oh, God, Leo," breathed Rosaria. He could hear her putting a coffee cup down on the granite counter. "Where would he go? Disappear back into the city?"

"Don't know. We've been calling all day. Searching down by the river, everywhere. I've got to make more calls now, Ro, but I wanted you to know in case you had any ideas. Ask Nuncie too, but keep it on the quiet. The media's going to kill us."

"I know. This is terrible, Leo. I hope you find him."

"Me, too. God, me too. I'll talk to you later. Bye, Ro."

Before Leo started to make the next call, Rosaria's number came up on his screen.

"I think I know where Joey might be," she said. "I'll take you there, but just you and me. No police cruisers, my car. That's the deal, okay? I don't want us to frighten him. Bring a couple of those big flashlights you guys have."

After a moment's hesitation, Leo agreed.

Rosaria picked him up at the station twenty-five minutes later. It was a crisp night, and the warmth of the car was briefly interrupted by a shock of chill air as Leo hopped into the passenger seat.

"Nice car," he said, looking out the window. "This isn't the way we should follow up on your hunch, but I'm desperate right now."

"I know, Leo," acknowledged Rosaria in a matter-of-fact tone as they made their way through the crowded neighborhoods, past the old football stadium and the bars on Grant Street. Rosaria shut off the headlights as they cruised to a stop at the end of the street.

The old shoe factory loomed against the night sky. Leo could smell snow in the air as he left the car and zipped up his jacket. There was a wind whistling steadily through the rusted factory gate, and the chain that locked the entrance swung with a steady rhythm as it hit the fence.

"I remember Joey used to come down here all the time to meet his Dad after work or bring him a lunch. Maybe I'm wrong, but I think he might come here sometimes," Rosaria said.

Holding their flashlights low and covered to get their footing on the uneven ground, but not high enough to call attention, they walked to the back of the factory yard around the tall chain link fence. A blurry moon, white as bone, largely lit their way. As they had anticipated, someone had cut an opening in the back of the fence near the marshes. Leo lifted the stretch of chain link, and they entered the concrete lot where the trucks used to load shoes from the production lines.

They made their way toward the main building across the lot, now broken and cracked with brown weeds and grass growing through chunks of concrete. They could hear faint voices and see points of light in the old plant. "Jesus, " murmured Leo. A small fire smoldered in a rusting metal barrel on the back loading dock. Whoever had lit the fire and warmed their hands on it had disappeared into the night as Rosaria and Leo approached. "This place could go up in a flash and take these godforsaken people with it."

They turned their flashlights on high as they entered the building. There was wary movement in the dark corners of the factory floor, a faint rustling beyond their lights. They heard a soft "Shit" as someone slipped out a side door. Blankets hung from the frames where the giant machines, long since sold to factories in South Asia and Mexico, used to stand. Small boxes and jars of foodstuffs lined the dusty grated windows. "Like a goddamned apartment complex in here," said Leo.

"Police," Leo called. "Looking for Mucci."

A long silence. Then a rough voice from the shadows. "Sole room upstairs."

They found the old metal staircase and started to the second floor. "Got to clear this place out," muttered Leo. "First thing in the morning. Disaster waiting to happen."

"Where are they going to go?"

"Not my department, Ro. They can't stay here. That's what shelters are for. This place was supposed to be sold and torn down by last year. Don't know what's holding it up." He kicked a random size-fourteen basketball shoebox on the stairs out of the way.

"Sal Mucci, Joey's dad, worked in the sole room," said Rosaria quietly and looked at Leo. He nodded. They were both silent as they got to the top of the stairs and stood staring into the cavernous space. Leo remembered from his own visits to his father at the plant that the sole room used to be a busy place, always steamy, almost unbearable in the summer. Noisy, clanking, with the stench of burning rubber. Sweaty men in strap T-shirts yelling over the machines.

Now, a vast empty space, the high-grated windows and massive frames standing sentinel. A long, sad gray shape was swinging quietly from the big middle frame where sole stamper #3, Sal Mucci's machine, used to stand. They didn't have to turn their flashlights onto the frame to know they'd found Joey Mucci.

Bill Kenneally opened his eyes. "Oh damn, damn, damn."

"Good morning to you too, slugger."

As he stood beside Bill's hospital bed, Father Hanrahan looked down and smiled. The priest's black suit appeared as if he'd slept in it, though his suit always appeared as if he'd slept in it. Taking in his surroundings, Bill was exasperated to discover that he lay under all the beeping machines and plastic tubing that he'd hoped to escape at the end of the line. Winking and blinking, they wound around his bed like cheery, unwelcome visitors come to help, when he just wanted them to go away.

"What're you doing here?" Bill mumbled.

"Wasted the Last Rites on you. God knows why. You're a lost old soul."

"What am I doing here?" Bill lifted his head slightly to look around him and then let it drop heavily back to the pillow. "Dammit."

Through the fog of painkillers, Bill could feel his body, already compromised by the vicissitudes of illness and age, suffering greatly from the violent assault upon him in his own kitchen. There wasn't a single location for the pain, if someone were to ask him to specify where it hurt. It hurt everywhere. His legs and his back when he'd bounced off the kitchen table and his head where it struck the linoleum floor. His whole body felt wrecked.

Bill moved his toes on one foot tentatively and then the other. He wiggled the fingers of one hand and then the other. Thanks be to God, all the digits responded. Maybe enough parts of him were still working that he could carry on. But dammit, that's not what he wanted. Words slurred, he licked his dry lips and closed his eyes tiredly. "Could have gone the way I wanted."

"In a brawl is what you wanted—is that how I'm to take it?" The priest wet a swab and leaned down to dampen the old man's lips. Afterward, he gave him a sip of water through a bent straw.

"This isn't what I wanted," Bill mumbled, his jaw jutting out slightly.

"Tough. You're back with us." Father Hanrahan crossed his arms, staring down at Bill. Bill wished he had the energy to tell the damned priest to get lost. "You're sulking, Kenneally. It's not a pretty sight."

Bill didn't respond.

"I told Terry to go downstairs for a sandwich, and I'd keep a watch on you, though I can't say you're the best of company." The priest put his hands in his pockets and smiled at Bill. "They put you in a coma to allow you to heal and now they've been gradually bringing you out. The doctor says he wishes he had your constitution, you old reprobate."

Bill made an indeterminate grunt in response.

Father Hanrahan walked to the hospital window and raised the blinds to look out on the reservoir, warming in the afternoon sun. "Before Terry comes back, we need to talk. We should probably let you recuperate before we bring this up, but I think you're tough enough to handle it, and the situation is urgent."

Bill kept his eyes closed.

The old priest continued, his voice growing weary. "We've had some troubles. Some you know about. Some not."

"Oh, my God. Oh, my God. Patrick, Patrick," Bill murmured, squeezing his eyes in pain. It was all coming back.

The priest adjusted his rimless glasses and put his big hand on Bill's arm. It was a warm and strong hand, built for comforting the afflicted. After some time, Bill's face relaxed, a tear making its way down over the folds of heavy wrinkles on his face.

"The DA's office got the package that Patrick sent them before he died, Bill. They'd like to talk to you about it. Patrick included a note that a certain William Kenneally of Malford would be aware of the situation. They've been calling to know when you'd be well enough to talk with them. Leo asked Terry and myself to alert them as soon as you gained consciousness."

There was a long silence before Bill opened his eyes, and spoke clearly. "Never better. Tell them to come along."

CHAPTER 21

hree days after finding Joey Mucci's body, Leo steered his car through the narrow streets of Lowell, one of his hands grasping the steering wheel, while he delicately sipped a large Americano from the Daily Grind with the other. He was taking the morning to meet with Captain Perrault of the Lowell police force as part of his role on the regional narcotics task force. Lowell's recent issues with a new wave of drug activity in the public housing projects were very similar to Malford's.

Leo couldn't get Joey out of his mind. Guy didn't have a chance. Never did. Leo should have locked him up the first night. What was he thinking? If he'd done that, Joey would be alive today. He'd screwed up. He'd just goddamned screwed up. Jesus.

Around him now, the red brick of the mammoth, defunct textile mills looked warm, and the canals glittered in the bright winter sun. Leo could almost hear the mills as they were over a hundred years ago, with the deafening noise of the looms. All abandoned for decades until brought back to life in recent years with lofts and tech startups. The great energy of change.

Neighborhoods of spectacular, well-kept Victorian homes overlooked the city, while not too far away, worn nineteenth-century workers' housing and large old homes haphazardly chopped into apartments jostled for space, stoically awaiting the city's rejuvenation to reach them. Porches sagged, and rusted mailboxes dangled from discouraged nails.

Leo drove by one of the city's housing projects where a small group of young people stood in front of square, stark brick buildings. The teenagers passed around the communal goblet of their generation, a red plastic Solo cup. Leo thought the cup probably held vodka and Pepsi or some other face-the-day liquid assist. Even on this chilly day, the girls wore light, short jackets over cropped T-shirts and low rider jeans. Boys stood with guarded faces—stark white or soft brown. Bravado and fear.

Not too different from his own city. Not too different from the project where Malachy Sullivan grew up and made his cash by pushing. And apparently still did.

Leo pulled in beside the Lowell police station. A statue of Officer Christos G. Rouses, killed in the line of duty while responding to a pharmacy silent alarm, centered the circular driveway in front of the building. In the lobby, Captain Norm Perrault welcomed his colleague from Malford and led him into a small, neat conference room with a UMass Lowell River Hawks hockey poster on one wall, and a Spinners semi-pro baseball team poster on the other. Perrault's voice still had traces of his parents' French-Canadian heritage.

"Thanks for coming over right away, Leo. Just throw your jacket over there." He gestured to a side chair. Then, the two men sat down, facing each other across the conference table. "You okay for coffee?"

"Yeah, yeah, all set, Norm."

"That's good. All we have is the shit in the workroom. Looks like you have better taste." Perrault nodded at the Daily Grind cup.

"Oh, I drink a lot of the workroom stuff all day. When I get a chance, though, I might grab one of these. Of course, I bury it all with sugar anyway." They both laughed. Then Perrault got down to business as he sat back in his chair.

"Anyway, yeah, so I'll give you the picture from our side and we'll go from there." Perrault leaned forward on the conference room table, his white shirt straining against muscular arms. "We've got the same epidemic—cheap H laced with this fentanyl shit, just like you have, like I said on the phone. And I'm talking $7 a bag here, dirt cheap. Forty overdoses the last month, three fatal. No needle. They snort it or smoke it."

Leo nodded and leaned back in his chair as he listened.

"Packaged in bright colors." Perrault reached into a bag at his side and pulled out three empty plastic packages in neon colors of green, yellow, and pink. "Isn't that pretty?" He fingered a fluorescent green packet. "Problem is, when they're gone to bliss land, they might forget to breathe or wake up. Then not so pretty. All the officers are carrying the Narcan." Perrault referred to the nasal spray used to reverse an opiate overdose. "But we don't always get there in time."

Perrault rubbed his hand over his short, military crewcut several times. "And you know, the part that we're stuck on—it's not the usual network. We know who the pushers around here are and we keep a lid on it as best we can. They're not in on this. Whoever sells is here and then they're gone, usually from one of the empty apartments in the projects. In and out. Different guy in a different apartment every time. And then, of course, nobody in the housing units knows anything. They're afraid, but they don't know who they're afraid of. They're just scared."

"From what we've seen, they should be afraid," said Leo grimly.

Perrault inhaled deeply, then asked, "Where's it coming from?"

"The fentanyl's not pharmaceutical grade. We think it's being manufactured up north, somewhere in Quebec, and coming down through the Saint Regis reservation," Leo responded. "You know they've been moving high-quality B.C. marijuana through there for years."

"Yeah, no secret."

"So, anyway, it's mixed with the heroin somewhere in upstate New York." Leo's finger traced a route on the surface of the table. "Around here, it looks like there's a group organizing things from Chelsea. The usual suspects, but there seem to be some different parties involved, too. Parties that make it easy to get into the housing projects—real easy. The projects are a good distribution base. The operation's well run. We think authority management is involved." Perrault raised his eyebrows at that. "Anyway, Lowell is apparently the next expansion opportunity for them."

"Fits what we've seen rolling out here."

Leo hesitated for a moment. "This is big. Confidentially, Norm, we're also looking at a high profile Malford businessman and the Housing Authority leadership there. If we're right, all hell is going to break loose when we crack this. You may need to keep an eye on your own authority management."

"Oh great. He's the Mayor's cousin." Perrault pulled his chair back and grimaced. "Well, that's the way it rolls. Good thing I'm almost at retirement. We'll have to keep it low-key—even in this building. This place is like a sieve for leaks on something politically hot like this. State Police will help you on the surveillance and make the move. They'll take most of the flack."

"We haven't made the decision yet, but we're thinking of bringing them in operationally on this. It's getting complicated, too big for us."

"Okay." Perrault sighed deeply. "Really made my day, Gelenian. Good news guy."

"My pleasure."

Later, as they walked outside, Perrault stopped at the smoking area. He took out a pack of Du Mauriers, shaking his head before he lit his cigarette. "Trying to stop. Tough to do. Down to about four a day." He inhaled briefly with pleasure and exhaled a cloud of smoke.

Slightly sweet, observed Leo as he breathed in the smoke. Here we are, thought Leo. Here we are. "Don't see those much around our neck of the woods," he said, looking down at the cigarette packet.

"Canadian. My brother-in-law buys me a couple of cartons of the king-sized Reds at duty-free every time he goes up." He held a cigarette out. "Sort of sweet, almost like a liqueur taste. You either hate them or love them, as they say."

Leo checked the cigarette pack Perrault had put on the stone wall behind him. "I hear you can get them by mail order."

"Yeah, but most people have family or friends bring them back a carton. Less expensive. You'd have to have spent a little time up there, I think, to get the taste for them, though."

"We bagged a couple of these at the scene of that nun murder you probably read about. Just kind of different. Caught our attention."

"No kidding? That's interesting. Listen, want to grab a bite to eat and we can talk some more?"

"Sure. Let's get a sub. I saw a Subway a few blocks back there."

Perrault laughed and gave Leo a light shove to the shoulder. "Hey, live a little, Gelenian. There's a good little French restaurant up on Merrimack Street— La Boniche."

"Good little French restaurant?" asked Leo, frowning. "Hey, Norm, do you know my chief? If Cullen catches wind of that, I'll never hear the end of it."

"Oh Christ, Cullen doesn't have to hear you had a good French lunch instead of a goddamned sub. Who's going to tell your chief? And what's it to him if you pay for it yourself? You can see a little of Lowell on the way too. We'll take my car."

Leo didn't respond, but found himself following Perrault as he pulled out his keys and strode toward the parking lot.

Perrault took the long way around and a couple of detours so that Leo could see the entrance to the National Historical Park in one of the old mills, Boarding House Park where the summer folk concerts were held, and a few other areas of interest. As they worked their way back to Merrimack Street toward La Boniche,

Leo glanced over to his right and noticed the Ward Eight Grill, a pub with a Rooms For Rent sign on the second floor. A stocky man in work clothes, with a coarse face and a head of black hair, was exiting the front door of the Grill. Leo felt some dim flame of recognition. Where had he seen that face?

At La Boniche, the two policemen had a long discussion over lunch—steak hache for Perrault and shrimp provencale for Leo. While neither Leo nor Perrault could make a solid link between the sweet-smelling Du Maurier cigarettes and the murder of Sister Aurelius, they agreed the cigarette stubs pointed to a Canadian or a frequent US visitor to Canada.

"There's some connection between these Du Mauriers and what's going on with the H," Leo said. "If I were to guess, I'd say maybe there was a transaction in the corner of the Immaculate school complex the night the nun was murdered. It's pretty hidden there, especially after dark. Maybe she walked into a transaction. Wrong place, wrong time."

"Possible."

"If she was just an innocent wandering into some business deal, it's hard to believe she'd be killed for it. They'd just take a fast walk away. But, you never know, sometimes these things go down funny."

Perrault nodded, and took a bite of his steak.

Leo looked down at the table for moment before he looked up at Perrault. "You know, Norm, we thought we had pretty much cleared up the nun murder with a local homeless guy. He said he just found her, but he had blood on him and he was acting whacko. Well, he was whacko, so that's not a surprise."

Perrault held his fork in mid-air. "Past tense? Was whacko?"

"Yeah, past tense. He offed himself over it before we indicted him." Leo looked out the window of the restaurant.

"Rough."

"Went to school with him. Big, weird guy. Never did anything like this before, but we figured he'd finally just gone around the bend and killed her. In the end, I guess he couldn't take it all and hung himself."

"Didn't have him in lock up? With a suicide watch?"

Leo moistened his lips and didn't respond for a few moments. "No, probably should have. We thought we could handle him in a halfway house while he was still a person of interest and put a tight case together."

"You make the best call you can."

"Yeah. Well, maybe I should have made a different one here. To tell you the truth, now I'm pretty sure the guy really did just find the body. He remembered the smell of the cigarettes and two shadows. We didn't give his account much weight." Leo paused. "He was so crazy, you know."

CHAPTER 22

osaria adjusted her schedule and came with her red rose to the schoolyard early on Tuesday morning instead of Wednesday. Settling onto the bench by the stone wall at the rear of the building, she waited. Within twenty minutes, she watched the Tuesday visitor approach.

The morning was unseasonably warm, and the snow was evaporating into a soft mist. Francie Sullivan's gray coat mirrored the spring-like fog over the schoolyard. A blue scarf, Francie's light brown hair, and a single white rose with a blue ribbon broke the gray monotone.

She stopped for a moment when she saw Rosaria on the bench. Something skimmed across Francie's face like a ripple across a smooth pond. Then, she resumed walking.

Francie placed the white rose in front of the grammar school wall and bowed her head in prayer. After some time, she looked up and came to the bench. She sat and turned her face to Rosaria. Neither woman spoke.

An image crossed Rosaria's mind of babysitting Francie as a kid down at Morrison Park. Pushing Francie on the swing, sun behind her on a cloudless spring day. Francie pumping her little legs as hard as she could. An adored only child, always slightly overdressed, even to go to the playground, with pink ribbons on her fat brown pigtails, matching flowered pink corduroy overalls, and sneakers.

Rosaria reached her hand for Francie's now and held it, her thumb stroking the side.

Francie closed her eyes. "This is so hard, Ro. A good woman."

"And old and vulnerable."

"I don't know if that's the worst part. It's just that—" Francie paused. "It's just that she was *so* good. She didn't deserve this."

Rosaria closed her eyes for a moment, deep in her own pain. "A lot of good people don't deserve the things that happen to them"

Francie nodded. She let out a long sigh.

They were silent for some time, looking straight ahead together. Each could hear the other inhaling the moist air in deep, sad breaths.

Francie removed her hand from Rosaria's and placed it on her lap. Without turning her head, Francie said, "I have something. Something to do with Aurelius's murder."

Rosaria frowned and shifted her body to face Francie. "I'm sorry. What did you just say? You have what?"

"I have something related to the murder," Francie said, a slight tremble in her voice.

Startled and confused, Rosaria leaned toward Francie to make sure she heard what she was saying. "Something related to the murder. Like what? And where did you get something related to the murder?"

"Never mind."

Rosaria moved her face closer to Francie's. "If it's related to how somebody killed Aurelius, you have to give it to the police. You should have done that right away."

Francie shook her head, a frightened but determined look on her face. "It's too complicated. I'll give it to you and you can bring it to them."

"Why me? It's you they'll want to talk to."

As if Rosaria hadn't spoken, Francie continued to stare straight ahead at the schoolyard. "Yes, I'll give it to you." Then, she turned to Ro. "But it has to be fast. It has to be fast or he'll know."

"Who'll know?"

"Half an hour at the reservoir across from our house, just at the turn where the big rocks are." Francie took Rosaria's hand and leaned forward to look directly into her eyes.

"Just you, Ro. I won't come if there's anyone else there. I'll deny everything if you go to Leo or the police before I tell you to."

She released Rosaria's hand. "Then I need to go. Get away from here."

Francie got up from the bench, stopped at the murder site to cross herself quickly, then walked across the schoolyard to her car.

Francie took great care that day putting some flatbread crackers and olives on the counter for Malachy's luncheon snack, and wrote him a note to check in the fridge for the smoked salmon, Brie, and San Pellegrino. She usually wrote *Love you* at the close of her notes to Malachy. She didn't do that today—and she wondered if he'd notice.

Some weeks before, Francie's world had begun its slow implosion. The Monday after the nun's murder. Malachy was leaving for work with Maisie. He poured coffee into a large travel mug and snapped his fingers for the dog.

"Bye, Malachy." Francie looked up from cleaning an already spotless granite counter.

Malachy didn't respond, but turned when he reached the back door. "Hear from Leo again?"

"No, no. He was fine."

"Good, there's a girl, Francie." He walked across the kitchen and gave her a kiss on the forehead. "There's a girl."

Francie still felt his lips warm on her forehead after he'd closed the back door, and could still inhale the smell of him—soap, a whiff of shampoo, and coffee. She wasn't sure she could remember the last time he'd done that.

Later that morning, Francie stripped the bed to wash the sheets. Malachy liked the sheets hung in the sun to dry, even in the cold, and then ironed before being put back on the bed. He'd had a special enclosure for a clothesline built behind the house. Francie enjoyed hanging the sheets in the fresh air, though she wished the fence wasn't there. She would have liked to look at the trees and small animals in the rocky woods behind the house when she was outside.

After the sheets were hung, Francie emptied the bathroom hamper and carried the clothes downstairs. As she was sorting the colors and whites for washing, she squirted a few spots with pre-wash spray. Sometimes when Malachy had spent part of the day inspecting his properties, Francie had to really work on the stains and dirt he could pick up on his clothes at the construction sites or old buildings. Out of habit, she checked the beige slacks Malachy had worn to the Daleys' party before she put them in the pile for wash.

Francie was about to spray a splash of brown spots near the cuff of the slacks when she hesitated. Mud maybe, but kind of an odd color—with a slight reddish cast. A little like menstrual blood, but a different shade. It *did* look like blood... perhaps Malachy had cut himself? Funny place if he did, and he usually noticed these things. Maybe he was too distracted. Things had been busy and he'd been at work late every night.

She touched the spot with her forefinger. A tiny current of clarity shot through her body. She knew what these brown-red spots were about. Francie felt a little dizzy and heard a low buzz in her ears. She was conscious of her breathing and the beating of her heart. Both slow and deep.

Her movements felt weighted, as if she were underwater. Francie put down the green bottle of pre-wash spray and lowered herself to sit on the floor. She leaned her forehead against the washing machine, feeling its soothing, cool metal surface. Images flowed around her—Malachy pushing her, losing the baby, his fists, his anger.

His anger, his anger, his anger.

After a few minutes, Francie slowly raised herself to a standing position, holding onto the washing machine for balance. She took a brown paper grocery bag down from a side shelf. Carefully folding the slacks, she slid them into the brown bag and placed the bag in the back of the broom closet.

The bag seemed to throb quietly in the closet. Almost like a living thing. Malachy was out at his properties every day, and she went about her own work with an odd serenity. Francie could feel the soft pulsating of the bag as she came and went. Something was shifting. She was surprised when she looked outside to find the trees in the same place. Everything the same, but not the same.

Rosaria had driven to the reservoir right after Francie left the schoolyard early that morning.

It wasn't long after she found the big granite boulders at the curve of the path that she saw Francie's gray coat as she walked around the reservoir. She held a brown grocery bag in her hand. Against the 1930's stonework of the reservoir and the hills, Francie was, for just a moment, an Italian Renaissance Madonna against a Tuscan landscape.

Rosaria stood to greet Francie, who looked behind her once or twice, her brown hair blowing across her lightly freckled face. Faint gossamer lines showed around her eyes.

"Is this it, Francie?" Rosaria gestured toward the paper bag.

Francie nodded and held the bag out. Rosaria took the bag, but didn't open it as she continued to meet Francie's eyes.

"The slacks Malachy wore to the Daleys party. I don't think he even noticed the spots near the cuff. Could be nothing, but I think it's important."

"What are you saying?" Bewildered, Rosaria raised her hand in question. "I don't understand."

Francie looked calmly at Rosaria, though Rosaria saw a slight tremble on her lips.

"I think there's blood on them." Francie took in a gulp of air and turned her head toward the water. Small waves lapped at the shore from the light winter wind. "We were at the party. Aurelius was there too, but—"

Rosaria sat back heavily on the boulder, glad for its grounding. She reached for Francie's hand and gently pulled the young woman to sit beside her on the boulder, her eyes fixed on Francie's face. "But what, Francie?"

"Malachy was gone for over an hour and a half. He got a call and left. I know he didn't take the car, because I went out to look for him, and it was still there, even if he wasn't. I didn't know where he was."

"And Aurelius?"

"I didn't see her. Malachy... he..."

"He what?"

"Hated her. I don't know why, Ro, but he did."

"Does Leo know this?"

"No, and I lied to him when he asked me if Malachy had been at the Irish-American the whole afternoon that Aurelius was killed. Malachy had called me after Leo left his office, and told me what to say before Leo got here. Malachy said he had left the Irish-American to meet someone. They had to straighten out a business problem. But it would just get too complicated if Leo knew Malachy was gone from the party for that long. He didn't have time to explain everything to Leo. It was easier if I just covered for him. Save everybody a lot of time."

Francie was close enough beside Rosaria on the boulder that their shoulders touched. Now, she stared out at the water.

"He'd kill me if he knew I was here, Ro. He'd really kill me. You don't know him." Scuds of wind rustled dull brown leaves around the boulders. Francie shivered.

"You should really have the police involved now."

Francie shook her head emphatically. "They couldn't protect me."

"You could come stay with me."

Francie gave a soft laugh and looked at Rosaria as she would a child. "I told you, Ro. You don't know him. If I went to stay with you, we'd both pay the price, believe me. No, I have my own plan. I know what I'm doing. Just give me a couple of hours before you give this to Leo."

"Okay, Francie."

A car horn nearby beeped briefly in a rhythmic two beat. Francie turned. Across the roadway, through the trees, a white and gold Veterans Cab stood waiting outside the Sullivan house, the cabbie inside craning his neck to see the front door of the house.

"I have to go, Ro. That's for me." She started to walk away, and then turned to embrace Rosaria. "You were always a standup, Ro."

"Good luck, Francie."

"Thanks. I'll need it. "

Their foreheads touched for a moment before Francie released Rosaria and walked swiftly across the roadway, signaling the driver to wait.

Rosaria stood watching, not knowing what was to come and worrying about Francie. The horror of what happened to Aurelius, never far away, became fresh again in Rosaria's mind. She wanted to fling the brown bag and its hateful contents into the reservoir.

Francie walked toward her house and up the long driveway. Once she entered the side door, some long minutes passed. Craning her neck, Rosaria stepped a little to the left and a little to the right to see if she could get a better view of the house. Maybe Malachy had been watching them. He shouldn't have been home now—mid-morning—but maybe he was in there. Rosaria listened for sounds and considered going up to the door. Francie didn't want the police, but two women were no match against such a man.

This was not a situation for waffling. Rosaria took out her phone and, tucking the brown bag under her arm, started to call 911. But, before she'd finished making the call, Francie finally emerged from the front door of the house with only a small travel bag in her hand. She walked quickly to the cab, opened the rear door, and got into the back seat. She raised her hand to Rosaria through the window. Behind the raised hand, an anxious and resolute face. Then Francie was gone.

Rosaria stood watching the cab's tail lights fade into the gray landscape, feeling the weight of the unopened bag in her hands.

CHAPTER 23

alachy opened the back door of his house, noting with annoyance that the door was unlocked again. When would that woman learn to keep things locked up? Anybody could just walk in here. *Jesus.* He'd tell her to do things. Simple things, over and over, and she said she just couldn't remember. Well, she remembered, all right. She just didn't *want* to do things. To spite him. That's what it was all about.

The kitchen was darkened with heavy blinds that shut out the light. Small insert lights over the counter glowed over a set of snacks.

"Francie?"

Maisie bounded across the kitchen floor to her water dish, her nails tapping loudly on the polished white birch.

"Francie?"

He noticed a slip of paper on the counter with Francie's neat handwriting. It lay next to a plate of sesame cracker breads and a jar of opened almond stuffed olives. *San P, smoked salmon, and Brie in fridge.*

"Well, Maisie girl, I guess a guy has to take care of himself. Nothing else to do all day, and she can't even stick around to make me a snack or a lunch?" Malachy took off his jacket and flung it on the chair. "Nothing goddamned else to do all day and she can't even make me a goddamned snack. Where the hell is she?"

He looked at the dog. "Maybe taking a nap, though God knows what she'd be tired from." The dog cocked her head, trying to assess the mood of her master.

"Francie?" Sighing heavily, he opened the refrigerator and prepared himself a late morning snack, spreading the cracker breads with the soft cheese and thin slices of smoked salmon. He popped open a can of San Pellegrino lemon water and looked around again. *Where was she?* Her BMW was still here. He took a sullen, hungry bite of the crackers and a gulp of the San Pellegrino, and then followed that with several of the stuffed olives. He carried a cracker sandwich and the lemon drink with him as he walked through the downstairs—the living room, dining room, and office, then upstairs through the vacant bedrooms, Maisie following him closely all the time.

"Francie, are you here?"

Malachy checked the hall closet for Francie's coat, which was gone. Then he noticed the cell phone on the counter. He checked her recent calls and her voicemails. Her mother. Of course, her mother. *Jesus.* A reminder from the vet about Maisie's shots. Here, Malachy made a note to check on Maisie's shot record later. A friend thanking Francie for the flowers. *Who was she sending flowers to now?* The woman thought she was her own sunshine committee, for Chrissakes. *Like I'm made of money.* Two outbound phone numbers he didn't recognize. He wrote them down. He'd have to call them later. *She'd better not be up to anything.*

He put the phone down and picked up his jacket, grabbing a few more of the olives. Malachy gave Maisie's head a quick rub and headed out the door. "See you later, girl. Watch the house." Better stop by the rectory and then make a visit to his nibs. He'd straighten Francie out when he got home.

That afternoon, Malachy Sullivan pulled his SUV into the lot next to the Immaculate Conception rectory. He noted Monsignor McDermott's new black Lexus in the back of the building, taking two parking places so that no one would park beside the car and possibly ding it with a carelessly opened door. The priest was drawing too much attention to himself, just wasn't thinking. Between him and that half-wit O'Toole, they'd screw this up yet.

Bad enough that O'Toole had upped his take from the Housing Authority again. *Jesus, the man's greed has no bounds.* As if he wasn't already taking a shitload of cash from the operation. Somebody was going to notice—and soon. He prayed O'Toole would escape an I-team investigation on television or a Spotlight series in *The Globe.* That's all they needed. *Time to get the fat greedbag in line.*

Malachy closed his eyes as he got out of the car. He felt a headache of some sort coming on and was a little light-headed. If people would just do what they're goddamned supposed to do, he wouldn't have this stress.

He rang the doorbell and heard the familiar soft chimes peal in the hall. He could hear Mrs. Fitzpatrick coming down the hall before she opened the door.

"Good afternoon, Malachy," she said warmly.

"How are you, Helen?"

"Well enough, Malachy. Well enough." She wore a maroon sweater over her white blouse and gray skirt, comfortable Easy Spirit shoes, and a small gold cross at her neck. Very motherly. "The Monsignor's in his study. He's expecting you. Would you like a cup of tea or coffee? Maybe a macaroon?"

"No thanks, Helen. I'm fine," Malachy responded over his shoulder, as he walked down the dim hall with its heavy furniture from another time. A large portrait of a resplendent Cardinal O'Connell from the last century dominated the end of the hall. *Now, there's the man,* thought Malachy.

They didn't call the bastard Number One for nothing. He was the king. *The Puritan has passed; The Catholic remains.*

Monsignor McDermott was working on his computer behind a large mahogany desk. A stack of downloaded college handbooks stood on the corner, a cigarette curling smoke in an ashtray on top of them. Malachy noticed an apparent new entry to the college target list for the boys. Georgetown. The admissions white boards dominated the sidewall, while on the bookcase behind the Monsignor was a picture of his proud parents. From Lowell, too, like Cardinal O'Connell. The Monsignor's father, stern and unsmiling in an ill-fitting suit, and his mother with a sweet face that looked very much like Helen Fitzpatrick's. A son given to the priesthood. Redemption guaranteed.

His eyes caught the photograph of some of the Monsignor's seminary mates— arms around each other's shoulders, their robes and hair tousled by the wind. Maybe on the grounds of Saint John's Seminary. All handsome young men. There was a picture of Malachy, too. He and the Monsignor on a long ago graduation day. The priest had been good to him. He wouldn't be where he was today without his help, but Christ, sometimes the old man acted like he didn't have a brain in his head.

"I could get that great Plum Island place again next summer." The Monsignor turned the monitor to show Malachy the picture of a large, blue Victorian summerhouse with a wraparound porch. "I think all that nonsense has blown over now and we can get back to normal. You remember the place. Right on the beach. Sleeps eight."

"Are you crazy, Owen? Are you frigging crazy?"

The priest blanched, and then waved his hands dismissively. "All that business has blown over now. The Chancery cleared everything up with those malicious rumors. Everything is on the up and up."

"When I said stop that crap, I meant stop. Full Jesus Christ stop."

Monsignor dropped back in the chair as if he'd been hit. "Okay, okay. Don't get carried away, Malachy." The priest looked toward the door, and got up to close it gently. "What's the issue you came for?"

"What's the issue? What's the goddamned issue?" Malachy's voice rose. "You haven't gotten the deal done at the Chancery the way you were supposed to. That's the goddamned issue." The priest frowned, pointed toward the hall and gestured to Malachy to lower his voice.

Malachy's voice was no less angry when he lowered it. "Look, I did my part of the deal with the Redevelopment Authority. You were supposed to be getting the final signoff from the Chancery. When that happens, you can take your cut. Build a new science center, buy a summerhouse on Plum Island, retire to California with your buddies—whatever you want—and we can be done. But," Malachy's voice started to rise again, "you have to deliver on the Immaculate. I've got the financing all lined up."

The priest reddened, raised his chin, and looked out the window without a response.

"What's happening, Owen? You've been saying for months they'd sign off any day. But nothing's moving. Nothing's frigging moving!"

"Malachy, these things take time. There are new people. This guy Leonard is a tight ass. Wants to go out for bid—"

"Go out for bid?" exploded Malachy. "You said this was a done deal. They'd give you the authority."

"They'll listen to reason." The priest's hurt eyes pleaded for understanding. "You're a willing buyer for the Immaculate with cash in hand and approval from the city. They'll come around."

"They'll come around? *They'll come around?* They'd damned well *better* come around, Owen." Malachy barely contained his rage as he walked to the door. "They'd damned well better. And fast, or there'll be consequences. You understand? There will be consequences."

The color left the Monsignor's face. He stood and approached Malachy to put his arm around his shoulders. "It'll work out, Malachy," he said in a soft voice.

Malachy pulled away and left the room in a fury. The priest had let him down. Left him hanging out there. *Christ.* He slammed the door, and let himself out of the rectory without speaking to Mrs. Fitzpatrick, who had a worried frown on her usually placid face.

"Bye, Malachy." Mrs. Fitzpatrick called after him.

Some minutes later, Malachy placed a call from the rectory parking lot.

"Hey, I'm coming up. Had to check on something here. A damn screw-up I have to work out."

"Anything I can help with?" The voice on the other end of the line was focused and practical.

"No, not on this one, thanks." Malachy stopped for a moment to take a deep breath and calm himself before continuing. "Anyway, we have some other things to talk about. O'Reilly's not getting the message. McPhail wants her done once and for all before he'll do any more business with us. Can you take care of that for me?"

"Done."

Malachy adjusted the car mirror to look at his face. He looked pretty pale. *Must be coming down with something.* "Good. This next round with McPhail is the big one. My last one. Then you can take over. You can be the king of the mountain. I'm done."

"About time, Sullivan." Malachy heard the resentment in the man's voice.

Malachy responded with a tired smile. "Yeah, I know. I've been too long at the fair. Your turn. You've earned it, buddy." He rubbed the side of his face. *Hope this isn't one of those viruses that lasts a week or more.* He didn't have time for that right now. "And we have to talk about O'Toole too. He doesn't know when to stop. He's like a pig at a trough. He needs a tune-up. Get that done this week before he does some other stupid thing."

"Got it. My pleasure." A dark chuckle at the other end of the call.

"Okay. Just a tune-up. Don't get carried away."

"See you at the Eight?" the man asked.

"Yeah, the Eight's good, but I can't eat anything. My stomach's queasy enough already. I must be coming down with something. Okay. At the Eight in about forty minutes."

Malachy closed the call and then made another, leaving a voicemail.

"Hi, honey. I'll be there tonight, maybe around 9:00. But I can't eat anything. Something wrong with my stomach." A wan smile came to his face. "Can't wait to see you, babe." Still smiling, he turned his cell off and started the car.

Later that night, Malachy parked his SUV some distance from the Gardens housing project and walked the few blocks to the first building. He rang one of the scratched doorbells beside a row of tattered scotch-taped name cards and then climbed the concrete stairs, holding the iron railing. He stopped for a moment, breathing out slowly as a wave of dizziness crashed over him. He still felt queasy— much worse than before.

He thought about heading back to his car and just going home to bed. But then he saw Rebecca Winthrop Linsky at the top of the stairs, holding the door open to her small, tidy apartment. And he was glad he'd come.

CHAPTER 24

eo took the crumpled brown bag from Rosaria with a deep sigh and a sour look on his face. He shook his head, then said, "Why the hell didn't you call me?"

"I told her I wouldn't. She wouldn't have given me anything if you'd been there. And if you'd talked to her, she'd have denied everything."

Rosaria was surprised to notice a look of hurt cross Leo's face. "I don't know about that. We were friendly once." Then, in a flush of embarrassment at his own comment, Leo shook his head and said, "Well, anyway, you should have called me. Where is she now?"

"I don't know. Took off in a cab."

He placed the bag on top of his desk. "What time was this?"

"Maybe eleven."

Leo checked his watch. "You took long enough to tell me. What kind of cab?"

"The white and gold ones."

"Veterans." Leo ducked his head out of his office and called down the hall. "Victor, call Veterans Cab—today, late morning—Sullivan house. One woman. Where did they take her?"

Rosaria watched as he walked around to his chair and sat down heavily, eyeing the bag sitting on top of his desk. Leo looked up at her. "Sit down, Ro." He gestured to a chair and opened the brown paper bag. "Okay, let's see what we've got here." He removed a pair of rumpled, light brown slacks. "Malachy's? Must be. They look custom made. Jerk."

"There's a DVD in the bag. I haven't played it."

Leo took the square plastic case out of the bag and removed the disc. He placed the disc into his ancient department-issued desktop and called out, "Hey, Johnson. Over here. Want you to see this too."

Leo inspected the slacks while he waited—and waited—for images to appear on the screen. He looked up at the computer screen several times as the machine laboriously started to process the information on the disc. "Damned slow piece of junk."

"Don't hit it, Leo. Bad enough as it is," commented Johnson.

The beginning was all blackness. Then, suddenly an image of Francie Sullivan appeared, erect in a ladder-back wooden chair. She was wearing a soft yellow sweater, her hair pulled back into a ponytail, revealing simple pearl studs in her ears.

"That's the office off their kitchen," Leo said.

Francie frowned as she spent some time adjusting the video. Then, she sat gravely still. She swallowed, closed her eyes and took a deep breath before she spoke. Her voice quavered at the outset and gathered strength as she continued. A slight tremor in her voice, Francie spoke without notes, but had obviously rehearsed these sentences in her mind many times.

Rosaria's eyes welled up as she watched Francie begin. She was remembering Francie as a sweet child, before she met that dark angel, Malachy Sullivan. She could see that Leo was captivated too, not just by the evidence or Francie's bravery in presenting it, but by Francie herself.

"My name is Francie Sullivan. I am submitting here possible evidence in the recent murder of Sister Mary Aurelius at the Immaculate Conception School. My husband, Malachy Sullivan, was wearing these slacks on the night of the murder. You will see, at the bottom of the right leg, near the cuff, a small splattering of blood. I believe the blood could be Sister's."

Leo turned the slacks over to see brownish red stains near the cuff of the right leg. He raised his eyebrows and looked up at Detective Johnson. Beside Leo, Rosaria sat very still, transfixed by Francie on the screen.

"Previously, I was not truthful regarding my husband's whereabouts the night of the murder," Francie continued. "I told Detective Gelenian that my husband was with me the entire evening at the Irish-American Club, attending the Daleys' fiftieth-anniversary party. This was untrue. I gave this untrue statement to Detective Gelenian because my husband told me to." She stopped and lifted her chin. "I was afraid not to follow my husband's instruction."

"Now, I want to tell the truth and to say that my husband Malachy Sullivan was not at the party for the entire time period in question. He was absent for about an hour and a half, between 4:00 and 5:30 PM approximately. I checked the parking lot for his car, and it was still there, but he wasn't. I watched for him from the window in the rear lobby of the club and thought I saw him coming back by way of Lloyd Street, which leads to the back entrance of the Immaculate Conception."

Francie paused. "My husband never liked Sister Aurelius. He always said she should mind her own business. She was always mouthing off, causing trouble, in the way. Someone should shut her up."

"Well, well, well," said Wesley Johnson, nodding his head and grinning.

"Be quiet, Johnson," Leo said.

Detective Johnson got comfortable in his wide-legged stance and continued to smile broadly.

"I can't stay here now. It's too dangerous for me. My husband," Francie hesitated, "my husband can be a hard man." There was a silence as she looked to the side, lost in thought. Then, they were surprised to see a slight smile on her face as the shadow of a dog's head appeared near the top of the desk, nudging Francie's elbow.

With her hand rubbing Maisie's head, she finished. "I would like to say that Sister Mary Aurelius was a fine woman, a good woman. She deserved better." A long sigh. "I hope this is helpful."

They were all silent when the screen went to black again. Finally, Leo turned to Rosaria. "Where would she go?"

"I haven't the slightest, Leo."

"Right. Okay, if you'll excuse us, Ro, we've got a lot to do here to follow up on this now. Johnson, you stay. Victor—in my office. Time to catch the big bad wolf."

An officer in an unmarked car had been assigned to park discreetly outside Malachy Sullivan's office—and another had been assigned to do the same at his home. Though the officer on duty reported no sign of Malachy or his SUV at the offices of Claddagh Properties, Leo and Wesley Johnson decided to visit there late that afternoon. They took the stairs up to the third floor to talk to Dorothy Murdoch, Malachy's office manager.

As Leo entered Malachy's office suite, he was no longer impressed with the overall statement of rich furniture, carpets, paintings, or the awards on the walls. The setting repelled him. He could almost smell the stench of something sinister, something musky, as if he were in a lair.

The diminutive Dorothy Murdoch stood to greet him. "Hi, Leo. If you're looking for Malachy, he's not here. He went straight home late this morning after his meetings in town ended early."

Close call for Francie this morning, thought Leo.

"He called here to see if I'd heard from Francie. She's usually home that time of day. He seemed concerned about her."

"I'll bet he is," said Leo.

Dorothy gave him a curious look. "Is there anything I can help you with, Leo?"

"No, no. Thanks. If he comes back, have him call us. We'd like to talk with him as soon as possible. Could I have his cell number?"

"Sure thing, Leo." Dorothy wrote the number on a high-quality, ivory-colored notepad with a small green Claddagh design near the top of the page. "There you go, but I think all the calls are going straight to his voicemail right now. Maybe he's busy."

As he took the paper, Leo wondered if Malachy allowed sticky-notes from Staples in the office or if everything had to be this level of quality. Pretty rich margins in whatever dirty side business Malachy was in.

"Thanks, Dorothy."

Leo started to walk down the hall from the offices, then turned back and quietly entered the suite again, just as Dorothy was picking up the phone.

"Don't do that, Mrs. Murdoch."

She flushed and put the phone down.

"Could I have the number of Malachy's *second* cell?"

Dorothy didn't look at Leo, but nodded, wrote another number down on a clean page from the ivory notepad, and passed it to him.

"Thanks. I'd appreciate it if you didn't call Mr. Sullivan today. You might even think about going home now." Leo reached into his jacket pocket for his card and gave it to Mrs. Murdoch. "Call me if he shows up."

"Yes. Okay, Leo." The woman met his eyes briefly and then looked down at her desk.

There was no answer on either of Malachy's cell phones, and the voice mailbox was full on his private cell. *Must be plenty of people who want to reach Malachy today*, thought Leo.

Shortly after midnight, Leo got the call he'd been waiting for.

"Just pulled in."

"Thanks. Be right there. Don't do anything, unless he tries to leave. If he does, hold him till we get there."

Only the kitchen light was on in the Sullivan house when Leo and Wesley Johnson pulled up, though the security lights flashed on as they came up the walk to ring the doorbell. The dog started to bark in the enclosed backyard.

A wan-looking Malachy Sullivan came to the front door.

"Is it Francie? Is Francie okay? Don't tell me something's happened."

Leo noticed a sweaty sheen on Malachy's face, and his unsteady stance as he held onto the doorframe. He talked in short bursts as he ushered them into the house.

"Don't know where she is. Had some business meetings tonight. Kept calling. Her purse is gone, but she left her cell phone. Why would she do that?"

Malachy stopped and looked at the two men when they stood before him without responding.

"She's okay, isn't she?"

"Francie's okay. We're here about the murder of Sister Mary Aurelius."

Malachy looked confused—and then angry.

"Shit. I told you everything I know already. Which is nothing. Nothing. Nothing. Where's Francie?" Malachy's face contorted. "Got these cramps. Jesus. Some flu or something. Been coming on all afternoon and it's really bad now. Where's Francie?"

"Francie's in a safe place, Mal."

"What the hell is that supposed to mean?" Malachy's voice got louder. "Where the hell is my wife?"

A frightened child in this big man, Leo thought. *He needs his mommy, but mommy's not coming home anymore.*

"We need you to come down to the station for a talk, Mal."

"Christ. I'm too fucking sick for this shit. I couldn't even take the dog out to pee. Wait a minute. I need to bring her in."

Malachy shuffled painfully to the back door with Wesley Johnson behind him. Maisie burst into the kitchen as he opened the door. The big dog greeted the policemen with all the affectionate exuberance of the hopeless watchdog she was and then settled beside Malachy. He had sunken into one of the kitchen chairs with his head in his arms on the table. The dog pushed her face into his arm and left it there. Leo and Wesley watched as the man wearily lifted his arm to pull the dog closer to his body.

"I need a doctor. Get me to a doctor." Malachy's facial muscles looked odd to Leo. Maybe the man was having a stroke. Leo called 911.

Later, as the EMT's loaded Malachy into an ambulance, his breathing was labored and his face was a frozen mask. Inside, Maisie was frantic. Wesley held her back by her collar. "Okay, girl. Hang on. It'll be all right now."

Leo reflected on that moment later. The dog had known it wouldn't be all right.

CHAPTER 25

n the end, it wasn't hard at all to find out where Francie had gone. Veterans Cab gave the officer who called the name of the cabbie who picked Francie up at her house that day. The cabbie in question remembered driving the lady to Wellington Circle. Very quiet, just looked out the window for the entire ride. Except for one phone call.

"Must have had another cell Malachy didn't know about. Maybe one of those prepaid ones, disposable," Victor suggested.

"Smart lady. Cabbie hear anything of the call?" Leo asked.

"Yeah, he said it sounded like someone was meeting her at an airport. He remembered that because he thought it was funny she had only a small carry case and didn't converse. Said to somebody on the other end that she'd be in about 3:45."

"Use a name?"

"Said something like, 'I had to, Charlie.' Something like that," Victor replied.

"Running off with some guy? Wow. That would take the cake. Serves the bastard right." Detective Johnson volunteered from the other side of the room.

Leo shook his head. "Doubt it. Sullivan had her locked up so tight, how would she ever meet anybody?"

"Internet," responded Johnson. "Happens all the time."

"She's not the type." Leo gave Johnson a sharp look of annoyance.

Johnson put his hands on his hips. "Give me a break, Gelenian. You've been in this business long enough. Nobody's ever the type, but it turns out they are."

Leo turned to Victor, his other officer. "Find out if Francie had any friends or relatives called Charlie. Ask her mother."

Some minutes later, the officer returned. Yes, Francie's mother said. Francie had a cousin named Charlotte, her sister's girl, nicknamed Charlie. The cousins had been very close when they were young, though less so in recent years. Francie's mother said that Malachy didn't care for Charlie. He said she meddled too much, and so the relationship between the cousins had become more distant. In time, Charlie had settled in Pittsburgh and married a fireman there.

"A woman of good taste," Johnson approved.

"Francie's got to come back," Leo said. We'll give her a couple of days, but she's got to come back."

———

Malford Hospital was high on the ridge above the city. The view of the reservoir and the surrounding woodland walkways from the patient rooms could give one the sense of being in a country sanatorium—perhaps an estate, thought Leo. You'd never guess you were in an old factory town.

As he parked his car and left it in the lot, Leo turned to the view and thought he could see Malachy's big white house on a small hill across the reservoir. *Fat lot of good all that does the sorry bastard now*, he thought. Leo pushed the revolving door into the lobby, and proceeded to Doctor Agarwal's office suite on the second floor.

"Thank you for seeing me, Doctor. Have you already spoken to Mrs. Sullivan?"

The doctor gestured to a chair for Leo, then came around to sit his own small frame on the corner of a desk. "Yes, thank you for putting me in touch with her. Mrs. Sullivan took it very well. Quite a shocking event. So sudden."

He shook his head and continued. "She gave me permission to speak frankly with you in whatever detail you may need." The doctor shifted his position. "By the time they got Mr. Sullivan to us, he was so far gone, there was really little we could do. Monsignor McDermott gave him the Last Rites the day after he was admitted and Mr. Sullivan was gone that night."

"How was the Monsignor? They were very close."

"Yes, I could see that. Monsignor was extremely distressed, so much so that we had to prescribe an anti-anxiety medication for him and send him back to the rectory in a cab. Mrs. Fitzpatrick is taking care of him." The doctor tsked sympathetically at the sadness of the situation.

"Mr. Sullivan kept asking for his dog, poor man. If we could have thought of any way to do it without having the hospital issued a citation for breaking protocol in a sanitary environment, we would have brought the animal in. There was no time anyway. Everything moved so fast, you know."

"He was really close to that dog." Leo puzzled for a moment to himself about someone as ruthless as Malachy having such a deep emotional bond with a tan boxer named Maisie.

Then, he broke that mysterious train of thought to ask the doctor, "So, what was the final diagnosis? What did Sullivan actually die from?"

"Botulism."

"Botulism? Food poisoning? From what?"

"Apparently some gourmet stuffed olives. A warning went out about them, but I understand that an opened jar of these olives from a shop downtown was found on Mr. Sullivan's kitchen counter. Pity. The shop thought it had completely cleared the shelves after they got the product warning, but apparently not."

Doctor Agarwal frowned as he continued. "Though I must say they do seem to have dropped the ball. They'd gotten the warning a little late it seems, since some of their customers had already heard about it on TV and online. Someone should have noticed Mrs. Sullivan making the purchase. Apparently it was a busy day. In any case, a tragedy all around. Mr. Sullivan apparently had ingested five or six of these gourmet olives. His wife said they were a favorite of his. He succumbed very quickly."

"A few bad olives can do that?"

"Oh yes, the botulism neurotoxin is potent and lethal. As little as one nanogram per kilogram can be fatal. It often appears in as little as twelve hours or even sometimes less after ingesting the toxin. All forms lead to paralysis, typically starting in the facial muscles and spreading toward the limbs. In its most severe form, like Mr. Sullivan's, it leads to paralysis of the breathing muscles and causes respiratory failure." Doctor Agarwal sighed. "Still, I think the food safety alert system failed us here. It's a pity you hadn't visited Mr. Sullivan sooner. If you had, this might have turned out differently."

Well, thought Leo, *maybe differently, not necessarily better.*

Staring into the distance, Rosaria was nursing her second cup of coffee and slowly nibbling on some crusty bread with Gruyere cheese when Leo came through the door of The French Connection. He worked his tall, angular body through the crowded shop to her small table.

He shook his head as Rosaria gestured to a coffee carafe in front of her. "What a week."

Leo stopped for a moment and looked at Rosaria. "You look like shit—pardon my French. Getting any sleep?"

"None. And you don't look like a prince yourself." Rosaria noticed he'd missed a spot shaving, and that he still had a tiny bit of shaving cream on his jawline.

"Well, as they say, you can't make this stuff up. The botulism Sullivan died from came from tainted stuffed olives sold here," Leo looked around the shop. "The health alert went out, and the shops were supposed to clear the shelves immediately. Johnson already spoke to the owners and the health authorities are coming in this morning, but I have a few more questions myself."

Rosaria was pensive as Leo spoke. She remembered something. Something she didn't feel good about.

Leo stopped when he saw Rosaria's face. "What?"

"Leo, I think Francie bought those olives the day I was here with Bill Kenneally, the day I was hit by the van. I saw them on the counter. She was in kind of a hurry, and I was on my way out, but I'm sure I heard her tell the clerk she was buying special treats for Malachy. 'For all he'd done,' she said."

The color seemed to drain from Leo's face, and he ran his long fingers through his hair. "Well, I guess we'd better talk to Mrs. Sullivan again. First, I'll talk to the manager here."

"Accidents happen, Leo." Rosaria looked at Leo closely, another larger message in her eyes.

"Sure they do, Ro. Sure they do."

She touched his arm. "There are gray areas."

There was a sad chill in Leo's eyes as he looked at her. "Not my call. Got a job to do." He stood and walked toward the counter where he asked the clerk for the shop manager.

Rosaria willed Leo to hear her thoughts. *Give it a rest, Leo. Francie saved herself and maybe did us all a favor, including you. Learn how to let some things go.*

CHAPTER 26

eo Gelenian had dressed quickly on getting the call about another overdose just after he fell asleep that night. He was still tucking his shirt in as he worked his way down the bank of the Mystic River. "So, who've we got here?"

"Meet Josiah Winthrop Linsky," Victor replied, drawing his notebook from his pocket.

"Some name."

"Yeah, we were saying."

"Winthrop was the first governor of the Massachusetts Bay Colony. Linsky's a bookie," said Leo.

"No shit? Well, there you go—a marriage made in heaven." Victor didn't look up, continuing to turn back the pages of his notebook.

The tall, white-faced boy lying near the water bore silent witness to the exchange, his ash blond hair radiating on the trampled snowy ground.

"OD'ed?"

"Right."

"You use the Narcan?" Leo rubbed the back of his neck.

"Yep, too late. Shame. Another one gone. A bunch of them were under the bridge, using a little, maybe some E, and drinking. Built a fire. Hanging out on a Friday night. He wasn't there at first. He was over at the River View." The officer pointed across the roadway to a neon-lit, low brick building that pulsated with the bass of heavy music. "His friends said it was really hot in the club, overheated and crowded. He'd had some E too. And, of course, they all were drinking. Anyway, they say he starts feeling dizzy and sick. Probably heat exhaustion with the E. Dancing, hot, crowded club."

"Right."

"So, one of his friends brings him over here to cool down, outside in the cold. And then he pulls out something he bought in the club and starts snorting. He slips away from the group, sits down next to the river, and must have started to shut down after a while. No one notices until much later, but when they come over to ask if he wants a ride home, he doesn't wake up." The officer lifted his chin to acknowledge the medical examiner, Heaney, heavily making his way down the banking. "All yours, buddy. Didn't touch him," Victor called.

"Good. You guys are slow learners, but you may be remedial."

"Good to see you too, Doctor Doom," Leo greeted Heaney.

Leo was turning away when Victor said, "The kids said Linsky was really feeling down tonight."

"Yeah, well, he can't get much downer than he is now." Leo looked at the small group of teenagers shivering near the bridge, pulling their collars up on their necks and their sleeves down to keep their hands warm. Stamping their feet in the cold. The girls were crying and holding each other. The boys looked vacant and stoned, their breath misting clouds in the cold. "Put those kids in the van and take them down to the station. Call their parents if you can find them."

As one of the officers started to walk up the hill, Leo called, "Feed them something and give them something hot to drink." He turned again to the group of officers. "Mother know?"

"Johnson's going over to get her. Rebecca Linsky. Waitress at the Strand over on Eastern Avenue. Know her?"

"Yeah, I do," Leo answered. "This is her only kid. Too bad. Nice lady."

"Probably not a bad kid either." Victor took a deep breath. "So that's what I wanted to tell you. My sister knows one of the Linsky neighbors. Word has it that the mother was real friendly with Malachy Sullivan."

"How friendly?"

"Oh, *friendly* friendly."

Leo frowned, absorbing this new information. "Sullivan and Becca. That hook-up's out of the blue."

"The kid here probably thought his mother finally found somebody that could turn out to be halfway decent, after all the losers she dated. Pretty lady with lousy taste in men. She made a whole lot of bad luck in her life and the kid's."

"Where do we think Josiah got the stuff tonight?" asked Leo.

"The club. One of the kids let slip that the guy selling in the club restroom got his supply from somebody distributing out of an empty apartment in the Gardens."

"Haven't we gotten a handle on that yet?"

"We've been all over the place. Nobody's talking. Even the usual sources have clammed up, ever since Fortunato got crushed by some big guy who showed up in the stairwell one night."

"One of Tuney's eyes is in bad shape. They may not be able to save it. Big guy never said anything. Kick to the face and the gut with a size extra-large boot, and then out the door. Something nice and visible. Everybody got the message. They're afraid."

Leo tightened his lips and shook his head. "This damned well better be the last kid we see like this from the Gardens. I'm going to talk to the Chief again about bringing the State Police in on this, not just with the task force, but operationally. Should have done that weeks ago." Leo held up his hand at Victor's objection. "It's out of control. Too big for us. We're not the only place around here with this new crap in the housing projects. I was just up at Lowell—it's all over there too. This is big. Bigger than us."

Leo took a last long look at young Josiah Winthrop Linsky. "I'll talk to the mother with Johnson. Call Freddie from the diner for me. I don't think she has any family and somebody's got to be there for her. He's the best she's got."

The next morning, the investigating officers reported they'd spoken to the housing authority and inspected the apartment in question. Apparently, it had been empty for two months, allegedly for repairs, though there was no sign of any repair being done. When the officers were there, a somewhat uncoordinated work crew showed up and began to pull the kitchen stove out for replacement. The apartment—like most in the project—wasn't in great shape, but to the officers there that day, the activity looked staged.

The occupants of nearby apartments were questioned. No one was aware of any activity in the apartment, never mind someone moving drugs. God, no—nothing like that. Saw nothing. Heard nothing. The kids themselves had clammed up when their parents arrived at the station the night of Josiah's death. The Chisholm kid who had let slip about activity in an empty apartment suddenly remembered nothing, and said he'd been misunderstood.

Leo talked to the Chisholm boy with his mother the next day.

"You told the officer that some guy was selling at the Gardens out of an empty apartment in D block."

"He made a mistake." The boy's mother hunkered down in a chair next to her son, her arms tightly crossed over a polyester Kmart uniform jacket. A heavyset, bulldog of a woman. If she could have moved her chair in front of her son to protect him from Leo, she would have.

"He can talk for himself, Mom," Leo snapped. "Brandon, tell me about the guy in the apartment."

"Didn't see nothin'. Officer heard me wrong," mumbled the boy beside her. A soft, fleshy boy with a pierced lip and floppy bleached blond hair.

"I think you're changing your story, Brandon. I think you were telling it right the first time." Leo leaned forward, rising out of his seat and placing his palms down on the top of the table. Brandon moved back in his chair. His mother moved forward to meet the challenge.

"The officer heard him wrong. He's telling you he didn't see nothin.'" The mother's mouth was set in a hard line.

"Who are you afraid of, Mrs. Chisholm?"

"Not afraid of nobody." The woman lowered her eyes. "Brandon didn't see nothin.'"

Defeated after an hour of similar, fruitless conversation, the detectives released the Chisholms from questioning for the moment.

Roger O'Toole, Director of the Housing Authority, was standing in the lobby of the station when they exited the interrogation room. Leo noted O'Toole's orderly rows of dark hair plugs, and wondered if anyone else still wore a Chesterfield coat during the business day.

"Hello, Leo. Good to see you. Just on my way up to drop in on Chief Cullen."

He turned to the Chisholms.

"Mrs. Chisholm, Brandon." O'Toole nodded genially at the mother and son. "Terrible business this, isn't it? I hope we can get to the bottom of this mess soon. Such a shame about the Linsky boy."

"Right, right, Roger. It's terrible," Mrs. Chisholm said. "But Brandon and me were just telling the detectives that we don't know nothin' about drugs being sold at the Gardens, do we, Brandon?" She forced a smile and nudged her son.

"Nothin.'" Brandon's bleached hair flopped side to side and over his eyes as he shook his head energetically.

"The officer must have misunderstood Brandon the other night. All a big mistake. Right, Brandon?" Mrs. Chisholm encouraged her son.

"Yeah, I don't know nothin.'"

O'Toole put his hand on Brandon's shoulder, where the hallway light caught the sparkle from the stone of a large pinky ring. "Well, we all make mistakes, Brandon, and we just do our best to make them right. These things happen. Isn't that the way, Detective?" O'Toole turned to Leo.

Leo tried to remember who O'Toole's connections were that got him this plumb civil service job. O'Toole raised money for influential people, and it was an open secret in City Hall that all the employees of the Authority were expected to make donations and volunteer for certain candidate campaigns. A housing authority post and a fat budget ready for the looting were just rewards for O'Toole's past services, and a down payment for future support. Some kid from the wrong neighborhood with the wrong color skin or the wrong accent robbed a convenience store of fifty bucks and got slammed, while O'Toole plundered hundreds of thousands of dollars and rode around the city in a Lincoln Town Car. *What a world,* thought Leo.

O'Toole turned Leo's stomach

Later, Wesley Johnson commented to Leo, "My mama told me to never trust a man with a pinky ring. Did you see the size of it? Good Lord."

"What do you think, Wes?"

"All lying. Afraid, you can see they're afraid. And not just of that fancy man that happens to be dropping in to see the chief."

"But O'Toole's involved. I know he is. You don't live the way he lives on a public salary, even with the size skim he's taking."

"Getting a cut for providing the base of operations."

"Of course," Leo said. "Someone will slip. Chief gave me the okay to bring the State in. They'll be here this afternoon."

Wesley raised his eyebrows. "Let the games begin."

"This looks like it's all of a piece to me. If we get anything to open it up even a crack, it'll be O'Toole that'll give the whole operation up. Squeal like a stuck pig if he gets a deal. Slimeball."

"Amen." Wesley Johnson started down the corridor before he turned and asked, "How's Linsky's mother?"

"How do you think?"

CHAPTER 27

hief Nicolo Cullen dropped his bulky, muscular body into his desk chair. The chair objected with its customary loud squeak. "No case here, Leo. Right, Shelly?"

Shelly Marquette, the young assistant district attorney, sat beside Leo Gelenian on the other side of the chief's desk. A small woman, professional in her tailored cream blouse and slim navy skirt, Shelly nodded and turned to Leo.

"Nothing here, Detective. The shop should have removed the jar of tainted foodstuffs. They missed it, and they'll be reprimanded and heavily fined, maybe sued. But Mrs. Sullivan—she can say she had no idea about the recall. Not everybody listens to the news every morning."

Ms. Marquette straightened her glasses and picked up her pen, lightly striking the desk. "And we know that Mr. Sullivan liked that product as a snack. Olives and almonds together. Tasty, healthy, low fat, and organic." The pen ticked on the table with each adjective. "We know Mr. Sullivan was very health conscious." Here the young woman paused. "And we know that Mrs. Sullivan was very solicitous of her husband's needs."

"So," she concluded as she put the pen down, "no jury's going to buy, without a reasonable doubt, that Mrs. Sullivan deliberately killed her husband. Also, I don't have to tell you that any jury would find Mrs. Sullivan personally a very sympathetic defendant.

"Even the newest public defender just out of law school could get an easy win off this. Piece of cake for a lawyer with any experience. We just don't have the resources to chase after a sure dead end for us, Detective."

Leo nodded and straightened his shoulders. He had to be upfront here, professional. God, it was so hard. Francie. He thought about the two of them as kids together and what she'd gone through since then. "You know there was a long history of domestic abuse there. She certainly had a motive."

"Oh, no doubt. I would have whacked the piece of shit years ago if it was me," the young woman responded. She and Chief Cullen both smiled. "But that doesn't make the case for us."

The Chief turned to Leo. "Let's just let it go, Leo." And, turning to the young woman, he added, "Thanks for coming out, Shelly."

The attorney gathered her portfolio and bag. "My pleasure, Nicky. Always good to see you. Glad to meet you, Detective." She gave Leo a surprisingly firm handshake with her small hand.

Leo started to get up to leave himself.

"Leo, stick around for a minute, would you? Thanks again, Shelly." Chief Cullen walked the young woman to the door, closed it, and came back to his desk. He sat and started to look over some papers on his desk as he talked.

"So, Leo, just to tie up all the loose ends on this, why don't you fly down to Pittsburgh and talk to Mrs. Sullivan? It would be better if you did that right away, before she comes home for the wake and the funeral. We want to make sure we get all the details. We'll need a formal statement when she gets back, but it doesn't look good to be having our first conversation while she's burying her husband." He looked up for Leo's response.

"We've got too much going on for me to take off right now."

"I'm not asking you to stay a week, just overnight. Besides, things may have taken care of themselves on Aurelius with Malachy and his shitty fancy olive snacks. We're operating on that assumption, though there's a lot of follow-up to do there. Part of that is a long conversation with Mrs. Sullivan."

Leo frowned. "You know, Chief, I told you that Joey kept talking about two shadows that night, and he remembered smoke. I never saw Malachy smoke. It's been bothering me. I think there's something there we need to follow. Maybe Malachy had an accomplice."

"Look, I don't know what to do with that, Leo. We don't have any evidence around that except a couple of random cigarette butts. Anyway, you know Mucci wasn't the sharpest tool in the shed the last few years. He said he saw two shadows, but one of them could've been his own. We can't do shit with what he remembered or didn't that night. Would never hold up. He was crazy and now he's dead."

He looked at Leo. "Sorry, just the way it is."

The Chief continued, "And on the Authority drugs thing, you and the State have most of the pieces in place. Still need to cement the O'Toole part. He'll spill his guts to get a break on the charges, and that'll be enough.

"You're the only one that can do the job right with Mrs. Sullivan. You know her the best. Christ, you've looked at that video statement of hers enough times to memorize it."

Leo reddened. "That's really important evidence."

"Didn't say it wasn't."

Leo was silent. He stretched his head to both sides a couple of times and bit his lower lip.

"Get out of here, Gelenian. I don't want to see you 'til day after tomorrow with a full report in your hand. You better get a flight tonight. Another storm coming in."

Leo walked to the door and, without turning, said, "Okay. See you." Then he left the office and closed the door.

A soft smile on his rough face, Chief Cullen delicately turned one of the pages on his desk calendar with his thick fingers and spoke to the empty door. "You're welcome, Leo."

Leo sat across from Francie in a coffee shop near the Pennsylvania Macaroni Company, a legendary Italian food emporium on the strip in Pittsburgh. The area and the traffic reminded Leo of the streets around the North End of Boston where the diaspora of North Enders returned—children and children's children who drove their SUVs and late model cars in from the suburbs, back to the old neighborhood to get some decent provolone, prosciutto, and homemade pasta.

Francie wore jeans and sneakers, and seemed much younger to Leo. "Never saw you in jeans before, Francie."

"Malachy didn't think women over seventeen should wear jeans and sneakers," Francie said flatly, giving Leo a look that could only be described as "Can you believe it?"

Leo allowed himself a smile. "I can believe that."

"My cousin took me shopping. I wore her hoodie when I went walking yesterday. Really nice and warm. I was going to buy one when we were out, but I think I'll wait until I get home. Maybe get a Pats hoodie."

"We need to talk now, Francie, but you know you'll have to give a formal statement when you get back. You can decide if you need a lawyer with you."

"Yes, I knew I'd have to do that. I have a ticket for the morning flight. Same one you're on. I talked to Kehoe's last night about the wake and the funeral. I can come to the station in the afternoon." She stopped to massage her shoulder. Weary. Matter of fact. Very weary.

"Good. That's good." Leo rested his arms on the table. "Okay, how did you know that the blood on Malachy's slacks belonged to Aurelius? "

"Did it belong to her?"

"Yes, of course it did. How did you know? Was it a guess?"

It took Francie a long time to answer. "No, it wasn't a guess. I just knew. Don't ask me how." She paused, thinking, and staring past Leo. "Does that make sense?"

"Not really."

Francie shrugged and then looked at Leo. "I think he was there and probably wanted it to happen, Leo, but I don't think he did it."

"Why not?"

"He was rough. You know he was rough with me." Leo couldn't fully read the expression on Francie's face as she said this. He thought he might have seen a mixture of shame, relief, and a certain dignity—all at the same time.

Leo nodded. It pained him deeply to think of Malachy's hurting Francie. The dimply son of a bitch.

"But I'll tell you—he couldn't actually kill somebody like that. That way, with a stone bashing someone's head in." Francie lowered her eyes, still looking stunned at the thought of Aurelius's end in the schoolyard.

"I find that hard to believe." *Malachy had seemed capable of that and a whole lot more*, Leo thought.

"Well, you believe what you want, Leo. It doesn't matter for Malachy anyway. He's dead." Her face said Malachy was a closed chapter. Francie picked up her purse. "You want to keep talking while we walk, Leo?"

"Okay, but let me ask you a question first. Did Malachy smoke?"

"Oh, never. That's what killed his mother. He was strong against smoking. He used to complain about someone he worked with that smoked around him."

"Interesting." Leo thought for a moment. "Okay, let's go."

Leo followed Francie through the restaurant as she moved, somehow regal even in her jeans, gracefully weaving around the restaurant tables on her way out.

Leo and Francie talked while they walked the city, the air crisp and bright. In the afternoon, they rode the cable car up the Monongahela Incline to Mount Washington and took in the broad vista of the city and three great American rivers meeting—the Monongahela, the Ohio, and the Allegheny. *Not exactly normal procedure*, thought Leo, *but she's talking.*

"Are you going to ask me questions about the food poisoning, Leo?"

Leo carefully studied the plaque telling the story of the Incline cable car before he responded. He sighed. "No, I don't think so, Francie."

Hands in his pockets, Leo looked out over the rivers and the city. He was quiet for some long moments before he turned to her in her jeans and down jacket, the sun on her hair and her dark blue eyes on his face. "What's done is done."

She nodded. "Thanks, Leo."

CHAPTER 28

uncie's brother Sevi ladled a lightly garlicked Italian fish chowder into blue Fiesta bowls in front of Rosaria and Francie at his dining room table. "I thought it would be better to have something not too heavy. You don't want anything heavy to eat when you still have hours to go with that circus. Just makes you more tired."

Rosaria remembered shopping with Nuncie to buy this dining room set when she was decorating her brother's new townhouse on the Fells. Now, Nuncie was dying, and Rosaria sat at the table with Francie and Sevi for dinner during the break between the afternoon and evening hours at Malachy Sullivan's wake.

"Francie's waking her husband, Sevi. Give it a rest. Don't call it a circus," Rosaria said.

"Oh, right," Sevi muttered before he looked over at Francie. "Sorry, Francie."

"It's okay, Sevi," Francie said softly as she sipped her tea.

Rosaria noticed Francie had taken a polite spoonful of her chowder, but wasn't really eating.

Sevi had invited Francie and Rosaria to his house for dinner. "You don't want to go to a restaurant and have all those people gawking at you or, God forbid, coming over to offer condolences. And you don't want to go to your parents' place. They need to go home and take a nap. They look tired. Come to my house."

"Francie's doing a great job, Sevi," Rosaria said between bites of warm Italian bread dipped in olive oil. If Sevi weren't so much like a brother to her, she could have fallen in love with him. What a cook.

Sevi nodded. "Yeah, must be hard. And you never know who knows what when they're coming through the line."

"Thank God, there's no word out yet. If we're lucky, it won't hit the street 'til after he's interred," Rosaria said.

"That'll be another tough time, Francie," Sevi said, giving Francie a sympathetic glance.

Francie met his eyes and shrugged. "Yeah, but I think I can handle it."

"One thing at a time, Francie," Rosaria said, putting her hand on Francie's arm.

Francie had asked Rosaria to be near her during the wake. "It would help me just to know you were there. I don't know how I'm going to do this."

That day, as Rosaria sat quietly behind her, Francie did do it. The line of mourners extended out the door and she'd stood for hours accepting condolences on the death of her husband. Rosaria had felt a rush of deep affection for Francie, as she watched the new widow accept accolades, one after the other, about her late husband.

All so unreal now.

She and Francie, together in a strange, hallucinatory dream as praise for Malachy flowed on. Such an exceptional man. Tragic, cut down in his prime. Especially that way. Terrible way to go. After all the good he did. Rosaria had to bite her tongue every time she heard another accolade for Malachy Sullivan.

For this brief moment in time, Malachy was still a solid citizen and philanthropist. All soon to be swept away and replaced with the reality of his roles as murderer and drug dealer.

Francie responded with graceful patience to the many questions. No, she didn't intend to sue The French Connection and the two sisters who ran it, nor did she intend to go after the little organic food company that produced the food product with the botulism that killed Malachy. These things happen. She knew nothing like that would ever happen again at the organic food company or the shop. She certainly hoped everyone would still patronize The French Connection and enjoy the fine food and service.

Rosaria asked Francie if she'd taken the medication the doctor had prescribed to help with the stress of her sudden widowhood.

"No, I'm okay," Francie had replied with an otherworldly serenity. Several times in the course of the evening, she'd said to Rosaria, "What's done is done," like a mantra. Now, there was only this river of people to get through. Well-meaning people who knew nothing of Francie's life or that of her husband.

People nodded in an understanding way when Francie said no, she didn't think she'd stay in the big house near the reservoir. Too many memories. Old women from the parish patted her hands in understanding. Yes, dear. It's so hard with the memories. And since you and Malachy didn't have children—here they cast their eyes down in apology—it's probably for the best. Maybe a nice condo over near the Fells, or perhaps you'd think about moving into your parent's house. You're staying there now, aren't you? Their kind old eyes would linger on Francie Dooley Sullivan's face as they held her hands. God love you, sweetheart.

One wise old woman knew better than the others. Perhaps she'd heard a new rumor, or seen a bruise, heard noises at night in the Sullivan house. Maybe she had her own history. Rosaria saw the woman grasp Francie's hand with her ringed, age-swollen fingers, and pull the young woman close to whisper, "The son of a bitch is gone to ground. Your best days are ahead." Rosaria and the woman exchanged a glance afterward. The woman whispered "the bastard" as she walked by Rosaria.

Father Hanrahan was not available, so a priest from Saint Joseph's, a neighboring parish, said the funeral Mass the next day. It was a high Mass with a spectacular "Ave Maria" as the Kehoe Funeral Home staff carried out the casket—the Mayor and the city council having declined the honor.

Rosaria had gone with Francie earlier when she'd ordered a large Celtic cross grave marker for Malachy. "He would have liked it. Just showy enough. My going away present." Later, when they went to purchase the cemetery plot, the cemetery official was surprised when Francie declined to purchase a plot for herself beside Malachy's on a small knoll under a maple tree.

Francie and Rosaria didn't speak afterward as they walked slowly down the winding paths and out the gates of Holy Cross Cemetery, arm in arm, that gray late winter day.

On the day of the funeral, after the Mass and the cemetery, when everyone had gone from her parents' house, Francie put on her sneakers, sweatpants, and new Pats hoodie and went for a long run by the river. She flew, her feet pounding on the cleared pathway, memories streaming behind her like dark ribbons lifting and falling in the wind. And she cried. Francie only cried when she ran.

She ran most every day. She avoided the running trails around the reservoir and instead ran through the Middlesex Fells Woods or by the Mystic River. She usually borrowed Maisie from Wesley Johnson and his wife, Tanesha, to keep her company as she ran. Wesley had raised his hand to take Maisie when Malachy died. After a period of animal grief and confusion, the dog was thriving. Maisie kept pace with Francie on her runs, and loved to sit close beside her, later, on a large flat rock after Francie had stretched, and both caught their breath. *Two widows*, Francie thought, *one human and one canine.*

Francie was staying in the guest bedroom at her parents' house. She told her mother she really couldn't sleep in her childhood bedroom with the daisy wallpaper and the maple bed covered with a white chenille bedspread. It would have been all too sad. She was only there for a few months anyway while she sorted things out and found her own place.

Sometimes at night, Francie thought she could hear her younger self moving around her old bedroom. That younger self was a stranger to her. She wanted to take the sweet girl in her arms and rock her to sleep. Poor, unworldly child.

Francie never went into the big house by the reservoir again. She hired people to go in and clean out the contents to give to the Saint Vincent de Paul Society, even her clothes and personal items. Francie wanted nothing. All tainted. All invisibly stained with misery. The house sold quickly. She took the first offer and opened a new checking account at the Malford Trust under the name Francine Marie Dooley.

CHAPTER 29

Several weeks after Malachy's funeral, Rosaria was calling ahead to alert Sevi that she was almost at the house in Gloucester. "I'm at the bridge." The Annisquam River glittered below as Rosaria drove over the bridge that spanned the river separating Gloucester from the rest of the world. She took the turn at Grant Circle and glanced at the insulated blue plastic containers on the car floor. They held a watery chicken and rice mush that suited Nuncie's diet now. One of the hardest parts of this cancer for Nuncie, a great Italian cook, had been leaving behind the pleasures of eating good food. Now, the cancer had triumphed and in what appeared to be her final weeks, even this watery mush was often beyond her.

A few minutes later, Rosaria pulled up to Nuncie's house and climbed the stairs over the granite rocks, balancing her delivery of homemade chicken mush. Sevi greeted her at the door, his long face sad and preoccupied as he took her containers.

"Hi, Ro. Don't know if she'll be up for this today. She can't even keep weak tea down. But I'll put it in the fridge. Maybe later. Go ahead—she's on the couch."

Nuncie's face looked wizened and jaundiced against the pillows on the couch. Her body, growing more insubstantial every day, lay under a lightweight ivory afghan. Nuncie didn't bother to wear her wig these days. "Too hot and itchy," she'd say. Only tiny wisps of hair haloed her skull, freckled with a few dark spots. Her eyes were closed.

Rosaria sat gently at the end of the couch and started to knead Nuncie's small feet. Nuncie didn't open her eyes and her voice was a whisper. "Everything's so fucking bad."

"I know, honey. I don't know what to say." Helpless and angry, Rosaria lay her head against the back of the couch and blew out a long breath.

"Don't get comfy," Nuncie whispered. "I have something for you to do."

"At your service." Rosaria leaned forward and smiled.

"House at the end of the point, just before Long Beach." Nuncie rested. Rosaria waited patiently. "Pete and Angie Blanchette." Another pause and rest, eyes still closed. "Remember Pete? He's younger than we are."

"Yeah, sort of. Blond. Good looking guy."

A smile lifted Nuncie's tired face. "I guess he was." Rosaria thought her friend almost chuckled. "Pete has some good info for you."

"What about?" Rosaria asked.

"Things at the Immaculate after we left." Nuncie rested for a moment, serious now. "Monsignor and the boys. Son of a bitch."

"Monsignor and the boys?" Rosaria felt a wave of weariness wash over her. "Why am I not surprised?"

"Everybody knew, but nobody knew." Nuncie gasped and caught more breath "Just talk to Pete."

Rosaria hadn't taken off her coat. She gave Nuncie's foot a squeeze, and then a quick hug and a kiss on the forehead before she headed for the door again. She thought this had all been put to bed, but now there was more. What a mess.

"Tell me when you get back," whispered Nuncie, again without opening her eyes.

As Rosaria reached for the doorknob, she heard another hoarse whisper behind her. "You're not the only hot shit sleuth around, O'Reilly."

Rosaria turned to see Nuncie's eyes still closed and the shadow of a smile on her yellowed face.

The little white house was actually a winterized cottage on a promontory over Long Beach. In the summer the beach was filled with families enjoying the sand and the waves. During the off-season, the line of cottages was boarded and quiet, the late winter wind whistling down through the front porches.

Today, the waves were good and there were a few surfers in their wet suits, sleek and black, riding the water like the seals swimming just beyond the beach or watching from the rocks. Rosaria could hear the calls of the surfers mixed with the cries of the gulls and the crashing of the waves. She inhaled deeply, the smell of sharp salt air and seaweed filling her nostrils.

A Marine Corps flag flew under the American flag on a tall pole in the yard, both snapping in the brisk wind. Lobster pots and buoys were stacked neatly on the leeward side of the house. Below, down a steep staircase built into the granite cliff, an ancient white dinghy waited at the ready on the rocks. In the water beyond, a battered but sturdy blue lobster boat rocked confidently on the waves like the old veteran it was.

Rosaria pulled her coat closer against the wind as she approached the house on a clamshell driveway. White shells crunched softly beneath her feet. Near the house, an aging black Honda with an Addison Gilbert Hospital sticker on the side window, and crystals hanging from the rear view mirror, sat idling, waiting for its driver. The fumes from the idling motor were blown away almost immediately by the wind. The high, deep scratch marks on the worn red front door of the house told her a large dog lived here also.

On her second knock, Peter Blanchette opened the door wide.

"Hi, Pete, I'm Rosaria O'Reilly, a friend of your neighbor Nuncie DiStephano. I think she told you I was coming by."

He greeted her with a warm smile. "Yeah, Sevi called for Nuncie and told me you'd be stopping down. Come in, come in." Behind Pete, a large golden retriever wiggled with pleasure at the prospect of a new visitor. "Calm down, Harry. Don't embarrass yourself in front of company."

Pete's close-clipped blond and gray hair framed light blue eyes in a deeply tanned and weathered face—the face of a fisherman, a fit, Marine Corps build.

The smell of freshly perked coffee filled the room, and Rosaria took in the view of the ocean from the picture window over a dining table. She entered the large open room. A Norwegian blue enamel woodstove, with a slightly crusted cast iron steamer on top, sat before a beach stone fireplace at one end. The fraying oriental rug of uncertain vintage in front of a dark red couch was covered with a light dusting of woodstove debris and dog hair. A pleasant woody smell mixed with the salt air and coffee.

On the ocean side, the dining room table with tall, mismatched oak chairs. A chipped white mug of hot coffee sat beside the *Gloucester Daily Times* spread over the table's worn surface.

"Nice." Rosaria observed to her host.

"We think so."

"I'm late. I'm late." A small, trim woman with an explosion of dark curls around her face burst from the side hall grabbing coat, hat, and purse—gently pushing the dog out of her way as he joined in the excitement. "Harry, get out of the way!"

She stopped when she saw they had a visitor. "Oh, hi. You must be Ro. I'm Angie." She offered her hand. "Sorry, have to run out. Have to take over for Theresa. One of her kids is sick. She had to go home. Don't forget to put the chicken in, Petey. Bye, Ro, nice to meet you." She gave Pete a moist kiss on the cheek and then she was gone.

"Nice to meet you too," called Rosaria to the retreating figure.

"That's my girl, always in a rush," said Pete with a grin. "Want some coffee?"

At Rosaria's nod, he walked into the kitchen area and poured another mug of coffee. This one was a deep blue and featured a crazy, toothy-looking fish and *Mad Fish Grille* on the side. Pete walked back with the mug and gestured toward the dining room table. Moving some newspapers, he put Rosaria's mug down in front of one of the oak chairs facing the ocean and sat at the end of the table. Harry settled himself noisily at Pete's feet. "Just a shame about Nuncie being so sick. Used to order lobsters from me—always having some kind of dinner with lots of people. Nice woman."

"Yes, she is a good woman," said Rosaria, looking out on the water as she sat at the table. "She's not doing too well right now, and doesn't have much time left."

"Tough. The good ones get slammed and some bastards live forever."

Rosaria gave him a small smile and nodded.

Pete sipped his coffee. "So, anyway, I'm not sure what Nuncie told you or what you need to know, Ro, but if she says I should talk to you, that's good enough for me. Angie went up to visit her the other day and happened to mention about when I went to the Immaculate. You know, since Nuncie's family owned that big bakery across the street from the school and all. Anyway, Nuncie asked if I'd come see her. She had a few questions."

Pete took a deep breath before continuing. "Anyway, I went over to Nuncie's and we talked. I have to tell you, I don't know why, but I told her things I haven't told anyone else. Maybe it was just her lying there—all wasted—looking at me so straight, being in her last days and everything. Kind of gets things close to the bone, know what I mean?"

"Oh, do I ever," Rosaria replied.

"To be honest here, I left that world and that time at the Immaculate behind and I don't like to go back, even in my mind." He pulled himself up in his chair and straightened his shoulders. "But, I promised. So, here we are. What would you like to know?"

"Thanks, Pete. I know it's hard. You know about Sister Mary Aurelius—Spike."

Pete nodded "Yeah, I heard right after. But why are you chasing this, if you don't mind my asking? Isn't Leo Gelenian taking the lead on this?"

"You remember Leo?"

"Yeah, he was younger, but I went to school with him. Smart kid. Too serious, but smart."

"That he is." Rosaria smiled, looked down at her coffee and took a breath before she spoke. "Well, Pete, I was close to Aurelius. I owed her big time, and I think she was chasing something, in her fashion. I'd like to finish the run for her."

He nodded and after some time said, "Okay, I get that. I'm good with that. I'd probably do the same thing. So, well—where to start?" Pete rubbed his head and the side of his face and began slowly. "You want to know about when I was at the Immaculate."

Rosaria nodded. "Yes. I do."

Pete looked out at the water. "Those were kind of weird days. To start, we had a tight little pack, with Malachy Sullivan and his best friend Dara McCarthy the top dogs. I guess that's kind of the way it usually works in seventh, eighth grade, and high school. I mean those packs that kind of run the show."

He ran his hand over his face. "I was a bit player. Part of the scene, but not locked in. The core group was really tight and a little scary, but I'll tell you," he put his elbows on the table and knitted his fingers in front of him, "the strangest part was that Monsignor McDermott seemed to be part of it. Does that make any sense?"

Rosaria didn't respond, but Pete continued.

"Malachy and Dara ran drugs, you know that?" He cocked his head and looked to Rosaria for confirmation.

"Yeah, I figured." Rosaria could feel a narrative coming into view, the smoke clearing away. She leaned across the table, closer to Pete, flattening the palms of her hands on the table. Two figures at an old oak table by the ocean, both in some kind of capsule, in another time with characters on another stage.

"You knew Dara?" Pete asked.

"Not really. Just saw him around town when I came home to visit. They were younger than I was. He seemed like a bully, hanging around the corner spa with his friends, terrifying the smaller kids."

"Yep, that was Dara McCarthy. Anyway, just to give you an idea of those guys, they gave a friend of theirs, John Michael Barrett, a bad batch of H on purpose because he mouthed off to Malachy and because they thought he was going to talk too much about their business."

Rosaria grimaced and dropped back in her chair. "You're not serious?"

"Of course, I'm serious. Who do you think you're dealing with here? Seriously bad actors." Pete looked away and took a sip of his coffee before he continued.

"But the best part—the part that's pure Malachy Sullivan—at Barrett's funeral, doesn't Malachy give the most heartfelt eulogy and carry the coffin with some of the other guys in his little club. Comforting the Barretts with hugs and sweet words. The Barretts thought the world of him, never knowing they were hugging the boy that murdered their son.

"So, that little scene will tell you everything you need to know about Malachy Ignatius Sullivan."

"What was up with the Monsignor?"

"What do you think was up? Suddenly one year we had some old guy from the parish council join the Monsignor and his priest friends when they took a bunch of us on the annual trip to Plum Island." Pete smiled. "Felt like somebody finally woke up and this old guy was a chaperone, but it was too late for some of us."

Rosaria closed her eyes for a moment. "I guess I'm not surprised. All those trips. How did this happen?"

"Oh, you know, the usual way. McDermott cared a little too much about certain boys, including me, especially boys whose fathers weren't around. He'd come on big time attentive and wanting to help you with your goddamned potential or something. Give you a few things, like the really good hockey skates your family couldn't afford. Getting closer all the time. And then, he's got you."

CHAPTER 30

osaria could feel a coherence emerging. A light tremble and a building
fury coursed through her body. Pete had clenched his teeth and was
quiet for some time. Rosaria watched his face. She could feel something
coming and didn't move. Around them, only the sound of the ocean, the tiny cries
of the surfers, and the wood crackling in the stove.

Pete held his coffee cup, still staring at the ocean. "It was Malachy and Dara
who brought stuff to Plum Island—different stuff, some E, speed, coke, and once
a little H. We all used. Made things easier."

Another long minute followed. "Joey Mucci came one time, and they gave
him something, almost just for fun. Like to play with him. He was way younger
than we were, already kind of weird. I don't know what it was they gave him. They
shouldn't have done that. Monsignor comes up the beach and sees us all there.
Starts chatting that way he does, knowing we're all high and out of it, and don't
know what the hell he's saying.

"Next thing we know, he's taking Joey behind a dune. We could hear Joey."
Pete's face reddened and a solitary tear started to roll down his weathered cheeks.
"We should have done something. We were all stoned, out of it. But we should
have done something." Pete wiped his face with a callused hand.

Rosaria heard herself whisper, "Oh God." Her own eyes teared. Beautiful
little Joey Mucci.

"The Monsignor brought Joey back to where we were sitting. It was so dark.
He didn't say anything, just sat Joey down. Joey was shaking and crying. 'There's a
good man.' That's what he always used to say afterward, 'There's a good man,' with
a finger to his lips, meaning we're not to say anything to the adults. Just between
us guys." Pete squeezed his eyes shut for some moments. "Then, he walked away."
Pete opened his eyes again.

"Some of us stayed out in the dunes with Joey for a long time, calmed him
down enough to bring him back into the house. Barrett stayed up with him all
night. Malachy and Dara could have cared less. Dara thought it was funny. He
was always a jerk. Malachy just went on as if nothing happened, but he seemed

to enjoy the show in some way." Pete stared out at the ocean. "Anyway, Joey was in bad shape the next day, with the shaking all over and crying. The priests got worried. They didn't know what the hell was happening. They were going to take him over to the emergency room at Anna Jacques Hospital up there. But in the end, one of them drove him home. Joey's parents brought him right to old Doctor Lamphrey. He said it was nerves. Joey had never been away from home. Just extreme homesickness. Do you believe that? Guy should have retired twenty years before he did. So, anyway, Lamphrey prescribed rest and some anti-anxiety medication. And Joey did calm down, but it was papering everything over."

"So that's what happened to Joey. Was that the end of it?" asked Rosaria.

"Oh no, went on for about half a year afterward. I feel bad saying I was kind of relieved, because if he had Joey, then he'd leave me alone. He used to invite Joey to the rectory for some private altar boy training or some other damned thing he made up. The Sisters and Joey's family thought it was an honor and Joey was afraid not to go, but he got stranger and stranger during that time." Pete smiled sadly. "He always gave Joey chocolate ice cream. After a while, the bastard got tired of Joey and moved on. I even forget who his next darling was, but by then Joey was totally screwed up."

Pete looked at Rosaria. "I can't even believe I'm telling you this. I'm going to keep going, but you should know it's making me sick. About that time, about myself."

"Do you want to stop, Pete? Is this too much for you? I can't imagine how hard it must be to bring all this up again." Rosaria was shaking her head, filled with concern for this tough ex-Marine fisherman re-living nightmares from the past—not on the battlefield, not on the open ocean, but in his own childhood parish at the hands of trusted adults.

Pete put his face in his hands. Rosaria started to get up to leave. He raised his head and without looking at her, gestured with his hand that she should sit. "Sit. I'm almost done. I'm going to finish this thing."

He took a deep breath. "Malachy used to laugh when he saw Joey headed for the rectory. It was sickening. We were just kids too, and Malachy was no one to fool around with, even then." Pete stopped and shook his head sadly. "It was Barrett who tried. He had too much heart, a little too soft and a little too brave to be around Malachy. He challenged Malachy about it all one day—Joey, the priest, everything. He said people should know about it. We always thought that was the reason Barrett got a special packet of bad H.

"Maybe Malachy let Dara McCarthy get offed too. Dara could be a real liability. One of those guys that doesn't know any boundaries. I think he annoyed the wrong people. He and Malachy had started working with a bigger supplier, tough bunch. They weren't taking any of Dara's crap. Knowing Malachy, I'm pretty sure he cut Dara loose and he's buried in some Peabody landfill."

"But, Pete, nobody ever told about Joey."

"Joey would never tell his parents. I wouldn't either. He thought they'd be too ashamed of him or something. They probably would have been. And the Columba Brothers, the ones that ran the high school? Well, the brothers weren't big into coddling. You had to take care of yourself. Except, Joey couldn't take care of himself, really."

"Did Aurelius suspect anything? Did she know?"

Pete paused. "I don't think she did directly, but I think she thought something was funny. That's why we ended up with that old guy chaperone at Plum Island one year. I'll tell you though, she'd come through the yard across from the girls school. It wasn't even her territory, but the brothers never stopped her. Anyway, she'd march into the yard with that look on her face and that stride. Walk right up to Dara and grab him by the collar if he was harassing Mucci.

"Dara was big. That took courage. That woman had it in spades. I'll tell you, he could have swung at her, but even Dara was afraid of her then. He'd sulk afterward and deny it, but he was afraid of her. It really pissed him off that she could put him down in front of everybody. If he could have, he would have whacked her."

"So, no one ever knew the full story?"

Pete shook his head. "Guys from the Immaculate at that time made a blood pact never to talk about what happened on Plum Island or the other stuff. We were all too ashamed. We've all been ashamed for twenty-five years.

"The whole sick atmosphere in those years just got to me. I couldn't get out of there fast enough. McDermott was going to get me a scholarship to the Cross, but I said no thanks. Somehow, I made it through high school and joined the Corps right after I graduated. Saved me. Then, I came up here, met Angie, and we've made a good life. Maybe not for everyone, but it suits us."

Rosaria looked around the little house and out at the ocean. "Looks pretty good to me. Could do a lot worse."

"Yeah. Like to think I took the right fork in the road."

They smiled at each other across the table. Pete took a final sip of is coffee, shrugged and put down his cup.

Rosaria looked at him. "Not an easy story to tell. I really appreciate it. Thank you, Pete."

He nodded. "Hope it helped a little."

"Would you be willing to talk to Leo Gelenian about it? Malachy's gone, but the Monsignor should be held to account."

Pete steepled his fingers and brought them to his mouth. He was quiet for a minute before he said, "It's a funny thing. For a long time, I thought it was my fault what happened with the Monsignor and me. You shouldn't, but you just do, you know." He turned to the ocean. "Now I see it for what it was."

He put his hands on the arms of the chair as he faced Rosaria. "Yeah, I'd be willing to talk now. It's the least I can do for Joey."

CHAPTER 31

onsignor McDermott scowled at the interruption. "Isn't Hanrahan around?" he asked Mrs. Fitzpatrick without looking up at her. "Can't he talk to her?"

"I'm sorry, Monsignor. He's up at the hospital, giving Communion and the Last Rites to Mrs. Connors," Mrs. Fitzpatrick responded.

"All right. Give me ten minutes."

Giving the Last Rites to Mrs. Connors. As if she'd ever done anything in her narrow, inconsequential life to need a ceremony to pass to the other side. A gray pantry mouse getting the Last Rites. And now, he needed to go through the motions of pastoral care once again, as if he were not damaged and destroyed beyond redemption himself. The grief over Malachy's passing enveloped him like a malevolent shade. He was smothered with it. He couldn't breathe sometimes.

His Malachy. He remembered when he first saw him in the schoolyard, so full of energy and life. He could still relive the moment when the boy had first turned to him. A dreamy slow motion image that played in his mind every day. The boy turning, his dark, almost black hair, damp from playing, his face flushed. The sweet nape of his neck sweaty under a crooked shirt collar. And that brilliant smile. If he'd ever had a son, it would have been Malachy... but now, Malachy was gone.

Malachy was gone and, Holy Jesus, now there was some parish woman sitting in his parlor. Maybe he should tell her to come back when Hanrahan was here. Hanrahan was good at these things. The man was as soft as a marshmallow. No wonder he'd been a drinker. He was one of those who felt all the pain and complications of people who kept dropping the detritus of their lives at the rectory door. As if a priest is some kind of magician who can, presto, make things better.

How often had the Monsignor felt the hand on his arm after Mass, "Could I stop by to talk later, Monsignor?" Or maybe just showing up at the door, "Can I have a few minutes of the Monsignor's time?" He'd prayed for patience and compassion, but more and more often as time went on, he'd wanted to shout, "No, you cannot! I don't want to know about all the problems in your crummy little life. I have nothing to give you. Nothing. Go away." And just shut the door.

He rubbed the nubby tapestry fabric of the armchair with his long fingers. Holy Mother, he was tired of it all.

Shut the door on the complaints about alcoholic sons, unemployed husbands too quick to raise their fists, interfering mothers-in-law, cancer-ridden spouses, children hanging with the wrong crowd. Former parish beauties sat before him in the rectory parlor, beauties turned coarse from the ceaseless work and strain of too many children with their overwhelmed child-husbands. Still wearing their hair as they did when they were in their prime in high school, now inexpertly colored a shade too dark or bleached a blond not seen in nature, ghoulishly girlish and inappropriate around their worn faces.

He'd listen with a practiced compassionate look on his face, nodding at the appropriate times, his mind elsewhere or lingering on the polished, worn heels or the knockoff bag. The stories that didn't change. They were all variations on the same themes.

Beside his desk, he had all the handouts. The AA group, the Right to Life offices, novenas for special troubles. Mostly, he listened and advised patience and prayer. He always ended with a blessing of the parishioner. Somehow, they seemed to go away satisfied.

But *that* one. Hanrahan, he couldn't just stop there. He was only supposed to be here to help with the Masses and those things. But him—oh no, he had to get too involved. He might take an appointment, have a conversation with a bruised wife and later put a hand on the shoulder of her husband at Church. "How're you doing, Frank? Stop in for coffee sometime." And the husband would know. Maybe he'd stop by for coffee, maybe not. He'd be furious at his wife for telling the priest, but keep his fists to himself for a while.

And then the endless money sob stories. The Monsignor had a little parish cash for such purposes, but he wasn't the bleeding Bank of Boston. God, the other one again. That one. Everyone knew Hanrahan was a soft touch. A word with the landlord about the rent in arrears or, Jesus, money out of his own pocket for rent or the oil bill or a gift certificate for Johnny Foodmaster from the supply he kept in his top bureau drawer. Mrs. Fitzpatrick complained about the people he started bringing into the kitchen for coffee and a sandwich. Monsignor put a quick stop to that. The rectory wasn't a damned soup kitchen—that's what the shelters were for.

Monsignor checked the calendar on his desk. Parish council tonight. He didn't think he could handle that either. They'd be fine without him. He thought he might start to weep, sitting there in cataclysmic pain while they discussed every damned little detail of the parish operations over and over. Finnegan, the budget king, loved managing the finances. More power to him. Certainly, it wasn't the Monsignor's thing.

Overall, the parish council ran the operation and things had gone smoothly. Except, of course, for that little difficulty some years ago, misunderstanding his outreach to some of the parish boys. Fortunately, the Chancery managed to clear everything up discreetly, though he knew it cost him whatever advancement he might have had in the archdiocese. He blamed the nun for that hellish experience and the freeze on his clerical career. The self-righteous harridan had raised the issue. Perhaps Monsignor should be spending less time with the parish boys. She had no inkling of the situation with the boys. The nuances of it. She was incapable of nuance. Made his blood boil all over again just to think of it. And she had tried to stir up trouble again. Thank God she was gone now. That had been taken care of. He was glad of the end of her.

He glanced over at the whiteboard on the wall with a satisfied smile.

This was his life's work. He'd accomplished so much here, bringing all those boys along. Everyone knew that. Now, they'd seen the fruits of his labor in the boys' success. He was so proud of them. This year, he'd met with each of the directors of admissions at five colleges while the boys were having their campus tours, and let the directors know that he had a personal interest in the application of each of his boys.

All the directors were respectful, saving Harvard's. The director there sent a young woman, hardly older than the boys themselves, to meet with the Monsignor. That was a low moment. A polished young woman who'd made him feel like a boy again, if only for a moment. A boy from the wrong neighborhood with the wrong accent in an old factory town. So, he'd been too aggressive, too arrogant with her. He was sure he'd appeared foolish and he didn't like to think about that. Perhaps their attitude would change, he thought, as more boys from the Immaculate scaled the wall of the institution.

The parish knew he was dedicated. He'd stayed up into the wee small hours to finish reading through the State Department of Education task force report on STEM education—science, technology, engineering, and math. Afterward, he'd pressed the high school to add more qualified math and science faculty. This initiative, like the new science lab and the nascent robotics competition club and coach, cost money, of course. And then with Malachy, dear, dear Malachy, he had found a way.

Monsignor knew that society, and indeed the civil authorities, would not understand or approve of his true source of funds for these initiatives and that he was engaged in dangerous liaisons in service of raising the funds. Occasionally, he wondered about that himself, but always decided that if there were ever a case of the end justifying the means, this had to be it. Generations of young men from the parish fulfilling their promise with the educations they deserved. They were starting with a disadvantage, as he had started with a disadvantage, as Malachy had started with a disadvantage, coming from homes that didn't know how to help them realize their talents and ambitions.

Yes, his work was a great source of satisfaction for him. The boys would thank him over time, and they would understand how much he cared for them and their dreams, even if somehow they became aware of how he supported their enhanced opportunities.

Besides, everyone knew that the kinds of people who bought product through their narcotics network would have just gotten it from somewhere else. Losers. At least their cash was not wasted—some of it went to a good cause.

The Immaculate hadn't been the worst assignment, but with Malachy gone now, he was done. Some lay people retired early. Why couldn't he? Except for helping the boys, he wasn't really cut out for this parish work. He should have been an educator, maybe a principal in a Catholic high school. Maybe he could have gotten his terminal degree and been the president of a good-sized Catholic college. He would have been good at that.

The Monsignor straightened his jacket. Perhaps he'd see the woman in the parlor and skip the parish council tonight. He looked in the mirror to brush his hair back and was stunned to see the haggard face looking back at him. He had to get a grip.

The Monsignor enjoyed his calling most when he was at the Cathedral with the other priests at high celebrations, all of them in their vestments, or when they were all together at some retreat on the Cape or even at the monthly poker games they each hosted. (Thank God, Hanrahan had declined to join the poker games. The whiskey would have done him in and the Monsignor knew the old priest just wouldn't have fit in.) Like a band of brothers the priests were then, a band of brothers on a mission. He remembered the thrill of one of his first Masses. Putting on the red vestments, the red of fire and blood, on the Feast of Saint Stephen, martyr. The light glittering on the chalice from the candlelight, his parents in the first row. He'd never forget it. He truly felt his calling to God in those days.

But then there was the thud of reality. His first pastoral conversation. It was a Mrs. Gallagher on a dull March day. The pastor, an older experienced priest, was out and the housekeeper asked him to take the visitor. The young priest had listened, watching the mother's worried face and noting the suit, too tight for her middle-aged shape. The Gallagher girl was pregnant. The boy didn't want to marry her, and she wasn't sure about him either. In his mind, he thought, what would you want me to do? A little too late to think about this now, isn't it?

Instead, he said they'd have to be married right away. Tell the daughter and the boy and his parents that Father McDermott said it had to be. Otherwise, it would be Catholic Charities. The baby would be placed in a good home. He said a prayer with Mrs. Gallagher and, after she'd left, wiping her eyes and thanking him copiously, he wondered what he had gotten himself into.

Now, if this new deal with McPhail worked out, even with Malachy gone, he'd have enough to give to the Immaculate for the science lab, and still have some to leave the priesthood without waiting until he was ancient and decrepit to get his tiny pension from the archdiocese. To hell with all the discussion and process and paperwork. He'd just pack his bags and leave, maybe drive across country. Go to Southern California and buy a condo near the beach. He had friends there. He could live his life without all these people around, everyone needing something, wanting something from him. Like an endless flock of pecking seagulls.

Monsignor checked his watch. Yes, he'd see this woman after all. Just steel himself, give this maybe fifteen minutes, whatever it was, and then skip the parish council tonight. Thus, lost in thought, he walked down the hall, put on his priestly face, and opened the parlor door. Rosaria O'Reilly sat on the edge of a heavily upholstered wing chair, staring directly at him.

She didn't stand as he entered the room. Such a difficult woman. One of those aging feminists. You had to pity whoever her ex-husband was. What a time he must have had with her before the divorce. You couldn't blame the poor bastard now, could you?

"Rosaria." The Monsignor nodded in greeting and sat opposite her.

"I had an interesting conversation with a man who went to the Immaculate High school about twenty-five years ago." Frontal approach, no prologue. No respect for his role. No *Monsignor*.

"Really. Who would that be?"

"Doesn't matter who it was. He's doing well, no thanks to you and Malachy Sullivan."

"What's that?" Such an angry face she could have. What was she starting on about? That was a long time ago. The Monsignor felt a light sweat building on the palms of his hands, and an uneasy feeling roiling in his stomach.

Rosaria leaned forward in her chair, her hands on her knees, looking hard at the priest with urgent green eyes. "You protected Malachy Sullivan's drug operation for years, and you probably still do. You broke Joey Mucci through abuse and who knows how many others. You stood by when Malachy murdered his friend John Patrick Barrett and probably Dara McCarthy. And," her voice caught, and he could see her eyes tearing, "and Sister Mary Aurelius. Did she learn about what was going on? Was that the story?"

It was as if he'd been punched in the chest. Almost took his breath away. He shook his head, involuntarily for a few seconds. He fought to gain control of his emotions. Take charge here. Stay calm. "What are you talking about, woman? Those are scurrilous accusations. Get out of here before I call the police."

She gave him a sweet, poisonous smile. "Oh yes, you do that. You do that and we can discuss your abusing boys and protecting Malachy all these years, pushing drugs to young people. And maybe what happened to Aurelius. You just call them, Monsignor."

Rosaria stood and walked up to his chair. In spite of himself, the priest leaned back in his chair, away from her. She was dangerous. With great will, he regained a modicum of composure. "That's a ridiculous story. I'm no pedophile. I'm no drug pusher. And the idea that I had anything to do with Sister's death is just appalling. You don't know what you're talking about. I think you have a problem. You've been drinking, haven't you?" He shook a long finger at her, furious that he had to crane his neck to look in her eyes. "You're nothing but a troublemaker, Mrs. O'Reilly. No wonder your husband left you. He has my deepest pity—the poor man, living with the likes of you. You're crazy, delusional."

The priest began to rise from his chair. When he did so, Rosaria continued to stand close to the front of his chair and didn't move, forcing him to slide clumsily sideways. Insolent cow.

The Monsignor stumbled out of his chair and then stood to his full, angry, hierarchical height, staring down at her. "This meeting is over. You come in here raving with awful lies and crazy accusations. An outrage. Get out of here this minute."

Rosaria crossed her arms. "This meeting may be over, but believe me, this conversation isn't over by a long shot, Mister."

Mister? He couldn't believe the arrogance of this woman. He wondered if she was mentally unbalanced. She was quivering with emotion. Yes, this could be dangerous.

The priest started to walk to the door that opened to the hallway. "This is all nonsense. Crazy talk. You're crazy." He waved his hand dismissively. "You don't know what you're talking about. You should leave now." He cursed the tremor in his voice.

Rosaria moved quickly and blocked his way. There was a wild look to the woman, her face flushed with fury. Monsignor saw her eyes move to a heavy brass eagle from the American Legion on the shelf near the door. A heavy piece within reach. Yes, she was crazy. She could kill him with that. The priest felt too stunned and disoriented now to defend himself, and the woman had all the strength of some fierce, mad rage. She could kill him. The Monsignor took it all in for a split second and he was filled with terror. He thought he heard himself whimper.

She reached for the brass eagle. Her hand had almost reached it when Mrs. Fitzpatrick knocked on the office door.

"Monsignor? Monsignor?"

He stared at the O'Reilly woman, his mouth too dry to answer.

Mrs. Fitzpatrick opened the door a crack. "You have a call from Mr. Finnegan. The budget meeting?"

Shaking, Rosaria pulled her hand back from the brass eagle without breaking eye contact with the priest.

Mrs. Fitzpatrick stood at the door and took in the scene. "Is everything all right, Monsignor?"

He cleared this throat. "No, it is not, Mrs. Fitzpatrick. Mrs. O'Reilly is leaving now."

Rosaria closed her eyes briefly, and took a long, ragged breath. When she opened her eyes again, her voice was low and firm. "This conversation might be over, but you can bet you'll have plenty of other visitors."

Monsignor McDermott felt dizzy. His skin felt as if electrical charges were running across the surface, and his voice came out higher than he expected when he shouted, "Get out. Get out. You're a lunatic. You don't know what you're talking about."

"Oh, I know just what I'm talking about. The game's over, you son of a bitch."

The priest went out the door without speaking, walking quickly past a stunned Mrs. Fitzpatrick in a jerky, uncertain gait. Dizzy and disoriented, the Monsignor stumbled toward the stairs. He paused, took a breath, and then climbed the stairs toward the second floor of the rectory with an erect posture and as much dignity as he could manage. Malachy. Malachy would know what to do. He stopped at the top of the stairs. But Malachy was gone. Oh God, what was he to do?

Rosaria watched the priest ascend the stairs. Then, she walked down the hall and out of the rectory without closing the big wooden doors. Tears coursed down her face.

Not quite knowing how she got there, she found herself in the front seat of her car. She sat there for about ten minutes while she tried to calm the tremors and the tears. Once, she looked up to see the Monsignor looking at her out of a second floor window—just for a moment before he quickly closed the curtains. His face looked pale, his eyes wide. Suddenly, he seemed very old.

Rosaria wanted to leave the parking lot, but didn't trust herself to drive. She could see the road to the reservoir across Pleasant Street and up the hill to the left. Yes, she thought she could manage at least that. She started the car, and tried to ease out into traffic, but pulled too close in front of an oncoming black pickup truck.

The pickup truck screeched to a stop, and the angry driver leaned on a very loud horn, keeping his hand on it to make a point. People turned in the street. Rosaria's whole body reacted in shock to the deafening horn. With some difficulty, she was able to control her foot, which instinctively wanted to hit the brake.

Rosaria signaled a left-hand turn, holding up traffic again. Now the driver opened his window and screamed. "Get off the road, you old bitch." Her head started to pound and her hands began to shake.

When a break in traffic came, she made her left-hand turn. The pickup truck driver gunned his motor and sped down Pleasant Street. He gave Rosaria the finger out of his window and hollered something she couldn't hear, but could only imagine.

Rosaria drove slowly up the gentle hill to the reservoir. She steered into a pull-aside near the water and shut off the car's motor. Then, she put her head on the wheel. Her body was trembling and her ears were ringing.

Breathe in. Breathe out.

Rosaria knew she should have called Leo before she went to the rectory. She was just so angry, she had to confront the monster herself first.

Breathe in. Breathe out.

She could have easily killed the priest. She could have killed him. She could have hit him with that brass eagle. Again and again. One blow for every damaged child. And the final blow for Aurelius. Rosaria could see herself doing it in her mind's eye. She could see the priest staggering and falling. She could see the blood.

Breathe in. Breathe out.

But you didn't, dear. You didn't. Even now, she could hear Aurelius, feel her strength.

There were ducks standing on the patches of ice on the reservoir and others swimming quietly in the gray water. Overhead, Rosaria could see flocks of seagulls gathering, flying in from the ocean for safety. Some were starting to land on the reservoir. There must be another storm coming.

Rosaria picked up her cell phone to call Leo.

CHAPTER 32

uring one major storm that eventful winter, Rosaria had settled on the couch with Archie, a cup of hot chocolate beside her and the weather raging outside her windows. She'd watched the news on television with scenes of the storm playing out across the Commonwealth. As often happens, the coast was particularly badly hit. The footage showing Gloucester and Rockport was dramatic. But much of Cape Ann is rocky—granite rocky—and was spared the worst of the impact. Further up the coast on Plum Island was another matter.

An Atlantic barrier island, or some would say an overgrown and constantly shifting sandbar, Plum Island was originally named for its beach plum shrubs, with their beautiful summer roses that grow around the sand dunes. Forty miles north of Boston, its long white beach is crowded with summer homes.

All built on sand. Endlessly shifting sands. Sands, which, depending on the tides and storms, could either shift imperceptibly over the years or pour out to sea in one major storm. For decades, the island sands were reasonably stable. But then there were more storms, bigger storms. Houses that were once more than a hundred and fifty yards from the ocean now had the ocean directly before their front porches.

In recent years, as the frequency and the power of the storms accelerated, great volumes of sand poured out with each storm, leaving old foundations exposed or sometimes collapsing whole structures, to be carried out in bits and pieces to the wide Atlantic. Dunes disappeared, the soft white sand coursing out overnight to leave flat, dark, and coarse bottom sand where a dune used to stand. Other storms might bring the sand back, but not in the same place. Instead, the sand might come back further down the beach, continuing to make the island longer and narrower. Or it might flow across to Crane's Beach, rebuilding dunes that had been decimated there decades ago, or perhaps accumulate at the mouths and upriver on the Annisquam and Essex Rivers.

It looked to Rosaria as if the news reporter on Plum Island could hardly stand and was in clear danger of being swept away herself in the wild, buffeting winds. Several of the old houses on the beachfront were in danger again. From the safety of a row of beach boulders, placed there long ago to brunt the oncoming ocean, the cameraman panned onto one small, older home. The waves cruelly pummeled the home's wooden supports before finally sucking enough sand out from under the house to collapse the front of it. The storm carried much of the structure away, leaving part of a back kitchen and an upstairs bedroom open to the elements. A refrigerator banged about in the waves, crashing into nearby houses.

Next to the smaller cottage was a spacious blue house, one of the originals, with a big wraparound porch and large picture windows facing the ocean. One of those beach houses that could accommodate eight to ten family members or friends in the summer, or maybe a few priests and parish boys.

As the giant waves crashed and pulled back from the beach, they sucked the sand from around and under the big blue house. Some, then all, of the supports started to wobble. The waves were relentless, powerful, and enormous. The sand poured and rolled from beneath and around the house. Violent, greedy waves sucked more and more sand with each pullback. The house itself began to break. The frame and the porch moved to the right. The walls started to crack. And then the porch fell into the waves.

For a moment, one large section of the porch was eerily level as it rode a titanic wave out to sea. It looked to Rosaria as if someone could sit with a cup of coffee on the porch, going for an ocean ride. Then, in slow motion, the porch went down, and disappeared into the roiling water.

"Oh, my God." The reporter could not contain herself as the front of the blue house on the beach began to collapse, and room-by-room was pulled into the ocean. Even the sand the house was built on and the dunes beside it were dragged out by ferocious, angry, biblical waves.

And then there was nothing left of the large blue house with the wraparound porch or the sand dunes around it.

Some hours later, the storm moved out to sea with remnants of the houses it had taken. The sand settled in slow motion, floating down to the ocean floor until the tides or the next storm carried it to a new home, perhaps to the Essex and the Annisquam. The ocean, spent from its fury, breathed quietly in gentle, rolling waves.

Sister Josepha looked puzzled. "Why don't you ask Sister Aurelius?"

Rosaria looked across the room at Mother Superior, who shook her head slightly. "She's not available right now, Sister," Rosaria answered Sister Josepha.

The elderly nun picked a few small yellow leaves off the woody stems of the geraniums in her bedroom window. The mass of plants with brilliant red blooms seemed almost vulgar in their muscular boldness beside the frail woman attending them. Outside, small patches of snow remained on the bare lawn of the Motherhouse and the dark limbs of trees silhouetted against a gray winter sky.

"It would have been sort of unusual mail for a nun here to receive. A regular bill from a bank to Sister Aurelius, for a safe deposit box, and perhaps they sent other communications. We just need the name of the bank," Rosaria prompted.

"Who did you say you were?"

"Rosaria O'Reilly, Sister."

"Did I have you?" Sister Josepha asked.

"No, I was in Sister Alvernia's class, Sister."

Sister Josepha turned to Mother Superior. "Did I water these, Mother?"

Mother Superior reached over and gently touched the soil of two pots with her fingertip. "Yes, Sister, you did."

"You can't overwater them, you know," Sister Josepha sat in a chair next to her geraniums and started to pick at folds in her navy skirt, the same way she'd fussed over her flowers.

Mother Superior had warned Rosaria that Sister Josepha, who'd managed the mail at the Motherhouse for many years and been legendary for her powers of detailed recollection, was no longer herself. Sister was rapidly losing touch with reality. Rosaria had thought it was still worth a shot to drive up to the Motherhouse and hope the old nun remembered something about mail Sister Aurelius might have received from a bank. Something, anything about the location of a safe deposit box matching the mysterious unmarked key taped inside Aurelius's copy of *The Meditations*. The local banks and the state banking commission had been unable to help. Sister Josepha was Rosaria's last prayer, and that prayer was apparently going unanswered.

"It would have been a bill from a bank," Rosaria repeated. "You don't remember—?"

Mother Superior put her hand gently on Rosaria's arm before she finished her sentence.

"Did I water these, Mother?" the nun asked again.

Mother Superior once again touched the soil of two pots with her fingertip. "Yes, you've done a fine job with them, Sister. They are well taken care of."

Mother raised her hand to a young nun in the corridor. "Sister, it might be a good idea for Sister Josepha to walk down to the solarium and check on the cyclamens. I don't think they're getting enough sun where they are. Maybe we should move them."

Sister Josepha looked up, her face brightening. "They like to be a little cool too, you know."

The young nun guided Sister Josepha out of the room. "And you can't over-water them," Sister Josepha advised her as they walked slowly down the corridor.

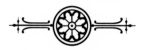

CHAPTER 33

osaria's knuckles scraped the doorframe as she and Sevi moved Nuncie's big bed into her broad living room, wide windows facing the ocean in Gloucester. "Ouch."

"I hope you appreciate this, Nunce," Sevi called to his sister, prone on the couch across the living room, face turned to them, heavily sedated but watchful.

"I'm sure she does, Sev," Rosaria said, followed by "Shit" as she dropped the headboard on her toes.

Forty minutes later, the freshly dressed big bed was set up facing the ocean. And such a night on the ocean. The full moon cast a glittering path of light over the gently rolling waves almost all the way to the rocks in front of Nuncie's house.

Rosaria smoothed the sheets on the bed, plumped the pillow, and pulled the light blankets back as Sevi carried his sister, a tiny child now, to the bed. Nuncie groaned as Sevi laid her onto the bed. Rosaria pulled an armchair beside the bed, along with an incongruous ottoman shaped like a bear, given to Nuncie by her nieces years ago. Sevi gently administered an anti-nausea medication to Nuncie while Rosaria walked across the wide, open house to the kitchen to make coffee, all while feeling strangely detached.

The door was firmly shut on any lingering thoughts of Malachy Sullivan, Monsignor McDermott, and their trail of abuse. Malachy was dead and McDermott had been put on leave as he was being questioned. Rosaria was determined that thoughts of them were not going to stain Nuncie's leave-taking day. Engrossed with Nuncie, arranging every detail of this day, the activity somehow held at bay thoughts of Malachy and McDermott, as it did the dark wave of grief waiting to engulf her on the loss of her lifelong friend.

Nuncie had declined a hospital bed, determined to die in her own bed in her own house, looking out at the ocean. She had also made other arrangements.

"Bottom drawer, left-hand side. Wooden box with the palm trees, the one from Kauai." Nuncie had always said that Kauai was what Paradise would be like for her.

There had been bad and angry days. "Christ, why me? All the jerks that get to have good, long, healthy lives and I get this damned thing."

And fear. "I'm afraid, Ro. I'm really afraid of this." And tears, many tears from both of them.

But this night, Nuncie lay in her bed, Rosaria in the chair beside her, both of them staring out at the moon and the sea, while Sevi rested in his bedroom. Nuncie's newly painted fire engine red toenails peeked from under the ivory afghan. Her hands, with freshly colored fingernails of the same color, lay flat beside her. The bottle of polish sat, along with Rosaria's coffee, a hairbrush, and a small bottle of Joy, Nuncie's favorite perfume, on a small table near the armchair.

After some minutes, Rosaria pulled a CD from her bag and placed it in Nuncie's sound system. She sat again as Luciano Pavarotti's voice swelled and filled the room. Nuncie nodded approval without looking at Rosaria.

Rosaria moved the armchair and bear ottoman aside to place a small end table next to Nuncie's bed, and carried another small table to the other side of the bed. Before she walked to the credenza for a bottle of Cabernet and three Adagio wine glasses, she texted Sevi. "Lift off." She filled one glass of wine for Nuncie.

Nuncie's souvenir box from Kauai, with an image of a serene palm-treed Pacific beach on its cover, sat on the end table next to a cut glass tumbler. Rosaria opened the wooden box and lifted out a one hundred milliliter vial of pentobarbital that Nuncie had mail-ordered from Mexico months ago.

Nuncie had researched it all, included the caution of an anti-nausea medication taken before the pentobarbital for any side-effects. *Nuncie was nothing, if not a planner,* thought Rosaria. She had even composed and signed a document testifying that she had made this end-of-life decision entirely on her own. As Rosaria poured the clear liquid pentobarbital into the tumbler, she thought about the sentence in the document that Nuncie had received no help in the process. Pretty much a blatant lie—but Rosaria could live with that.

Rosaria heard Sevi padding down the hall. She looked up to see him stop as he entered the room, a sad smile on his face for the Pavarotti and the wine glasses on both sides of the bed.

Rosaria gave Nuncie's shoulder a light touch. "Okay, pal. Here we go." Nuncie nodded.

Sevi came to the side of the bed. Together, Rosaria and Sevi gently lifted Nuncie's head up while they both held the glass tumbler to her lips. Nuncie drank the clear liquid, with only a few drops escaping onto her nightgown. A rush of stunned grief swept through Rosaria's body as she placed the tumbler back on the end table, but there were no tears yet and her hand was firm. Still, she gave Sevi a long, anguished look when she handed him Nuncie's glass of wine. Sevi's hands shook slightly as he held the glass and tears began to stream down his face.

He gave Nuncie several sips of the wine before, exhausted, she closed her lips and shook her head. Sevi slowly lowered his sister back onto her pillows.

It wasn't hard for Rosaria to slip into the big bed near Nuncie on one side and for Sevi to do the same on the other. Nuncie had declined to a mere wisp, nestled between the tall, robust bodies of her best friend and her brother.

Rosaria poured a glass of wine for herself and one for Sevi. They each held the wine in one hand and one of Nuncie's hands on the other. And waited. Rosaria could hear the sound of Sevi sobbing mixed with the music and the ocean. She herself was filled with grief, wonder, and the peace of promises kept. Once, before Nuncie slipped away, Rosaria heard her murmur.

"Thanks."

Maria Annunciata DiStephano was waked at Kehoe's several days later. Rosaria approached the casket. Nuncie was wearing her red eyeglasses and a slight smile on her face. Her mother's crystal rosaries in her hands seemed out of character, but otherwise she looked the height of fashion in her blond wig and sapphire blue Saint John suit. Rosaria remembered the day they'd chosen the suit, Nuncie in her bed against some large pillows, Rosaria taking candidate outfits out of the closet, rejecting one after the other, settling on the sapphire Saint John suit which would best set off her blond hair.

"Atta girl, Nunce," Rosaria whispered as she traced the red frames with her finger. For a moment, she saw the child Nuncie had been, so many years ago, with her little bossy face. Playing Red Rover or jacks, calling out girls who cut into the jump rope line. Hands on hips. "Cutter! You get to the back of the line, Sheila. Mary Claire was before you." And they always obeyed.

Kehoe's funeral parlor was not cold. She could see people taking sweaters off in the side rooms. But Rosaria was chilled, cold to the bone. She'd had more than a year to get used to Nuncie's leaving, but the loss was no easier. She only knew that, like Aurelius, there was some part of Nuncie that would always live in her, a part of her being.

Perhaps she'd start wearing some round red glasses in her friend's memory. Nuncie would get such a kick out of that. And make that gravy. Yes, she'd make that special gravy.

Although Nuncie's family had requested donations to the Sister of Jeanne d'Arc order of nuns or the MGH Oncology Center in lieu of flowers, there were banks of flowers as well. The Sons of Italy and the Gloucester Fishermen's Wives sent lavish floral arrangements. The telephone company retirees association sent an impressive piece and there was even a tasteful bouquet from The French Connection.

The old people came in the afternoon. Neighbors from Nuncie's childhood street in Malford and her new neighborhood in Gloucester, retirees from the phone company where Nuncie had worked, and people from the shoe plant who'd known Nuncie's father and frequented the bakery for decades before the plant closed.

A number of nuns from the Motherhouse came, a few of them stopping Rosaria to pat her arm or hold her hand. Sister Katherine James gave her a long embrace, whispering. "Aurelius was right about you, Rosaria. And I'm so sorry about Annunciata." Mother Marguerite stood back, giving Rosaria a warm, sad smile and nodding her head slightly.

There was a hush in the crowd as Mr. Stone arrived. The Stones had owned the athletic shoe plant for years before the business became unsustainable with foreign production. Mr. Stone was, as always, impeccably dressed. Very small now, he walked with a slight limp and a careful dignity. The old man stopped and looked about him with a distracted air, struggling to remember. He came alive as he saw familiar faces from long ago. His driver by his side, he stood beside Nuncie's casket, nodding slowly as if agreeing with a comment she'd made.

Then, he walked to each of his former employees in the room, greeting each by name with increasing confidence and vitality. "Bea, Johnny Mul, good to see you looking so well. Hi, Lena. You're looking well, Lillian." After some time, Mr. Stone took his driver's arm and walked with the same careful dignity to the black Cadillac outside. "He was a good boss," someone said, and the group murmured their assent. Later in the afternoon, the old people left, each exhausted by the effort of coming, each affirmed in the memories of their long lives, and went home to bed.

The evening crowd was much bigger, with Nuncie's many friends and all her nieces and nephews paying their respects and socializing in the side rooms. Rosaria and Nuncie's classmates from the Immaculate came. Nuncie had kept contact with them far more than Rosaria. Now, they arrived in high-end cars from the prosperous suburbs of Winchester, Andover, Marblehead. Sleek and fashionable, kids all graduated from good schools. New grandchildren named Joshua or Olivia or Taylor, or even Apple or Hunter. No Mary Margarets or Roccos there.

They were all so pleased to see each other. Laughter and high chatter graced Nuncie's going away. Nuncie would have had such a good time that night herself. Maybe she did. Rosaria could almost see her laughing along with the group, could almost hear her funny little cackle. And this was the way the classmates would see each other in diminishing numbers over the years, ghosts of their departed friends somehow present in the conversations.

Nuncie had specifically requested that Father Hanrahan minister her services, but when he arrived to say the rosary, there was much whispering, wondering, and conjecture in the side rooms of the funeral home. The parish was still coming to terms with the fact that the Monsignor was on administrative leave pending the investigation of a number of serious charges and irregularities.

The conversation stopped, however, as Father Hanrahan began the rosary. Then, the old priest's deep, resonant voice and the chorus of mourners carried up in a mesmerizing rhythm, into the late winter night sky over Malford. *"Pray for us sinners now and at the hour of our death..."* repeated over and over again.

CHAPTER 34

osaria thought there was probably something to the old belief that the spirits of the recently departed were still very present to their closest companions and among their earthly possessions.

As she packed boxes of Nuncie's well-used cooking utensils to send to her niece in California, Rosaria ran her hands softly along the worn wooden spoons, feeling her friend in each smooth surface. She had asked Nuncie's brother Sevi if she could keep her friend's old red pantry stool for herself. Not that she needed it. She was certainly tall enough to reach pantry shelves. But she remembered so often watching her petite friend standing on the stool to reach a can of plum tomatoes or a jar of roasted red peppers, all the while vigorously expressing a strong opinion about local Gloucester politics or a neighborhood imbroglio.

Rosaria had come down to Gloucester to help clean out Nuncie's house as Sevi prepared to put it up for sale. Rosaria and Sevi worked side-by-side packing Nuncie's many craft materials for her nieces, and bagging clothes and linens for some lucky customers at the local thrift shop. Occasionally, Rosaria or Sevi would silently hold up an item, like the kitschy "Moon River" music box Nuncie had loved, smile for moment, and then continue packing.

Rosaria was sleeping these few nights in Nuncie's old bedroom near the kitchen, with its views out to the ocean. Sevi slept in one of the downstairs bedrooms where Nuncie had hosted her nieces and nephews during the summer months.

She was glad she could take this time from work—having explained to her boss that her sister had died and she had to take a few days off. The man knew so little about Rosaria's personal life that he wasn't aware she had no sister. Still, he was relatively gracious in his condolences and flexibility, given that Rosaria knew the end of the quarter sales numbers were gnawing at his guts. She'd heard some rumors about big changes at the firm. Perhaps he was afraid of not keeping up with promises he had made to the board. In any case, on reflection, Rosaria realized that she didn't care. She just didn't care.

Now, she was living in Nuncie's presence, among her things, in her house for the last time. She could feel Nuncie at her shoulder, wryly commenting on this or that, redirecting the disposition of certain items. She was always so damned bossy. Rosaria even thought she occasionally felt a brief embrace. She could almost feel Nuncie's head against her arm, not reaching her shoulder, in an affectionate hug.

Before dawn, on the last morning, with the last bags for the thrift shop lined up in the front hall, Rosaria made herself a strong cup of coffee in the French press and pushed aside the slider to step onto the frosty outside deck facing the ocean.

The sky was still dark, with just a tiny sliver of murky sunrise on the eastern horizon. The water was unsettled, a dark, surly gray, and choppy. Might get rough that day, but the lobster boats would be putting out soon anyway, with that quiet, rhythmic hum of their engines in the water that Rosaria loved to hear. She had always liked to watch the boats in the dawn light from this deck. She went inside to get her long storm coat and a refreshed cup of coffee, so that she could stay on the cold deck to see the boats begin the day.

Rosaria returned, setting her cup of coffee on the edge of the railing post and fastening the first button of her heavy coat against the wind. Her lungs hurt a little as she breathed the thick, cold ocean air. She heard a soft sound behind her—probably one of the neighborhood cats. She started to turn, but then she heard the first boat of the morning. Rosaria searched beyond the rocks until she saw a small blue lobster boat heading out. She wondered if she should wake Sevi up to enjoy this. No, probably not. Waiting for lobster boats in the early morning darkness would not be Sevi's idea of a good time. Rosaria smiled.

She heard a soft crunch again, something on the frosty grass. More alert this time, she turned. As she did, Rosaria was jerked backward. A powerful, black-fleeced arm around her neck squeezed her throat, cutting off air, her instinctive scream smothered by the gloved hand covering her mouth and nose. Her own hands were useless in pulling at the muscled arm pressing against her throat.

Rosaria was a big woman, but she was easily lifted and pushed down the short flight of stairs from the deck. Her head slammed face-first against one of the giant boulders next to the stairs. A flash of pain and then all was darkness.

A short time later, Sevi came out to the back porch. Waking up to the pleasant smell of Rosaria's pot of coffee, he'd poured himself a cup and walked out to the porch to share it with her. But Rosaria wasn't there, though her still-warm coffee cup was sitting on the railing. He looked for her in the yard and down on the rocks. Not there. She must have decided to take an early morning walk on the beach.

As Sevi opened the door to the kitchen to go back inside, he happened to notice a hefty lobsterman carrying gear in a blue tarp, headed for a boat moored near the rocks. It must have been a strange kind of gear in that tarp, the way it folded so softly over the lobsterman's shoulder. The lobsterman threw his gear, so precious to his livelihood, carelessly and roughly into a tangle of pots and ropes on the deck. And what mess of buckets and tools. Hell of a sloppy lobsterman.

———

Rosaria had the worst headache of her life. She still had her storm coat on, though it was unfastened below the top button, and the wind blew through her thin sweater. She saw blood caked on the sweater and spatters of vomit. She could taste the blood and vomit in her mouth. When she put her hand to her face, it hurt. Her nose and cheekbone felt mushy. Now too, her bruised body ached from the pressure of the ropes and gear underneath her as she lay prone on the deck, a blue tarp flapping loosely around her.

She shifted and leaned up on her shoulder so that she could see where she was. On a lobster boat—near the open stern. The open stern lobster boat design, like a backless clog shoe, made it easier for the lobsterman to pull up his pots or bait and drop fresh ones. Or maybe to drop an inconvenient, nosy woman into the frigid water.

Rosaria felt the uneven pulsing of the boat cutting through choppy ocean water. The sky was an unremitting gun metal gray. She could see from the open back of the boat that the ocean was the same—gray, turbulent, and unsettled.

Rosaria hitched herself up further and, out of breath, she leaned against a heavy plastic bin with a primordial fishy smell that made her stomach even queasier. As she gained her bearings, she looked toward the wheelhouse. A big man in a watch cap turned the wheel, muscles working under his black fleece pullover. The man's black-gloved right hand had a cigarette between his middle fingers on the wheel. Occasionally, he brought the cigarette to his mouth. Sensing movement, the man turned. His face was heavy and angular. A wide slash of a mouth.

Rosaria felt oddly calm—drifting in an unreal, dream-like state. Just barely conscious. God, her head ached. When she looked at the man again, she saw a look of exasperation cross his face. *He thought he'd done me in,* she thought, *and here I am, squirming in the back of the boat like a half-dead haddock.* She saw the man's frustration at this uncompleted task of extinguishing her life. She mused in a confused, dreamy way that the man's working life likely consisted of a number of assignments like this one, killing people. Just a job.

She could see him considering what to do next. For a few moments, he alternated between steering the boat—not wanting to put it on autopilot in the increasingly rough sea, and glancing back at her. As the man looked at her, and she slowly regained her senses, Rosaria studied him. Such a hard face. She wondered if it ever relaxed in friendship or laughter.

Why did she think of another time and place when she looked at that face? A jumble of images flooded her mind. Street hockey down at Morrison Park so long ago when she was home visiting her parents. Boys laughing, pushing each other, eating Devil Dogs from the corner spa. Malachy Sullivan with his wild laugh, taking a big boy's Devil Dog and popping it into his mouth, eating it as he laughed and ran. The other boy, also laughing and running, catching up to Malachy and wrapping his big arms around his quarry, lifting Malachy as he choked down the chocolate mess in his mouth.

A name came to her. Dara McCarthy—that other boy—throwing Malachy into the hedges. Dara McCarthy throwing Malachy. She sucked in a painful breath. *Dara McCarthy's not lost in Alaska and he's not buried in a Peabody landfill. He's here on this fishing boat.* The open smile of his youth had gone from that wide mouth. *Where did it go?* Rosaria wondered in her daze. *When did it become a tight smile on a hard face?* She saw now that the man knew she'd finally recognized him.

His voice was not as deep as his frame would have suggested and it had a heavy smoker's rasp, but Rosaria recognized it over the hum of the boats' engine. If she closed her eyes, she could see him as a teenager. Why hadn't she seen this before? This was the man she saw behind the wheel of the dark van that hit her in Malford Square, the man who slipped out the side door at the bar in Chelsea, who stepped from the work van when she was walking Archie to Christopher Columbus Park. The adult Dara—so out of context, so changed, so rough. Now, in this strange, semi-conscious state, she could see him more clearly.

He blew smoke from his mouth. "Got in a little trouble with the wrong people a long time ago and headed up north. That ended up good for business, though." Then, his mouth twisted in annoyance. "But you and the damned nun. Busybodies. Never changed. Always butting in. You and the nun. Can't mind your own damn business." Dara's back was to her as he rummaged through a tool cabinet near the wheel. There was a lull in the wind. He turned to her. "But this is what happens when you don't listen, Ro. I gave you fair warning. But you just wouldn't listen."

Rosaria started to shake as Dara casually chose a crowbar from the tool cabinet. She began weeping wordlessly and couldn't stop the shaking. Dara hefted the crowbar in both hands, feeling its weight.

"But did you stop? Oh no, not you. McPhail was right. We should have done you right away." He slapped his hand with the crowbar.

"Aurelius?" Rosaria's voice was breaking. He didn't hear her over the water and leaned forward. "Aurelius?" she sobbed again.

"Christ, that nun. She was never going to stop. Writing to the Chancery and planning to go to the police after she figured things out. But, first—" Dara gave a sharp sound that was somewhere between a bark and a laugh and looked at Rosaria in disbelief, "—first she lets the priest know she's going to get him this time. Crazy old bitch. Just had to do it. Have the last word with him. See what I mean?"

Dara looked at Rosaria for confirmation while slapping his hand with the crowbar again, and talking louder against the sound of the building wind. "Jesus. So, the priest gives it to Malachy to take care of. But I took the job. Malachy was there, but I took the job." Dara laughed. "Malachy never got his hands dirty."

Dara talked as he closed the door of the wheelhouse cabinet. "What did she think would happen? She asked for it. Broke like an eggshell. Messy though." Rosaria squeezed her eyes against the horror of Aurelius dying this way in her old schoolyard. "And you. Just like her." Dara steadied himself with one hand on the side of the boat. "Did you think we wouldn't find out you went sniffing around? Pissed McPhail off. Wrong man to piss off, Ro. I have to take care of you before he'll work with me, now that Malachy's gone. That's the price of entry."

Dara straightened his shoulders. "They'll never get McPhail. No one will testify against him, including you, and he's got enough high-up friends. They won't forget him." He shifted the crowbar in his hand. "I'll be fast, and then a deep sleep out there." He nodded toward the ocean. "Only hurt a few seconds. Too bad I didn't get it done before."

She made herself look in his eyes, made herself speak. "Dara?"

For the first time, he flinched. She used his name. He ran his tongue along his teeth and twisted his mouth. "McPhail says you've got to go. You're a pain in the ass."

"Dara."

"Don't Dara me. Your own damn fault. Just wouldn't get out of the way."

The boat lurched. Dara grabbed the gunnels. Rosaria pitched to the side between two heavy wooden ribs where a bait bucket of salted herring tipped, covering her with small fish that stared out at the world in permanent surprise.

The wind was starting up again. Dara widened his stance for balance as he came toward her, the crowbar providing ballast in his right hand as he negotiated the heavy ropes lifting and flopping on the deck in the strengthening wind. As the boat pitched again, Dara's foot caught in one of the ropes and he fell against the pots.

"Shit. Jesus Christ." He had to put the crowbar down and lean forward to unwrap his foot.

There was a sudden, loud jolt. A wave crashed over the deck, the sudden storm worsening. The boat seemed small against the rising waves. Rosaria was pushed further between two supports. She held desperately to the wooden ribs, her hands like claws, getting out of the way of the lobster pots that were poised to slide toward the open stern of the boat and the freezing ocean water.

Her vision was blurred with the swirling water. Thundering noise shook her body. She could still see Dara's watery shadow pulling the ropes away from his feet. Rosaria looked around wildly. She maneuvered to the side of wooden pots near the boat's stern, all looped together by heavy ropes. Then, gathering her courage, she threw herself against the pots closest to her, pushing with every ounce of strength she had.

The pots didn't move. They were too heavy and she was too weak. She had no more strength. She saw Dara look up from the ropes, furious when he saw her pushing at the lobster pots. She couldn't hear him above the noise of the ocean and the boat, but his face was contorted in some kind of roar or snarl. Sobbing, she pushed again as she saw him stand, almost loose from the ropes. More, just a little more. Oh God, she couldn't move them. They wouldn't move.

Until they did. The pots started to slide to the stern, slowly at first, dropping heavily into the freezing water. Pulling the ropes, pulling each other. And pulling Dara McCarthy. Over crashing waves, Rosaria thought she heard a cry, maybe a curse, but water roared around her head too fiercely, too thunderously for her to know.

When Rosaria could see again, Dara was gone. The boat rocked wildly. Soaked and shivering, she couldn't feel her ears, hands, or feet. Her head ached, her stomach churned, her lungs hurt from screaming. Rosaria collapsed in despair and looked up to see a solitary gull, buffeted by winds, far above her in the gray sky.

With no one at the helm and the weight of heavy, loose ropes, the wooden pots and now the deadweight body of a big man pulling at it from underwater, the boat had turned sideward to the waves. The boat lurched, buffeted by the force of the water, rolling Rosaria violently about the deck. She grasped at a side bench and crawled beneath it.

Her mind swam. *No one knows I'm here. I can't die here. I won't die here.* Rosaria started to inch her way from under the bench toward the wheelhouse, as the relentless motion of the boat knocked her against the side over and over again. Across the deck, she saw a lifejacket. Too far. Too dangerous to cross the open deck. Another great, angry wave threw her back. Dazed, with the ocean roaring in her ears, Rosaria crawled forward again—avoiding the pot ropes, which were straining with a dead weight caught below.

She reached the edge of the wheelhouse. She saw the wheel whipping back and forth with a wild randomness. She was too frightened to reach up for the wheel, knowing she could not control it. Still struggling to move forward against the motion of the boat, she reached the tool cabinet and tried to open the door, but it wouldn't give. She pulled and wept and pulled and wept as the motion of the waves threw her repeatedly against the side of the wheelhouse. On the third time, the door opened, and in the rummage inside, she saw the handle of a flare gun.

Crawling along the side of the boat, holding the gunnels with one hand and the flare with the other, Rosaria reached the open deck. She didn't know if she knew how to use it, but she released the lock, pulled the trigger and shot once into the air. Her arm hurt too badly to lift or to aim properly. The boat rocked again. The flare went far to the side. Who would see it in this storm? A small boat, a tiny flare on the open ocean. She shot again—higher. A third time. Higher still. A hopeless cry into the void. She let her arm collapse and wept.

CHAPTER 35

 metal frame was holding her head and neck up. Leo thought it looked like the stand for the Foley Food Mill that his mother used to make applesauce.

Rosaria's faced was badly battered. Her nose and right cheekbone broken, her eyes swollen shut and her neck discolored with a violent purple bruise across it.

But she could talk. "They find him?"

"Oh yeah, wrapped in the ropes under the boat. He'd been nibbled at a lot. Eyes were gone."

"Ugh." Leo thought Rosaria closed her eyes, though it was hard to tell since they were so swollen already.

He shrugged. "Can't think of a better ending for the son of a bitch."

"Dara McCarthy. Holy Mother. What a nightmare. Did you know him?" Rosaria asked.

"Not really. He and Malachy were older than we were. I saw him around. A guy you'd try to avoid if you're a younger kid. Walk on the other side of the street or take the long way home. He'd knock you around just for the fun of it. He and Malachy were always close."

"Figures. So much for rumors. Guess Malachy didn't let him be offed after all. Where was he?" Rosaria's eyes were still closed.

"Guess he got into trouble with the wrong people around here and took off up north. Didn't go to Alaska. Went to Quebec. Got friendly with some sources for the fentanyl. So, he got in touch with Malachy. Malachy and Dara already had their own operation down here with McDermott. The three of them decided to make a deal with these guys up north and came up with the plan to use McPhail as the heroin source for the mix, and then O'Toole to distribute through the projects. Sweet arrangement. It was Malachy who thought up the special colored packaging. Real marketer, that guy."

"I didn't recognize Dara, Leo."

"No, he got to look like the guys he hung out with up there. Bikers. Rough bunch. When he came down here, he pretty much holed up in Lowell where he wouldn't be likely to see anybody from Malford. He only came down around Boston on business—to see McPhail or make a visit to keep someone in line."

"I thought it was over. I thought I was gone."

"You almost were. We couldn't believe how you did him, Ro."

"Yeah." Rosaria opened her eyes, a slight smile on her lips. "I did him, didn't I?"

"Who sent you the flowers?" An explosion of color, two-dozen long-stemmed yellow roses, sat on the window ledge.

Leo read the card. "Detective Belkin? Solly Belkin sent you flowers? I'm impressed. He's a legend."

"Guess so. He wants to take me out to dinner."

"Don't take the T."

Rosaria winced as she snickered. "Besides, I'm a legend now too. Bald Jewish cop—why not? But it'll be a while before I can chew right." Rosaria shifted herself slightly on the bed so that she could see Leo better. "So, anyway. I saw *The Globe*, but I'm a little fuzzy on things with these pain meds. Tell me more."

"Oh, you probably saw that O'Toole spilled his guts, gave it all up right away when they offered him a deal," Leo said. Rosaria nodded. "All McPhail's friends in government couldn't drop him fast enough. He's done for, and once he's in the can, he's been such a bastard, he won't last two weeks."

"I tell you, Leo. The first time I saw a picture of McPhail in *The Globe* after his arrest, I couldn't believe it. He looked like some fat kid, like somebody's bachelor cousin come to watch the Pats games on Sundays and to eat you out of house and home. If everything hadn't been so awful, and it wouldn't have hurt so much, I would've laughed."

It was a sweet spring evening. The windows in Rosaria's hospital room looked out at the red brick townhouses of Beacon Hill. In the center, the golden dome of the State House caught the sun's last rays.

"Leo?"

"Yeah?"

"I think Aurelius would have been proud of us."

"No doubt in my mind, Ro."

Route 3 North was clear and empty on this spring day. A flute played a slow air on the car's sound system and Rosaria was contemplative. And alive. Miraculously, she was alive. Bill Kenneally was right when he said that the bruises still on her face and her broken nose made her look like the loser in a welterweight boxing match. She'd lost the peripheral vision in her right eye and occasionally experienced a disturbing shimmer in her line of sight—all from the grievous *insult to the brain,* as the doctors said, that Dara McCarthy had given her when he smashed her head into a granite boulder on the Gloucester shore.

But, with time and work, perhaps all that would be resolved. Maybe not perfectly, but enough. At least she was alive.

She'd finished Aurelius's last mission, with great pain and loss, but she had completed it. She had kept her promise to her best friend in her final days and seen her out as she'd wanted. The fallen angels Malachy Sullivan and Dara McCarthy were dead. Francie had escaped a nightmare of abuse and perhaps was on the cusp of finding a life. Monsignor McDermott and Roger O'Toole were on trial, and Augustus McPhail was not far behind.

Against all odds, with her life in complete turmoil, she'd not only met but exceeded her corporate sales goals. Rosaria was sure she had a handsome bonus and yet another promotion in her future. But she had also heard whispers that her firm was a buyout target of a major competitor. If so, perhaps this was the time to hang it up.

Time for something else. Hard to know what that might be, but she was sure it would not have anything to do with making quarterly numbers. That world, so long her mooring, felt like a prior life. So good, so rich, so adventuresome. But it was enough now.

She'd been to Leo's for a roast leg of lamb the night before and wasn't entirely surprised to find Francie Dooley in the kitchen with him. Leo was an excellent, if fussy, cook, and Francie was relegated to chopping vegetables. Rosaria had watched as Leo stood close to Francie, hand on hers on the knife to show the correct chopping techniques. Francie had looked up at Leo with a barely suppressed laugh on her lips. Leo saw the look and threw up his hands in mock surrender. "Okay, okay. You know how to do this. Do it your way."

Sometimes, there are happy endings, Rosaria thought. She might just be witnessing one.

Rosaria took the Lowell Connector and swung off the highway onto Gorman Street and into the crowded neighborhoods of the city. Listening to her GPS navigator, she easily made her way to Father Morissette Boulevard and, after executing some hard parallel parking maneuvers, succeeded in pulling into a tight parking space between two obese SUVs.

She looked over her shoulder to the back seat where she could see Archie snoozing deeply on his doggie blankie, an old afghan she'd bought at a charity auction years ago. Judging it warm enough to leave him in the car for fifteen minutes, she cracked open two windows to make sure he had enough fresh air. Then, after struggling for a few minutes with a broken parking meter, she left a quarter sticking out of it, hoping for an understanding parking officer.

The Franco-American Workingman's Bank stood about halfway down the block. A few days before, she'd received a bill for a safe deposit box from the bank. The bill had arrived at the Motherhouse, addressed not to Mary Aurelius SJd'A, but to her given name, Mary Agnes Burke. Mother Superior had forwarded the bill to Rosaria with a note, "I think this will give you answers, Rosaria. We'll talk afterward. God be with you."

The mysterious safe deposit, finally.

In an unusual move, the order had relinquished the role of executrix to Rosaria in deference to Aurelius's wishes, expressed to Mother Superior at some earlier point "in case something should happen." Rosaria thought that serving as executrix in this case was a formality, given that Aurelius had no earthly goods to administer. But perhaps there were arrangements the old nun had wanted someone close to her to attend to.

Rosaria entered the heavy wooden doors into a small workingman's bank. The touches of cheerful modernity in colorful graphics and advertisements around the interior of the bank were surely introduced by a consultant to bring the bank up-to-date. Rosaria found them jarringly dissonant with the solid early twentieth-century architecture and fixtures. *Why couldn't they just leave well enough alone,* she thought as she stood in the lobby and looked around.

An assistant manager came out of his office to greet her. "Help you, ma'am?" Rosaria saw the man's gaze linger on her battered face.

"Yes, thanks," said Rosaria, pulling out the small brown envelope with the safe deposit key, and handing it to him. She gave him a wry smile. "Accident."

"Boy, it must have been a tough one."

"It certainly was."

"Well, let's see what we can do to help you here." The man slipped the brass key out of its small brown envelope. "Old one. Even the envelope is old. Haven't seen these in a while. Do you have some identification for me?"

"Yes, I have that and the legal paperwork. The owner was a close friend of mine. I'm the executrix of the estate."

The manager checked the paperwork. "Oh, I remember this one. The old nun had this box. Did something happen to her?"

"Yes, she died some months ago."

"Same accident, by any chance? "The manager cocked his head in sympathy,

"Sort of." Rosaria answered, looking toward the safe deposit area, hoping not to have to discuss this anymore. She was starting to feel a wave of emotion coming on.

"So sorry to hear that. She seemed like a high-quality person."

"That she was, thank you." Rosaria turned away. After everything, why was she still so weepy? Why didn't he just show her to the goddamn box?

"I apologize for prying," he said quickly. "My condolences for your loss."

His kind eyes rested on her ruined face for a moment. "Well, everything looks in order. Let's go to my office. I'll sign where I need to and we'll get my keys. Then, we'll go back and get you the box."

Some minutes later, the manager led Rosaria through a large brass grated door to a narrow corridor with safe deposit boxes on both sides. He turned to Rosaria as they approached a far corner of the area.

"Again, I'm sorry about your friend. Were you one of her students?"

"Thank you. Yes, I was. We all miss her. She was a great teacher."

The manager removed a medium-sized box and placed it on a small table. "Well, here you go. I'll leave you some privacy." And then the man left Rosaria with Aurelius's safe deposit box.

There were only two envelopes in the box. Rosaria opened the first marked *His Eminence* in Sister Aurelius's firm hand.

> Dear Eminence,
>
> I write to you in great sadness but with an equal sense of urgency regarding a grave situation at the Immaculate Conception parish in Malford. I've long believed that Monsignor McDermott of this parish was involved in the abuse of certain parish boys. I reported this fact to the Chancery decades ago—with only a small measure of success, I might add, Your Eminence. This grieves me deeply to this day.
>
> In addition to his abuse of certain students, I have now come to the conclusion that Monsignor McDermott used his stature in the community to protect a group of boys who were distributing drugs from the parish high school. I'm convinced that he did so because of his close relationship with the young man who organized and led the operation as he does currently.

I believe that young man, Malachy Sullivan, now grown and a successful real estate developer, never left the drug distribution business and that his network has likely grown far beyond the reaches of a small Catholic high school. It's also my firm belief that Monsignor McDermott is still involved with this business, using his share of the profits in an unholy, misguided effort to enhance the finances of the Immaculate Conception boys' high school. This, like the abuse of the parish boys, is clearly a matter for the law enforcement authorities, as well as the Chancery.

These circumstances are of great concern to me, as I'm sure they are to you, Your Eminence. I bring this grave situation to your attention and will contact the civil authorities, knowing that this travesty will be addressed with the urgency it deserves.

Yours in Christ,
Mary Aurelius, SJd'A

Rosaria's heart sank. She should have thought about Lowell, Aurelius's birthplace, and her given name when she was trying to trace the safe deposit box key. So obvious now. And here, Aurelius had it all laid out for them in this letter. Rosaria took a long breath and ran her hand across her forehead. When there are so many questions in a time of crisis, it was something like, she supposed, the fog of war. It's hard to know where to focus. If she'd just been more thoughtful, not rushing around so much, if she'd just considered the possibilities more carefully.

And the Chancery. The Chancery must have received this letter. Rosaria wondered how there could not have been an immediate response. But the Chancery was an old, slow bureaucracy, used to handling things discreetly out of the public eye. Perhaps not knowing what to do with these stunning accusations, instead of acting, they had discussed, consulted with lawyers. Of course, too, the Monsignor had friends at the Chancery. Someone would have quietly alerted him. He would have denied all, saying the nun was suffering from dementia and had always been a borderline personality. Then, he would have told Malachy before Aurelius went to the police and the Chancery followed up with her. At that point, the die was cast.

Rosaria felt a rage building. The Chancery must have wondered about the circumstances when they saw the news that Aurelius had been murdered. Perhaps they were relieved. They should have come forward with Aurelius's letter, but they never did. Well, she was certainly going to call someone at *The Globe* and make sure that letter was published on the front page, even before she gave Leo a copy. She didn't want him to hold it up for some evidential process. She wanted this out there *now*. Rosaria's heart was beating with a building fury. The Chancery had sacrificed Aurelius. She'd never say that was their plan, or that they were not likely horrified and pained, or that the leak about Aurelius's letter to the Monsignor was condoned. But they stood aside quietly, never coming forward when Aurelius was murdered.

Rosaria's anguish and anger were interrupted when she glanced at the contents of the box again. A second large envelope sat at the bottom of the safe deposit box. She was surprised to see her name on the envelope in Aurelius's distinctive script. In the corner, Aurelius had written, *Caritate perpetua, Filia.* Love everlasting, daughter.

Feeling as though she were moving in slow motion, like seconds had stretched into minutes, Rosaria picked up the heavy envelope. It was not sealed. She lifted the corner and caught a glimpse of a blue ribbon. Tied in the blue ribbon were valentines, all the handmade valentines she'd given Aurelius as a child, all the birthday cards. And, as time went on, the clippings of her notable achievements as a student athlete in high school and college, her awards over the years, notices of her short-lived marriage, and later, her professional successes. And, at the bottom of the packet, an official document, fragile from having been opened many times.

Two pictures were wrapped in the document. One was a small, faded image of a serious young girl with a large ribbon to the side of her long dark hair in the fashion of the day. The faint and spidery script on the back read "Mary Agnes Burke—Grade 6, Saint Jeanne d'Arc Parish." The second picture was of Rosaria, taken on a school picture day in fifth grade at the Immaculate, her long dark hair loose, and her face serious. The face of Sister Mary Aurelius looked out from both pictures.

Rosaria unfolded the document further. The birth certificate read of a baby girl born to Mary Agnes Burke of Lowell, *Father Unknown*.

CHAPTER 36

osaria spent the next couple of days in a disoriented state. Something, *everything* had changed. She felt as if the world had tilted on its axis. She wished she could talk to Nuncie. Maybe she'd call Leo. No, that wouldn't be the same. In the end, she called Mother Superior to ask if she could stop by her home for a short visit.

"Yes, Rosaria. I'm glad you called. I was going to call if you didn't."

Rosaria met the nun at her door and was once again struck by the woman's natural style. Even with her windblown hair and red cheeks, Mother Superior had a certain elegance that many women spend a fortune for and never achieve. The nun took off her coat now and rubbed her arms for warmth. A pearl gray scarf with a soft blue pattern and a small wooden cross lay against her ivory turtleneck.

"Brisk out there with that wind." She walked over to the living room windows and looked out on the harbor with appreciation. "Very nice."

"Never gets old," said Rosaria. "Come have some tea. It'll warm you up."

The nun smiled and took a seat at the dining table where Rosaria had laid out a plate of Madeleine cookies and a pot of tea.

"How lovely, Rosaria. This reminds me of my childhood. Did you make these Madeleines?" She tasted one. "Perfect."

"I did. I like a good rich cookie with a strong cup of tea."

"You're a woman of secret talents. I'm not surprised."

Rosaria acknowledged the compliment with a smile and a nod.

Mother Superior looked out on the harbor again. "You know, I once lived in an apartment that had a view like this out to the Saint Lawrence. Well, different, but a similar feel. I used to watch the container ships coming and going when I had my morning coffee before work. It was quite beautiful in all the seasons."

She turned to Rosaria and noted the surprise on her face. "Oh yes, we do have lives before we take our vows, Rosaria. I lived in that apartment during the years I was Marguerite Fontaine, barrister and solicitor in Quebec City with a successful intellectual property practice."

"Forgive me, Mother. Of course, I think we forget."

"Some people think we're born with a short veil and a pair of round wire glasses." Rosaria laughed. "Well, I suppose so."

"We all come to this vocation from other lives. Sometimes, quite eventful lives." She smiled and looked at Rosaria levelly.

"I can imagine that, Mother."

"Yes, you'd often be surprised." The nun picked up a cup of tea. "And, please, Rosaria, don't call me *Mother*. You can call me Marguerite."

Rosaria returned her smile. "Okay, Marguerite. That's a little more comfortable for me too."

"Good. So, now we'll talk." She took a sip of her tea and put her cup down.

Rosaria leaned back in her chair and waited. Only the Chelsea clock ticking and the muted sounds of the harbor outside the windows. Now, she hoped there would be more answers.

Mother Superior spoke carefully. "Aurelius and I were friends with something of the same character and interests. I loved her deeply." The nun looked down, clasping her hands and brushing her thumbs together. "But we only talked about her situation and yours twice."

Rosaria waited in the heavy silence before the nun continued. "The arrangement for her to teach at the Immaculate was by all measures unusual and probably risky. But it was one which was beneficial for all the parties involved at the time."

She looked up at Rosaria. "Though I have to say that we had no satisfactory plan for how we were to deal with your future feelings. We just had to have hope and faith that you would understand and in some way appreciate the situation. The O'Reillys asked us not to divulge the arrangement while they and Aurelius were alive. I was uncomfortable with that, but agreed with reluctance. They and Aurelius were the only people who were aware of the arrangement, other than myself. Now the O'Reillys are gone and," she stopped for a moment, "so is Sister Aurelius."

Rosaria was shaking her head slowly from side to side, eyes closed, trying to absorb it all. Maybe she shouldn't have been surprised to find something like rage building. It all made sense now, but they never told her. *They never told her.*

"Perhaps this keeping of secrets is unforgivable, but I hope you will find it in your heart to understand and find some measure of compassion yourself. Our motives were the best and Aurelius loved you very much, as did your parents."

Rosaria lowered her eyes and took a deep breath.

"You'll want to know about your biological father."

Rosaria raised her face to the nun. "Of course, I would want to know about my biological father." An edge to her voice. *They did this to her, all of them.* Never told her, even in adulthood. The whole lot of them keeping secrets from her. She'd never pursued finding her birth mother. Her parents had told her that her mother was a young teenager who'd gotten into trouble and moved on with her life.

Mother Marguerite looked at Rosaria steadily. "I can't imagine how difficult this is for you." She looked out the window at the water briefly and continued. "I'm afraid I don't have much to tell you there. I do know he was a married man with children. A police officer who had his beat in Aurelius's neighborhood of triple-deckers in Lowell—back when she was Mary Agnes Burke.

A policeman. Interesting.

"Sometimes they would talk while Mary Agnes watched her brothers and sisters playing by the street outside. Mary Agnes sitting on the front steps, him leaning on the street lamppost. He made her laugh and she started to look for him in the afternoons. She saw him sometimes in church with his wife and children. She imagined herself with him in place of his wife."

The nun looked steadily at Rosaria for a moment. "This was a young girl, remember, who had heavy responsibilities for her age, raising her brothers and sisters. She'd lost her own mother far too early, and poor Mr. Burke was so overwhelmed with trying to hold his family together financially and otherwise, that he had nothing left to give Mary Agnes in terms of affection and attention."

Rosaria was carried back to another time and place in her mind. Aurelius as Mary Agnes Burke, a child.

"One day, this policeman said he liked the way she was wearing her hair—shiny and dark, pulled back in a blue ribbon. He asked if she ever walked down by the river. She didn't, but now she did sometimes when she could get away. Three times she walked and he wasn't there. The fourth time, he was."

A rape. Statutory rape. The nun must have read the horror on Rosaria's face.

"Aurelius never thought of it that way, Rosaria. Today we would, and it surely was. She never did."

They were both quiet for some long minutes.

"Those were hard days for unmarried mothers. Mary Agnes was not allowed to see or hold the baby. Later, the woman from Catholic Charities told her that the baby girl had gone to a wonderful couple that couldn't have children of their own. Aurelius told me she had wanted to feel some comfort for her child and happiness for the parents, but felt instead great emptiness in herself and in the world."

Rosaria took a long, deep breath—pained now to think of Aurelius as a young girl. A young girl on her own after losing her baby.

"Afterward, she worked in a woolen mill in Lawrence and lived with an aunt there until she applied to the Jeanne d'Arc order of nuns. The nuns at her school had been very good to Mary Agnes and her brothers and sisters after their mother died. Adopted them in a way. They gave them extra food, which convents had little of themselves in those days. Brought the younger children into the school and cared for them far before they were of age to be in school.

"Again, those were different days. People just did what had to be done. I'm sure that when Mary Agnes applied to the order, there were long and complicated discussions, but these were women of great heart. I have to say that most orders would not have shown this charity and understanding, but those women did at the time. I'm very proud of them." Marguerite Fontaine's eyes filled and she turned away in embarrassment. "The order took months to decide before accepting her, but in the end, they did."

She looked over at Rosaria. "Are you okay, Rosaria? Do you need a break?"

Rosaria rose from her chair and picked up a bottle of whiskey from the credenza. She offered the bottle to the nun, who shook her head, and then Rosaria poured a shot of the whiskey into her now cold tea. "Go on," she said.

Mother Superior closed her eyes and raised her face for some moments, perhaps in a short prayer, before continuing. "Adoptions then, of course, were closed and everything was highly secretive, but because she was a resourceful young woman, Aurelius found where her little girl had been placed. The adoptive parents were a middle-aged factory supervisor and his wife in a shoe factory town north of Boston. Aurelius learned the O'Reillys had named the baby Rosaria." Here, the nun chuckled. "She told me she had hoped the woman was not overly pious. And it did turn out, as you know, that your mother, Mrs. O'Reilly, was very devout."

A wry smile from Rosaria.

"Aurelius told me that she'd been content with her first teaching assignment in Methuen, content in the kind of numb way she lived those years. She was stunned when I called her to her next posting, to teach seventh grade at the Immaculate in Malford.

"I was aware of Aurelius's history, you see, through my predecessor, Mother Julian. The story broke my heart." She took a Kleenex from the pocket of her navy skirt and looked away for a moment. "Aurelius was an unusual person. If anyone was equal to navigating a complicated situation, Aurelius was. I felt something had to be made right for this good woman and," the nun looked closely at Rosaria, "her daughter." Rosaria felt a tiny electrical shock at the spoken words *her daughter*.

"So, I took a risk. I had a quiet conversation with the O'Reillys to raise the possibility of Aurelius's coming to teach at the Immaculate. You know how kind your parents were."

Rosaria nodded. They were that. Good and unselfish people. And she had been such a difficult child.

"Given their permission and Aurelius's acceptance, the order assigned Aurelius to the Immaculate, with the stipulation that her relationship with you would never be divulged in their lifetimes, and that she would not develop what was called an 'unhelpful' focus on you. This last was difficult, but she managed outward appearances. Internally, I know, it was another matter."

Rosaria saw the nun hesitate. She could see her debating internally whether to go deeper, and deciding to do so.

"She told me she disciplined herself to only the occasional, teacherly touch. Just straightening your hair for a school picture would sustain her for months. Aurelius had a poetic side, as you know. She told me on the day we talked that the secret was like a small, soft animal always purring near her heart. I often thought of that description after Aurelius died."

Rosaria felt her own heart contract.

Gathering strength, the nun continued. "She told me about her first day at the Immaculate. She was on the school playground, with the children lining up for classes. Her eyes scanned the youngest classes and she knew you immediately. Taller than your classmates, standing with your arm around your friend—a small, dark blond Italian girl. Nuncie, of course. Long, dark braids with curls at the ends, what Aurelius said was your father's mouth, softer and fuller than her own thin lips. But you had her strong-boned face and green eyes. She described them as a dark gray green, like the ocean on a certain kind of cloudy day. And that's how I would describe Aurelius's own eyes."

Grief, anger, and wonder coursed through Rosaria. She felt chilled and pulled her sweater more tightly around herself.

"Aurelius told me that, through some act of will that day, she'd called her own students into the big brick school, with only one backward glance at the first grade class processing into the other doorway. That night, she told me she fell on her knees in the privacy of her room at the convent and wept in gratitude. She said a litany of gratitude every day of her life after that."

By the time Mother Superior had finished her story, dusk had fallen and Rosaria had not turned on any lights. The two women sat in the shadowy light without speaking for some time.

Then, Mother Superior asked, "Would you like me to stay, Rosaria?"

"No, I'm good," Rosaria replied, while still staring out the windows at the harbor.

"Well, I doubt you're good, but I understand. I'll leave you now and call you tomorrow. Would you like me to do that?"

Rosaria couldn't bring herself to respond.

The nun rose and put on her coat. Before she left, she put her hand on Rosaria's shoulder. Rosaria didn't move. "We meant for the best, Rosaria."

A tiny nod. "I'm sure you all did."

"And you had each other in your lives."

Rosaria looked up at the nun. "Yes, we did."

"Shall I turn on some lights, Rosaria?"

"No, thank you."

Mother Superior left Rosaria sitting in the shadows as she closed the door to the apartment. Outside on the water, the lights of a ferryboat marked its steady progress across the harbor. Archie laid his head on Rosaria's feet. She closed her eyes, breathing deeply, and after some time found stillness, something like peace.

THE END

ACKNOWLEDGMENTS

he haunting image of an elderly nun walking across an abandoned schoolyard at dusk came to me a few years ago, and just stayed with me until I had to write a book about it. I have many people to thank for that writing journey.

I am indebted to my publisher, Barking Rain Press, who took a chance on yet another unknown author with a tale to tell and gave me a great team to work with. My outstanding editor, Melissa Eskue Ousley, buoyed this first-time author all the way with enthusiasm and skill, making the book much better. Thanks also to Barbara Bailey for eagle-eyed proofing, and to Craig Jennion for a creative and suitably spooky cover. I was in good hands through the entire process.

I've been fortunate in teachers—all talented and generous writers themselves—starting with the Seascape Workshop angels Hallie Ephron, Roberta Islieb, and Hank Phillippi Ryan, who gave me the spark to write this book. Gotham Writing Workshop teachers Greg Fallis, Carter Sickels, and Carole Bugge, writing group leader Susan Oleksiw, and Grub Street Launch Labbers Lynne Griffin and Katrin Schumann. I'm privileged to have worked with all of them.

What a blessing loyal family and friends are! My late brother Tom and my brother Jerry toured me through all the Boston neighborhoods we see in the book and were enthusiastic early readers of the manuscript. My brother Bob was also a supportive beta reader, as was my true-blue sister Jane Compagnone and her Pittsburgh friends Mickey Gatto and Mary Panczcyk.

Heartfelt thanks to my steadfast book club posse who read the early manuscript—Fiddle Walton, Marcia Smith, Jody Newman, Brigid Menzi, Sandra King, and Jean Vnenchek—and to Joanne McMahon and Kate Jackson, as well as Sisters in Crime and its subgroup of Guppies (the Great UnPublished).

My husband Bill and our children—Maggie, Nick, Katherine, and Mary—thanks for always being there with loving support and encouragement in my aspirations. (And to Archie the dog for warming my feet under the desk in the cupola.) You are the world to me.

And, finally, thanks to you—the best kind of reader—who takes the time to read acknowledgments.

COMING SOON FROM
MARIAN MCMAHON STANLEY

Buried Troubles

The long reach of grievances and secrets from Ireland's troubled past ends the life of an Irish journalism student in Boston and threatens the stability of the Irish political landscape.

WWW.MARIANMCMAHONSTANLEY.COM

MARIAN
McMAHON STANLEY

Like her protagonist, Marian McMahon Stanley enjoyed an international corporate career with a Fortune 500 company and, more recently, a senior position at a large, urban university. A dual citizen of the United States and Ireland, she is a proud mother and grandmother of four adult children and a growing number of grandchildren. Marian writes in a small town outside Boston where she lives with her husband Bill and—just as in *The Immaculate*—a Westie named Archie. Currently, she's hard at work on her next mystery. You can find out more about Marian on her website, or on Twitter, LinkedIn, or Facebook.

WWW.MARIANMCMAHONSTANLEY.COM

About
Barking Rain Press

id you know that five media conglomerates publish eighty percent of the books in the United States? As the publishing industry continues to contract, opportunities for emerging and mid-career authors are drying up. Who will write the literature of the twenty-first century if just a handful of profit-focused corporations are left to decide who—and what—is worthy of publication?

Barking Rain Press is dedicated to the creation and promotion of thoughtful and imaginative contemporary literature, which we believe is essential to a vital and diverse culture. As a nonprofit organization, Barking Rain Press is an independent publisher that seeks to cultivate relationships with new and mid-career writers over time, to be thorough in the editorial process, and to make the publishing process an experience that will add to an author's development—and ultimately enhance our literary heritage.

In selecting new titles for publication, Barking Rain Press considers authors at all points in their careers. Our goal is to support the development of emerging and mid-career authors—not just single books—as we know from experience that a writer's audience is cultivated over the course of several books.

Support for these efforts comes primarily from the sale of our publications; we also hope to attract grant funding and private donations. Whether you are a reader or a writer, we invite you to take a stand for independent publishing and become more involved with Barking Rain Press. With your support, we can make sure that talented writers thrive, and that their books reach the hands of spirited, curious readers. Find out more at our website.

WWW.BARKINGRAINPRESS.ORG

Barking Rain Press

ALSO FROM BARKING RAIN PRESS

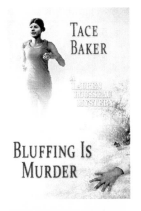

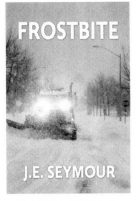

VIEW OUR COMPLETE CATALOG ONLINE:
WWW.BARKINGRAINPRESS.ORG

CPSIA information can be obtained at www.ICGtesting.com
Printed in the USA
BVOW05s1546250516

449534BV00001BA/9/P